Brett was proving to be hard to dismiss

She'd never realized until after he'd gone just how quiet the house got at night, or just how strange it was not to hear another human voice for hours on end. She had not heard so much laughter, or been so tempted to it herself as in the two days spent in Brett's company. It had been a strange feeling, but it had been good.

Jane didn't believe him when he'd asked if he could come back. And she didn't believe the kiss he'd taken, seeing it only as the tactic of a sophisticated man. But what Jane also couldn't believe was the shock of realization that she wanted to respond. For a heady instant she wanted to know the full aggressive pressure of his mouth. Did she want Brett Chandler to come back? She had no idea. Jane only knew that his appearance and his departure had changed something around her.

ABOUT THE AUTHOR

Sandra Kitt is the librarian at a major museum in New York City. She and her husband live in a Victorian house in Prospect Park South, an historical district in Brooklyn. As well as being a writer, Sandra is also a free-lance graphic designer and has just illustrated her second book with Isaac Asimov.

Books by Sandra Kitt

HARLEQUIN AMERICAN ROMANCE

Don't miss any of our special offers. Write to us at the following address for information on our newest releases.

Harlequin Reader Service
901 Fuhrmann Blvd., P.O. Box 1397, Buffalo, NY 14240
Canadian address: P.O. Box 603,
Fort Erie, Ont. L2A 5X3

An Innocent Man
Sandra Kitt

Harlequin Books

TORONTO • NEW YORK • LONDON
AMSTERDAM • PARIS • SYDNEY • HAMBURG
STOCKHOLM • ATHENS • TOKYO • MILAN

My sincere thanks to Ms. Carol Martin,
CBS News Local, New York City
and
Mr. Chuck Belensky, Engineer,
Grumman Aerospace, Bethpage, New York

Published January 1989

First printing November 1988

ISBN 0-373-16280-4

Chapter One

Jane frowned in concentration over the paper in her hand, quickly assessing the words and thoughts. Was she really making a point? Did she really have something worthwhile to say? Was anyone going to care? At one time she'd thought so, when she was younger and full of energy in her quest for truth. Of course, that was before she'd discovered that truth had shades of difference to it, and was not always absolute.

The sudden silence distracted her. It was very quiet in the room and brought into sharp focus her sense of isolation. It was also cold. She had forgotten to raise the heat in the small two-story house, and winter was making itself felt. Jane had always hated winter. It was gray. Even the holidays, too many of them spent alone, held a questionable joy. She didn't like winter's noises any better: wind that moaned and gusted in anger...the eerie silence of falling snow...wheels spinning uselessly on ice in an attempt to move....

Jane tilted her head and caught the sound, muted by the wind. First there had been an awful grinding of metal, and then a thud. She peered through the frosted pane as if expecting to see the source of the sounds, but the night was black and there was silence again.

Behind Jane a body lumbered into an upright position and padded slowly to the window. A head was pressed close to the glass, black eyes searching the darkness beyond. Jane turned and smiled ruefully at the alertness in the dark face.

"It's all right, Jones. The wind does strange things at night." She briefly stroked the head in answer to the small whimper, and turned back to her P.C. screen.

She began typing again, the gentle clicking of the keys drowning the ghostly sounds from outside. Jones pulled his hind legs under his body and sat in front of the window, continuing to keep watch. The head was still, the eyes focused, the gentle breathing and lolling of his tongue the only sounds he made.

Jane ignored the animal and forged through the rest of the first draft of her work. She had no sense of the changes going on outdoors, least of all the one important one that set Jones to whining again in a low tone, and his tail to swishing on the floor. Finally the animal got up and came to stand next to her. He was not one to make noise unnecessarily and waited patiently for Jane to notice him.

"What's the matter, boy?" Jane crooned. "Did I forget to feed you?" Turning off the P.C. and standing, she touched the dark head again and started from the room. "Let's go see what we can find in the kitchen for dinner."

Jones turned to follow, trotted past her and headed toward the outer door. But Jane turned right off the foyer and went into the kitchen. She opened a pantry door and seriously reviewed the shelves.

"What'll it be tonight? Kalcan with chunks of tender chicken, or fillet of beef?" she asked, amusement in her voice as she read the selections. But the dog was still by the door, staring at it as if it would open on its own.

"Jones!" Jane called lightly. "Come and pick something for dinner!"

In response, the dog let out a low deep bark of frustration.

"Oh, you want me to choose, hmm?"

Jane took a twelve-ounce can of dog food from the shelf and opening it, dumped the decidedly unappetizing contents into an aluminum dish on the floor. "Come on, boy," she coaxed. "It's getting late. After dinner you'll take one quick turn around the yard and then we'll get some sleep."

Talking to the animal was no longer any stranger than berating her computer when it occasionally went catatonic and swallowed her typed copy. She cursed it, of course, and then tried to retrieve the data. She expected no response from the P.C., but was surprised when Jones didn't gratefully attack the dishes on the floor.

Jane stuck her head out of the kitchen door and spotted the animal in the hall. "You know the routine. You eat first and then you go out."

The dog came over to Jane and looked up at her. He barked in answer and wagged his tail. Then he came up easily on his back legs and placed his front paws on Jane's chest. Straight up, he was almost as tall as she was. But his effort to gain her complete attention only made Jane smile.

"Yeah, I love you, too. But it doesn't change anything." She gently pushed him away with one last pat and headed back to the kitchen. "Now stop fooling around. Your dinner is getting cold," she quipped.

Jane quickly assembled a sandwich from cold cuts in the refrigerator and made a pot of hot tea. She sat down at the small table, but had only just taken the first bite of her dinner when Jones came over to her. He sat down next to her chair and simply stared at her.

"Forget it!" Jane mumbled as she chewed. "Go and eat your own dinner."

Jones looked at the waiting food dishes on the floor, but at that moment did not have canned dog food on his mind.

He sat and contemplated Jane's every move, occasionally looking over his shoulder to the door. All the same, it was obvious his mistress was not about to be rushed. When Jane gave every indication of lingering over her tea, Jones lost patience. The sound was low in his throat at first, starting as a half moan and whimper. Then he suddenly bounded effortlessly to his feet and began to bark to gain Jane's attention. It worked.

Jane had never been a person to relax completely and easily become complacent. She lived alone, isolated by choice, and the reasons were never far from her thoughts. Her heart lurched in her chest, and the beat grew fast and painful. Fear gripped her and brought an instant replay of threats from the past. Was she overreacting? Slowly Jane lowered the mug to the table. She rose and cautiously followed the animal. His sounds and movements made it extremely clear that he wanted to go out. Somehow Jane knew with a sinking heart that it wasn't a case of nature's call. There was someone out there.

One of the worst storms Montauk had ever recorded was raging outside in the late December night. It was three days after Christmas and her two nearest neighbors were away visiting family. There was Oliver, of course, but she remembered he'd been invited to a drinking fest in town with some of his cronies. By rights there should be no one else around. Jane released the breath that had caught in her throat. No one in their right mind would be out unnecessarily in this weather, even to get to her.

"Jones, there's nothing out there." But Jane wasn't totally convinced. She knew the animal's instincts were much sharper than her own. If there was nothing out there, then something at least was definitely wrong.

Leaving the dog barking by the door, Jane walked purposefully from room to room, gazing futilely out each window to locate the source of the animal's excitement. She could see nothing. The dog continued to bark.

"Stop that!" Jane said sharply. "Someone would have to be crazy to be out there, Jones." *Or drunk,* she thought. *Or hurt.* She stood still and considered the possibility. And then she recalled the faint sounds outside nearly an hour and a half ago.

Her good sense told her she knew better. But curiosity got the better of her. Jane had not completely eliminated the possibility of danger to her person, but like the dog, she now *had* to investigate. She also reasoned that in the final analysis, Jones would not let anything happen to her. It had never struck Jane as odd that she so readily placed confidence in her dog. Unlike her fellow human beings, Jones had never disappointed or hurt her.

"You win," she said with a sigh as she opened a hall closet and reached in for a bright red down parka. "Let's go see what's out there...and it'd better be more than a rabbit!" Jane pulled on a pair of sturdy boots. The dog had stopped its barking and stood waiting for her. Jane turned back to the closet and reached for a long-handled emergency flashlight on the top shelf. She dug through other tools until she found a heavy crowbar. She hadn't the first idea how it was supposed to be used, but felt it would make an adequate weapon if need be. So armed, Jane reached for the door and pulled it open. Jones forced his big body past her and disappeared into the darkness.

"Jones! Come back here!" Jane shouted. For an instant she recalled a hot summer night of unexpected danger, when she had unwittingly been drawn into an intrigue that had ended tragically...simply because she had responded to her curiosity.

Jane pulled the door shut behind her. The sudden cold slammed into her chest through the open parka.

"Jones!" she called again plaintively, but got no answering bark. She turned on the flashlight and swung it in an arc around her, finding only white flecks of snow past the beam of light. She could see nothing else.

Jane took a few tentative steps, following the holes made by the dog's paws. The snow was blinding. Her hair whipped around her face, quickly becoming damp and tangled. She found herself leaning into the wind, against its force, but never thought of simply returning to the calm and comfort of the house right behind her.

"Jones! Here boy...come here!"

Jane continued slowly, not sure which way Jones had gone, but knowing something or someone out here had his complete attention. She'd moved only about twenty feet when she tripped and with a small startled sound, dropped everything as she went sprawling. Jane grunted and landed flat on her stomach in soft snow. She pulled herself up and reached for her flashlight. Now she realized the folly of coming out without a hat and gloves. The dog popped out of the darkness to bark and circle around her. She felt instant relief upon seeing him. "Oh, Jones! Where were you, boy? What did you find?"

It was clear to Jane he had discovered something and wanted her to see it, too, so when he trotted off again, Jane was right behind him. She could barely see through the storm and her loosened hair felt as though it were being torn from her scalp by the strong winds. Her hands were nearly numb from the cold and her face began to sting from the wet flakes on her skin. Once more she lost sight of the animal and veered in the wrong direction, but Jones retraced his steps so she could find him.

Jane realized that they were now crossing the narrow private road that bordered the back of her house. Immediately beyond that the land dipped into a deep ditch of low scrub pines and tangled vines. Jane stopped and swung the

light, not venturing any farther. Off to her left Jones began
barking again and she turned the light in that direction. She
found herself looking at the rear lights of a vehicle of some
kind about fifty feet down the road. Its front end was firmly
against the base of a tree and sloping down at a sharp angle.

It was a sports car in charcoal metallic gray and had
Massachusetts plates. The engine was still running and the
driver's door was open, but a quick glance inside told her it
was empty.

Jones was thrashing through the snow-laced bushes, and
slowly Jane stepped downward toward the front end of the
car. Still some distance below that, the animal was whining
and digging. Jane began to cautiously work her way down
the slope. About fifteen feet down she gasped and stared in
total disbelief at the body lying at an awkward angle in the
brush with snow lightly covering it.

"Dear God . . ." she breathed, and then took two more
steps toward the figure. Jane dropped to her knees and ran
her light over the long male figure. Hesitantly she reached
over him and worked her hand under his jacket and against
his chest. There was a strong heartbeat, although his
breathing was shallow.

Jane let out a sigh of relief and tried to see what had happened. The man's dark head lay against the base of a partly
hidden stone, and she discovered a wide and bloody abrasion through his hairline at the temple. There were a number of smaller scratches on his right cheek. She couldn't be
sure if anything was broken, but he groaned and rolled his
head in pain. Jane had no idea what to do next. She had no
idea how long he'd lain unconscious, but he was not dressed
to stay out in this fierce weather much longer without serious consequences.

Setting the flashlight in the snow and angling it to shine
on him, Jane used her cold-stiffened hands to move hur-

riedly over the still form to look for further injuries. She tapped his cheeks lightly and shook him gently to try and bring him around, then suddenly felt herself sliding and reached frantically with her booted feet for a hold on the ground, but gravity and the slippery snow only aided her descent. As he witnessed the plight of his mistress, Jones set up a frantic barking again. The prone figure next to Jane began to move.

"Jones!" she cried helplessly as her legs went out from under her. She twisted sharply and instinctively grabbed the arm of the unconscious man next to her. Her body slid down the slope. The other body rolled as well, its heavier weight adding momentum. It only took a few seconds, but when Jane came to rest again, her back was pressed into a thicket, and her unconscious companion was half across her, his head on her rib cage. Jane heard a deep moan from him and felt his feeble attempts to lift his body.

The flashlight had fallen nearby, and stretching out her right hand, Jane grabbed it to look around. Her burden now lay motionless on top of her. She could still see the car and knew she hadn't rolled that far below it. Jones was prancing about.

"Jones, I'm okay!" Jane said, flashing her light above her. Jones stopped his barking but his tail was moving in agitation and his tongue hung out of his mouth. He whined softly and Jane completely empathized with him.

"Another fine mess you've gotten me into," she grunted to herself, trying to shift her body while she cradled the head and shoulders of the stranger pressed against her.

Suddenly he groaned again and slowly lifted a hand toward the gash on his head. Jane grabbed his hand away. "No, don't touch it," she whispered, beginning to shiver. "Can you hear me?" she asked. Almost imperceptively he nodded against her chest. "Then don't worry. We'll be okay as soon as we get out of here." But she had no idea how they were going to get out.

"Jones...help me!" Jane called to the dog.

For another moment the dog stood over his mistress. Then he pivoted and took off into the night. Jane gasped, wanting to call after him. She didn't want to be left with this injured stranger pinned to her chest. What if he died? she thought in a sudden panic. But the stranger in her arms burrowed his head against her, seeking warmth.

Jane tightened her arms around him, and she stroked her hand through his wet and frozen hair. "It's all right," she whispered softly. "Someone will come soon." She tried to pull a corner of her open parka over him to protect his face, cocooning him inside her jacket. The action sent a subtle feeling cascading through her—one of softening, of feminine nurturing. Suddenly she felt needed, quite aside from the fact that this man's life might well depend upon her. It was a responsibility that dredged up painful memories from the past.

The man turned his face a little, so that his mouth and chin were pressed into the cable-knit sweater covering her breast. Jane felt invaded against her will and by a power she couldn't identify. And even though she was not sure what any of these disturbing sensations meant, she enclosed the silent man in her arms to keep him safe.

She couldn't remember the last time she'd held a man. But this man, this stranger without any identity, reminded Jane that she herself had never been the object of anyone's care or tenderness. Suddenly on a stormy night, by pure chance, someone's well-being depended on her very existence. The irony of it made her sad, and she tightened her arms around the man.

"Hurry, Jones," Jane breathed feebly from frozen lips. This man was touching her too deeply, too quickly, and she couldn't handle it. She had made the decision years ago to stop being what she couldn't be, to stop wanting what she couldn't have. In three full years she'd never regretted her decision or her way of life. It was insane that in a mere twenty minutes the loneliness of her world should come crashing down on her, so that she was holding on to this man for her own sake as well as his.

"Help me, Jones. Hurry," Jane groaned now through her chattering teeth. She had an overwhelming feeling that she, too, needed saving.

BY THE TIME Jane heard the dog bark again, she was beyond feeling anything. Jones leaped down the incline, reaching Jane to sniff at her and lick her cold face.

"Good boy...good boy," Jane managed. A light flashed above her.

"Jane! Jane, are you all right?" came a booming voice, and a bear of a man came into view to tower over her.

"Oh, Oliver... I—I'm so g-glad to see you! I—I'm fine. J-just so... so cold...."

"Are you sure you're not hurt?" the anxious voice bellowed.

"Yes...yes."

"What are you doing down there, anyway?" the voice asked in mild impatience.

"There's a man down here, Oliver, and he's hurt...."

The big man was already cautiously making his way down the slope, his light bouncing off the darkness around him as he tried to see Jane. He stopped within a foot of her and surveyed the scene.

"Should I ask what you're doing in a ditch with an unconscious man on top of you?" he asked in a teasing tone while still seriously assessing the situation.

"No!" Jane said petulantly. "Just please get us out of here before we freeze to death!"

"Okay, okay....Take it easy," he stated calmly as he knelt in the snow next to Jane. The stranger again seemed to be coming around, and tried to lift his head. "Whoa...just be still now," Oliver said to the man, finding the wound and probing knowledgeably for others. "That's quite a cut you have," he murmured, almost to himself. Then Oliver shifted and tried to slide his arms under those of the injured man.

"Is he all right?" Jane asked as Oliver partially lifted the man away from her, allowing her to pull herself upright. It was very painful to move.

"I don't think it's serious," Oliver said, grunting as he maneuvered the limp form.

"What can I do?" she asked her rescuer.

Bending, Oliver draped the body over a brawny shoulder, then got to his feet. "Here...you take the light and help me get my footing. Move, Jones!" He motioned the dog out of his way and slowly began the ascent to the road.

"Be careful!" Jane gasped once when Oliver missed his step and seemed to fall forward. He'd stumbled over her crowbar, which she now quickly retrieved.

"Was that concern or advice?" Oliver chuckled. "Don't worry...I've never lost a patient."

When they finally reached the top, Oliver continued slowly down the icy road in the direction of Jane's small house, with Jones at his heels. Jane turned off the motor of the car and closed the door, then followed, much more slowly. The door to her house was wide open when she got there. She walked into the foyer, closed the door and looked around.

"Oliver?" she called.

"Up here," came back the muffled answer.

Jane followed the voice up the stairs to the second-floor bedroom. Oliver had placed the man on the double bed and already had his jacket and shirt open as he examined him quickly for pulse and heartbeat. She forgot her momentary

shock at finding that Oliver had put the man into her bed.
Her eyes were noting his strong jaw and firm masculine
mouth. The hair, nearly black, was wet and plastered to his
scalp. The wound on the side of his head was raw and the
skin at his hairline had turned a purplish black. He was
moving his head, his dark brows drawn together in pain.

Jane was shivering almost uncontrollably. "Is...is he
going to be...be okay?"

Oliver's head was bent intently over the man. "Oh, yeah.
He's probably got a mild concussion, but being out in the
cold for so long didn't do him much good, either."

Jane moved slowly into the room, noting the broad chest
of the prone man, the dark layer of thick curling hair that
rose and fell with his deep breathing. He turned his head in
her direction and the eyelids rose heavily so that his eyes
found hers. She swallowed and absently brought her clasped
hands up to her chest. She continued to stare.

"You'd better get out of those damp things," Oliver said,
casting a brief look in her direction before lifting one of the
stranger's eyelids. "Take a quick shower. And while you're
doing that, I'm going to run over to my place and get a few
things."

Jane came out of her trance. "But...shouldn't we call the
police or the hospital?"

Oliver stood and crossed his arms over his chest as he regarded his patient with a frown. "Probably. But it wouldn't
do any good tonight, anyway. I doubt if a police car or an
ambulance could manage the roads any better than our
friend here."

Jones padded to the side of the bed and looked at the injured man, then quietly sat back on his haunches.

"Jones seems to think he's safe enough. Looks like you're
going to have company for tonight." With that, Oliver
turned from the room and started down the stairs. "I'll be

back shortly. Go take that shower and get into some dry clothes,'' he said sternly just before he closed the outer door.

Jane nodded absently, but she couldn't seem to move. She felt a premonition wash gently over her. Her instincts had never steered her in the wrong direction, and now her inclination was to call Oliver back and tell him she couldn't allow this stranger to stay. Instead, Jane advanced slowly upon the bed to stare as Jones had done. She had to be sure if what she'd felt earlier had been real. With a kind of resignation Jane reached for the quilt at the foot of her bed and carefully spread it over her visitor, knowing deep inside her, the way one just sometimes knows these things, that her life was about to change yet again.

OLIVER TOOK a healthy gulp of coffee and squinted over the rim of his mug at the open wallet, trying to read the fine print on the identification card.

"Brett...Al...Alexander..."

Jane passed the older man a pair of framed half glasses that were sticking out of his shirt pocket, and watched him scowl disagreeably as he set them on his nose.

"Brett Alexander Chandler, it says here. He must be someone important," Oliver mused dryly. "Nobody but bankers and movie stars have three names."

Jane let a small smile appear at the corners of her mouth. She was sitting opposite Oliver at the kitchen table, her raw chapped hands wrapped around her own hot drink. She'd had her shower as Oliver had instructed, and was now dressed warmly in a velour robe, with her freshly shampooed hair drying under a terry-cloth turban. She'd rubbed generous amounts of face cream into her sore and tender cheeks, and right now they were shiny and very red.

Since they'd found the stranger's wallet, Jane had been waiting to find out exactly who was sleeping in her bed. Although Oliver had talked and questioned as a matter of course, he'd received no answer from the patient. And then, for all his nonchauvinistic sensibilities, Oliver had still banished her from her own room as he stripped the injured man of his wet garments.

"Is he from Long Island?" Jane asked smoothly.

"Nope. If this is to be believed, he's from somewhere near Boston."

Jane raised his brows at him. "Why wouldn't you believe it?"

Oliver looked briefly at her before shrugging indifferently. "I don't know. He could be a spy."

Jane laughed at the ridiculous idea. "Sure...and he's wandering around Montauk, Long Island during a horrible storm dressed in formal wear for an assignation, right?" Jane's eyes sparkled with amusement as she shook her head at Oliver.

"Let's see now...." Oliver removed several folded papers and put the wallet down. "Maybe we'll find a phone number or the name of someone to contact."

"Why don't you just try Information?" Jane asked absently, eyeing the wallet with interest.

"Good idea!" Oliver approved. "I always knew your research ability would come in handy someday." He laughed and got up to head for the phone in Jane's small study just off the living room.

She could hear Oliver's commanding voice on the telephone, but she paid no attention. With her hand she cautiously turned the open wallet toward her so she could read the other information displayed there. Oliver would not have considered the rest of it important. But Jane did.

Brett Alexander Chandler was thirty-nine years old. He'd be forty in June of the new year. He was six feet, one inch tall and weighed a lean one hundred seventy-five pounds. His hair and eyes were listed as brown. Feeling only slightly guilty, Jane looked through the rest of the wallet, reasoning that she had a right to know as much about him as she could. After all, she had to stay the night alone with him, and who knew if he was safe? She ignored the fact that his head was bashed, that he was unconscious and hardly capable of harming anyone. Nor did Jane choose to question the deeper gut need to know more about Mr. Chandler.

Actually she was surprised at the limited amount of information his wallet contained. There were a number of business cards, one from Inland Estates, a large real estate conglomerate that Jane was very familiar with. There was also a card for a private prep school in Pennsylvania. All in all, none of it shed any more light on Brett Chandler, although she was curious to know his connection to Inland Estates, especially since they were currently embroiled in litigation over land development. She heard Oliver hang up the phone and hastily pushed the wallet away. She didn't want Oliver to think she was being nosy.

"Well, there was a phone number for him all right, but...no answer. Either he lives alone, or his family is with him somewhere in the area, or he's visiting alone. Take your pick."

"What about the other papers you found?" Jane asked as she poured him more coffee.

"Nothing revealing. Just the usual things like Social Security, Voter's Registration, American Express ... a platinum card, no less. Oh, and there's a written note that reads, 'See you at Christmas' and it's signed Jonathan."

"Are there any pictures?" she asked.

"Men don't carry pictures in their wallets, Jane." Oliver brushed aside the idea.

"*You* don't," Jane said easily. "Men do if they have families or girlfriends."

"By that reasoning I guess he has no family and no girlfriends. No pictures!" he concluded.

Jane sighed, feeling vaguely let down. She definitely wanted to know more.

"Look..." Oliver said with a huge yawn. He took off his glasses and began replacing the papers in the wallet before carelessly tossing it back onto the table. "It's nearly three o'clock in the morning. B. A. Chandler isn't going anywhere for the next thirty-six hours, at least. He'll come around in the morning, when the pain medication and sedative I gave him wear off. I'm sure he'll tell us everything we need to know about him, including why there are no pictures in his wallet."

Oliver yawned again and began dressing for his short journey home, about a half dozen houses down the road. Jane turned to him with a final thought. "But Oliver...what if he wakes up in pain? What if he gets worse?"

Oliver grinned at her broadly, but nonetheless headed for the door. "Just give him two aspirins and call me in the morning. 'Night."

There was a momentary blast of cold damp air before the door closed. Jane stood there with a wry smile. She was constantly amazed by Dr. Oliver Seymour's flippant attitude and questioned how anyone had ever taken him seriously as a doctor.

Jane shivered in the chilly hallway, curling her socked toes under. She knew she might just as well go to bed herself. She'd made up the sofa to sleep on, but wasn't really inclined to go to bed, even though dawn was virtually around the corner. Oliver had said her houseguest would be okay, but she felt compelled to check on him once more, anyway. She started back up the stairs.

In the three years Jane had been in this house she'd never had any visitors to speak of, and certainly no one to stay overnight. It felt odd to have not only an unexpected and unknown guest, but one who was male and who'd inadvertently commandeered her bed. Jane slipped quietly into the darkened room. At once Jones got up from the floor. He'd stationed himself next to the bed, and whether it was due to habit or because he was keeping an eye on the stranger, Jane could not tell.

"Is everything okay?" she asked in a whisper, and Jones raised his snout to sniff into her warm palm. Jane's eyes found the long body that seemed to take up all the room in her bed. His dark hair had dried and was attractively tousled over his forehead, hiding the large gauze pad at his temple. He was well into a day's beard growth, and Jane found that attractive, as well. But the thing that surprised her most of all was her own interest in this man named Brett Alexander Chandler from somewhere near Boston.

Jane felt something in the feminine center of herself, an awakening and stirring that was surely inappropriate. Maybe it was because she had held him in his weakest, most vulnerable moment that his life mattered to her.

She openly contemplated the sleeping man. From the moment she'd held his limp form there had been an immediate affinity with him. It was the vulnerability. In this man she could feel emotions she hadn't thought most men capable of. Jane had never known a man who could be weak, hurt, unsure, gentle or compassionate. Vulnerable.

Even Oliver possessed a certain hard-core, larger than life profile that had nothing to do with his size. He was a big man, powerfully built. His size could be intimidating, as could his demeanor. But Oliver never threw his weight around, so to speak, and treated everyone the same, man and woman alike. What he expected from one, he expected from the other. *Which probably explains why he's never married,* Jane thought ruefully.

There were obviously men who managed very well alone and who preferred it that way. Oliver was like that. And there were apparently men who needed people only insofar as they could be used. Her father was like that. Those were

An Innocent Man

the only two kinds she had ever known. *So...which one are you, Brett Chandler?*

Jane asked the question silently, cautioning herself about the stranger. But somehow she sensed that he was neither like Oliver or her father. This man had been hurt. Not in the physical way that was evident now, but in the mental and emotional way that is sometimes beyond a person's control. She had seen it and recognized it for a brief moment when their eyes had met.

The man on the bed moved and uttered a soft moan. In the dim light Jane could see that his face and shoulders were moist with perspiration from a fever. Watching him she struggled with a desire to help make him comfortable that alternated with the feeling it would be wiser just to leave him alone until Oliver looked him over in the morning. But she found herself slowly unwinding the towel from her hair. The heavy twisted locks fell to her shoulders as she approached the bed. Awkwardly she leaned over and touched the terry cloth to his face and began gently dabbing at the moisture. He moved his head, but didn't awaken as she continued on to his neck and shoulders, again feeling that melting sensation inside her chest and stomach.

Drowsily his eyes struggled open and fixed their lazy gaze with precision on Jane. They locked on her for an infinitesimal moment, then his lids closed once more. Jane laid her open hand against his bristled cheek, and the stranger settled into sleep.

Jane hugged herself, running her hands up and down her arms to ward off a sudden chill. She could feel a melancholia descend upon her. She thought briefly of going to her study on the first floor and trying to work it out on her P.C. But she knew it would be a waste of time. She rarely produced good copy when she wrote during emotional stress or confusion. Instead, she settled into the high-backed Queen Anne chair, drawing her feet up onto the seat. Jones came to stand before her, finally lying down on the floor. Jane absently stroked the dog's head.

She didn't understand why it happened, but suddenly she was reminded of her father. Perhaps it was because her father was a shadowy, two-dimensional figure like the black and white picture of himself that sat framed on the bureau across from her bed. And the man in the bed, for all that he was a stranger, was so vividly real. Maybe it was because her father as a person had no more depth for her than the studio-posed image, while she felt a connection to Brett Chandler.

He now slept peacefully. Even Jones was sleeping quietly at her side. Jane had to acknowledge the irony of the situation. She was the only one who was fitful and out of sorts. Only she was reacting as if the unconscious man could actually pose a threat to her. Only she was both fascinated and suspicious of him, and he'd not spoken a single word to her. But only she knew and remembered with hurt, even anger, that she had to be very careful who she gave her trust and empathy to.

Chapter Two

He felt as if someone had taken a sledgehammer to the side of his head. It was throbbing painfully, particularly near the temple. He gritted his teeth against the unbelievable pounding and slowly lifted his hand to investigate. Fingers that were still stiff from the cold tentatively touched the wad of gauze over the eye but quickly withdrew when a searing burning sensation shot through his head.

Brett groggily realized that he was tucked snugly under several warm blankets. He also didn't have on a stitch of clothing. He shifted slowly, wanting to sit up, but only managed to drag his upper body far enough to half prop himself against two pillows. His mouth felt dry as cotton, and there was a lack of energy as if he'd been drugged.

It had been foolish to leave the yacht club in such a storm, but he had not wanted to go to begin with. A business dinner with the board of directors of Inland Estates was not his idea of how to spend the Christmas holidays. He wanted to be with his son. Certainly the respected company his father, and his father's father before him, had built from scratch was not to be ignored, but Brett had hoped that he'd done his part in maintaining the family heritage. He could not really complain about the course his life had taken. It might not have gone the way he would have planned, but it had been privileged and comfortable. The decisions he'd made had invariably been for the benefit of others. He had given up a career and even denied himself true love. Yet the thought that he might be complaining, in spite of having so much, made Brett restlessly deny his feelings.

Brett moved his head on the pillows and struggled to open his eyes. He saw at once that the double bed he lay in was an old-fashioned four-poster, and the warm bed linens were in a delicate flowered print. There was a fragrance to his surroundings that was decidedly feminine, like flowers. On his right was a small night table with a lamp and a stack of books and papers. There was an additional pile of newspapers and magazines on a low stool. Along the wall next to a lace-covered window were a bureau and wall mirror. The bureau top was neat and orderly with the trappings of a female occupant, including a stack of freshly laundered underwear that hadn't been put away yet. On the wall opposite the bed was a bookcase nearly the height and width of the wall. It was well stacked with more books, papers, loose-leaf binders and albums. There were no little knickknacks or objets d'art along the edge of the shelves. Just one framed photograph of a handsome middle-aged man, smiling rather urbanely at a studio camera. Brett couldn't make out the inscription in the lower right-hand corner.

He moved his head to the left. He blinked into the dimness, his eyes heavy-lidded, and found the huddled and curled-up figure of a woman in a high-backed chair. She was wrapped in a thick wool afghan up to her chin. One elbow was resting on an arm of the chair, and her cheek was propped against the folded fingers of her hand.

Brett couldn't see her face, and the strain of trying made his head throb so badly that he felt nauseous. But he could tell she had an incredible mass of thick fire-lit hair that was wavy. Her mouth was slightly open in peaceful if not exactly comfortable sleep. He knew with a certainty that this was her room and her bed and she had been displaced for his sake. He wondered now exactly where he was. But against his will his eyelids began to droop. He let them close and felt his head spinning crazily, as if he were falling into a deep, comforting black vacuum.

Brett drifted back into oblivion, and hoped he wouldn't awaken to find that the sleeping beauty in the calico chair had only been a dream.

WHEN JANE HEARD the moan she thought it was Jones shifting on the floor in some doggy dream. But the moans turned to a grunt and a very groggy expletive at just the time Jones placed his paws on her folded legs and licked her hand to bring her awake. Jane opened her eyes, was instantly alert and sat up.

Brett Alexander Chandler had managed to sit up, on the side of the bed. He was holding his head with one hand while reaching with the other for a bedpost, trying to pull himself onto his feet. When he did try, there was an unsettling shout from behind him that startled him into dropping back to the mattress. Brett uttered another oath and squeezed his eyes shut.

"Don't move!" Jane called. She fumbled her way out of her covers and stood up. Taking note of his lean hard back, naked except for a tangle of sheets around his hips and thighs, Jane quickly reached his side. His face was pale and pinched with pain. She watched him waver unsteadily.

"You really should lie back down," she advised calmly, wishing that Oliver would suddenly appear.

Brett lifted his head and opened his eyes to squint painfully at her. The first thing Jane noticed was that his eyes were not just brown as his driver's license had stated, but a startling hazel with distinctive flecks of gray and green.

What Brett noticed was an oval face that was flushed from sleep, with a spot of deep pink where one cheek had rested on her hand. Her eyes were a bright sea green, but wary as she met his examining gaze. And he had been right about her unruly mass of red-gold hair. Brett could also see that whatever other physical attributes this woman had were hidden beneath a crewneck cotton sweater much too large for her. Her state of dress reminded him that he wasn't dressed at all. Discreetly he reached to pull the sheet over his naked middle and once more braced himself to stand.

"You're being very foolish," Jane said as he finally stood up.

"It wouldn't be the first time," he muttered through clenched teeth, attempting to wrap the sheet around the lower part of his swaying body.

"Look...if you'll just lie back down, I'll get you whatever it is you need," Jane suggested.

Brett took hesitant steps toward her. "I don't think you can get me what I need," he grunted.

"Well, what is it?" Jane asked anxiously.

Brett looked at her briefly. And Jane could have sworn he tried to smile. "The bathroom," he said significantly.

"Oh," Jane responded, but stood rooted. Understanding won out over caution, and she reached out an arm to lend some support to his efforts, sliding it around his waist.

Brett looked down at the tousled head tucked against his armpit, and gratefully dropped an arm over her shoulders. Then he spotted the menacing black animal standing squarely in the doorway and eyeing him unflinchingly. He certainly knew better than to assume that all dogs were harmless house pets, especially when they were as big as this Labrador retriever.

"Jones, it's okay. Move now," Jane said in a firm voice, and the dog obediently moved out of their way.

"Bodyguard?" Brett asked in a hoarse voice.

"No, just a companion," she murmured. "Just a few...more steps," she panted, beginning to feel his greater weight on her small frame.

"Thanks," Brett whispered as he lifted his arm away and stood in the bathroom door.

"You really shouldn't be left alone," Jane said logically.

Brett began to close the door, but there was a definite spark of amusement in his eyes. "I think I can manage this on my own. But I'll call you if I need you," he said—and closed the door.

Jane stared at the door, feeling both foolish and annoyed. But she waited patiently until it opened again. Then there was a moment while they both physically confronted each other. He was much taller than she'd thought he would be, and every bit as masculine. She tried not to let her eyes wander over his bare hair-covered torso or the firm full line of his mouth with its grooved corners. Now that his hair was dry, it was clear that it was peppered with gray.

Jane had forgotten how she'd dressed the night before, but now this stranger's silent appraisal, every bit as open and frank as her own, seemed to say there was still a lot of her apparent behind this ridiculous garb. High rounded breasts pressed through the cotton sweater. Long legs tapered into slender ankles. Brett surmised that she was not a very young woman. There was character and experience in her face, in the eyes that were assessing and clear. A mouth that in its firmness now lacked the sensual softness he'd glimpsed as she slept. There was also something very careful about the way she held herself. A little apart and aloof. Yet she seemed more accepting than embarrassed by the present circumstances.

"Thanks for waiting," Brett said hoarsely, breaking the trance between them. "I think I can make it back on my own."

She shook her head. "I doubt it. And I'd rather not have to try and lift you up from the floor if you faint." Brett didn't protest anymore as she helped him back to the bedroom. He obviously wasn't going to let his pride make a fool of himself.

Slowly he sat down on the bed with his eyes closed against waves of throbbing pain and nausea. "I . . . I'm really sorry to . . . impose on you like this. And I'm grateful for all your help."

The apology was unexpected, and Jane responded with a small shrug of her shoulders, absently pushing her hair away from her face. The motion caused her sweater to rise over her thighs, and Brett's gaze was automatically drawn to their smooth shapely length. Silently he lamented his inability to fully appreciate them at that moment.

The pale light coming through the window reminded them both that the sun was rising. Brett slowly began to hunt around the bed for his clothes. "I'd better get myself together and be on my way."

"I'm afraid that's not possible." Jane spoke calmly, watching as he furrowed his damp brow and glanced around the room, looking for his clothes. "Oliver said you were in no shape to go anywhere."

"Oliver?" he questioned.

Jane ignored his inquiry. "Beyond that, you'll never make it past the door, and your clothes are still damp from last night."

He stopped his search to look at her. He liked the sound of her voice. It was low and smoothly controlled. She was not easily intimidated. For a moment he considered that he would like to stay. But there were people who would want to know why he had not returned to them.

"Look . . . I appreciate your concern, and all the trouble you went to for me. But I have to go. . . ." He stopped talking and just sat there. Finally his weakened state got the better of him, and with a muttered oath he sank back between the sheets. Jane came forward to adjust the covers over his panting chest.

"I think Oliver should look at you first and decide if you can leave or not. In the meantime, I'll get you something to drink and maybe some aspirin." He now lay unmoving, with his eyes closed. Jane stood and headed toward the closet, stepping over Jones's prone body in the middle of the floor.

"And what if I insist on leaving?" came the gravelly voice from the bed. There was no challenge in his voice at all.

Jane turned to look at him, her arms holding jeans, a blouse and sweater and fresh underwear. "Jones," she called quietly, and the great dog came to stand before her with his tongue lolling out of the side of his mouth. "Guard him!" She pointed imperiously to the man on the bed, who watched her with interest through barely opened eyes. Then Jane pointed to the floor. "Mr. Chandler is *not* to leave this room."

Brett chuckled silently at her earnest commands to the dog, but responded, "You have the advantage."

Jane nodded and glanced rather haughtily at him. "Jones is well trained. He'll do as I say."

"No...not the dog."

Jane looked quizzical.

"You obviously know who I am. Who are you?"

Jane was not often inclined to tell people her full name, but for an instant she nearly blurted it out to this stranger.

"Jane Lindsay," she stated simply.

He continued to view her through heavy-lidded eyes. "Jane..." he repeated with a curious softness to his voice. "Are you really going to keep me prisoner here?"

"I didn't go to all the trouble of saving you last night so you can foolishly kill yourself this morning. You'll have to wait until Oliver gets here."

"I really won't need Oliver's permission, you know. Whoever he is," Brett said with the first hint of authority in his voice.

Instead of answering him, she gave a final command to the dog.

"Stay!" The dog slowly lowered his body right across the doorway, effectively blocking the entrance. He looked impartially at the man on the bed and then at Jane. "Good boy," Jane crooned, gave her guest a triumphant look and walked from the room.

"Your round, Jane Lindsay." And all the way to the bathroom to wash and dress Jane could hear Brett Chandler chuckling in genuine amusement. The sound curved her mouth in a reluctant smile.

JANE STOOD at the window, sipping slowly from her mug of tea. It had stopped snowing during the night, but the wind still howled outside and it was very cold. Her eyes were following Oliver's approach as he walked from the sports car belonging to Brett Chandler that was still crazily angled off the embankment. She was wondering why he'd found it necessary to search the disabled car so thoroughly.

Jane had phoned Oliver as soon as she'd dressed, to tell him his patient and her houseguest had regained consciousness and was getting decidedly antsy. When she looked into the room, however, Brett Chandler was much more subdued, and obediently took the two aspirins and water she gave him. He fell asleep again almost immediately. Despite his declarations to the contrary, Brett Chandler wasn't fit to go anywhere.

Oliver had promised to come over, and Jane had poured herself a second cup of tea when she glanced out the window and spotted Oliver. Yet when she'd gone to open the door, Oliver had continued on toward the silver car, not noticing Jane in the doorway.

She assumed Oliver would check to make sure the car was okay, possibly see if there was any luggage. But Jane had been a bit shocked to witness Oliver's search. She had no idea what he might be looking for.

Finally Oliver started back in her direction. Jane held the door open and Oliver walked in with a bellows of frosty air surrounding him. His cheeks and nose were ruddy from the cold and some condensation had frozen in his gray mustache and trimmed beard.

"I have coffee on," Jane said, stepping back as Oliver stripped off his sheepskin coat. From the inside pocket he removed a stethoscope and a small leather pouch, laying his things on the hall table.

"I brought a change of dressing for the patient and another sedative."

"I don't think you'll need it," Jane offered, as Oliver blew on his cold hands and strode into the kitchen.

"Oh?" He poured coffee, giving Jane a quizzical look.

"He was pretty alert when he came to this morning. Thanked me for my hospitality and said he had to leave."

"Has he contacted anyone as to his whereabouts? Made any phone calls?" Oliver asked sharply. Again Jane was struck by the nature of Oliver's curiosity about the man upstairs.

"No. He just seemed to feel he was imposing. I told him he couldn't go anywhere until you'd given the okay, or else I wouldn't be responsible for what happened to him. I had to leave Jones standing guard over him to make my point."

Oliver chuckled, his eyes regarding Jane with surprise. "Oh, you did, did you? What's he up to now?"

"Sleeping," Jane said as Oliver walked past her, gathered up his equipment from the table and started up the stairs.

"Well, let's go see how he's doing...."

"Oliver," Jane stood at the foot of the stairs looking up to the big man who now paused halfway up to look back on her. "What were you looking for in his car?"

For a split second Jane again saw surprise in Oliver's gray eyes. "Just checking to see if he'd left anything important, before I call the towing service in town to come haul the car out of that ditch." He didn't wait for any response, just continued up the stairs. Since his answer made perfect sense to her, Jane quickly put the matter aside. When they reached the room, Brett was just coming awake.

"Good morning!" Oliver roared, and chuckled as Brett winced at the boisterous greeting. Jane came in more quietly, again very physically aware of him. Oliver sat on the edge of the bed, his trained eyes quickly looking over Brett's countenance. His coloring this morning was a bit healthier.

"I'm Dr. Oliver Seymour. How are you feeling?"

Brett quirked a brow. "I'd kill for a cup of decent coffee." He gave Oliver a lopsided grin.

Oliver laughed, and even Jane was charmed. This man was not a complainer.

"Well, I guess that means you're gonna live. Let's see how you're doing here, then we'll see about getting you something to eat."

Oliver began with a preliminary exam, and proceeded to change the gauze pad taped to Brett's temple. All the time Oliver was performing his small chore, Brett's gaze continually sought out Jane across the room as she watched what was happening. She couldn't help thinking how handsome and roguish he appeared with his strong unshaven face and disheveled hair. She did not flinch from his gaze. It was openly curious. But Jane was smart enough and old enough to know that it was easy for that kind of interest to be superficial.

"Anything else that still hurts?" Oliver asked as he gathered his equipment.

Brett warily closed his eyes and tilted his head back against the pillow. "No. I just feel like an explosion went off in my head and the dust is still settling."

Oliver nodded. "That's an accurate way of putting it. I wouldn't recommend trying to move for a while. You're none the worse for your adventure last night, but by tomorrow you'll feel more the thing."

Brett was shaking his head, and ran his hand through his thick hair. "I have some very important business to take care of and people to see. I was on my way back from a meeting last night. I didn't expect to end up in a ditch."

Oliver thoughtfully scratched his short beard. "Well, we couldn't call anyone for you last night. Couldn't find any names or numbers. Sorry. We had to look through your ID."

Brett waved the apology aside. "I understand...."

"Of course, you should call your family or whoever, but as your temporary doctor in charge, you need at least another twenty-four hours of rest."

Brett was shaking his head again, now with a small show of impatience. There was also a sound of impatience from Jane, and both men turned their heads to look at her.

"Unless you're planning on tying Mr. Chandler to the bedposts, I think we should let him go if he wants to, Oliver."

There was a silence in the room except for the panting of Jones, who had quietly and unobtrusively made his way back upstairs and was seated in front of Jane. They presented an unusual united front, the attractive observant woman with her riot of wavy hair and exotic green eyes, and her brute of an animal. Beauty and the Beast, Brett thought to himself.

Oliver struggled against a smile. It was unusual for Jane to show much emotion about anything or anyone around her. It was not indifference, just a way of protecting herself. Oliver found it interesting that she was so pointedly vocal about this stranger.

Brett was also surprised. He narrowed his eyes at Jane, seeing a slightly different woman than the one he'd found this morning upon waking up. This one facing him now was defensive and critical. Brett wondered about the confusing change.

"I think the lady would like to see me leave...."

"I think the lady doth protest too much," Oliver murmured.

"Mr. Chandler is a grown man perfectly capable of seeing after himself, although it hasn't been demonstrated so far," Jane said quietly in a caustic tone. In truth she was stunned by her outburst, too. But she had a sudden compulsion to see Brett Chandler gone while she was still in control. She didn't like the onslaught of feelings she'd experienced since meeting this man just a few hours ago. Even Oliver had done strange things since his arrival. Brett had a presence that commanded attention. And she'd known too many men who'd taken unfair advantage by being charming.

Jane blinked when she realized that both men were staring curiously at her. She realized as well how quickly she'd let her own personal confusion over Brett Chandler's presence escalate into an unreasonable outburst. Slowly Jane got hold of herself.

"I...I mean," she began, appearing suddenly vulnerable. "I don't want Mr. Chandler to think we're keeping him here against his will."

"Would you rather he left? I'm sure we can make arrangements to have him picked up and moved," Oliver said rather formally, and it was enough to make Jane feel properly chastened. She wanted to remain indifferent, and Oliver wasn't going to let her.

Jane frowned slightly at the sense of having been outmaneuvered. "Of course not. That is...if you think that...if it's better for..." Jane opened her mouth to say more but felt as though she was putting her foot in it. She gave up in defeat. "It's up to you," she said to no one in particular. Then she lifted her head proudly and turned to leave the room. After a second's hesitation Jones quickly trotted along behind her.

In silence Oliver went back to placing things in his bag, while Brett stared at the open doorway. He was considering the astonishing range of emotions that had played over Jane Lindsay's features; he found it intriguing. If he left he might never have an opportunity to get a sense of who she was, this woman who had come to his aid but who was so uneasy in his presence.

Brett finally made a decision. "I think I'll take your advice and stay until tomorrow," he said to Oliver.

"Good," Oliver replied, heaving up his body from the edge of the bed.

Brett studied him. "That is, if you're *sure* you don't mind."

Oliver began to laugh softly. "This is Jane's house, not mine. And no, I am *not* her husband, father or lover."

"I'm sorry," Brett said easily. "I just wasn't sure...."

"Forget it. I'm just a friend who lives down the road."

Brett lay back and regarded the other man with interest. "A doctor friend from down the road. What kind of doctor?"

Oliver folded his arms over his brawny chest. "I'm a retired pediatrician."

Brett was surprised. It was hard to imagine this huge man dealing gently with the fragile bodies of infants and small children.

"I do a little clinic work at the hospital in Southampton, but basically I've given up private practice."

Brett thought the big man too young for real retirement. He couldn't be more than fifty-five. "Why did you give it up?"

Oliver pursed his lips. He shrugged negligently. "Malpractice insurance was getting to be too expensive to maintain. Too many people had taken it into their heads that if they didn't get a perfect child, it was obviously the doctor's fault."

Oliver did not sound angry about this, but Brett did sense regret. "And what's the other reason?" Brett asked astutely, knowing there was one.

Oliver was openly impressed, and a look of respect filled his eyes. He thought carefully for a second before speaking.

"I was seeing far too many children who weren't truly wanted by their parents. Too many people never should have been parents in the first place. They were either unwilling or unable to give what I call quality attention to their kids. I didn't feel I could change anything I saw or make a difference. So I gave it up."

The doctor had touched on a sore topic with Brett—the lack of time he spent with his own son. Sometimes circumstances were not quite as clear-cut as Oliver seemed to think they should be. Sometimes people had less control over their lives than they thought they had.

"Are you married, Doctor?"

"Naw!" Oliver laughed. "Too grouchy."

"Children?"

"Too careful."

"You're a pediatrician, and yet you don't like children?" Brett asked, puzzled.

"I am a pediatrician because I *love* children. But being their doctor and being their father is not the same." Oliver scratched his chin and frowned. "I guess I really wasn't sure how good a father I'd make. So...I never tried."

The subject was carefully changed.

"How did I get here?" Brett questioned.

"I think the dog knew something was wrong and managed to get Jane to follow him to where you had the accident. Jane found you hurt and unconscious and sent Jones to get me."

Brett raised a brow. "It sounds like I was very lucky. Smart dog."

"Yep. I did what I could to make you comfortable last night. You weren't in any real danger so I didn't take you to the hospital. But like I said, Jane and I couldn't find anyone to call for you."

"What about my car?" Brett asked.

"Well, it won't start, but I don't think there's any real damage to it. I called a garage in town and they're going to send a tow rig to pull it out of that drift as soon as the road's clear."

Brett nodded wearily, running his hands through his hair. "I really appreciate your help."

"I didn't do much. It's really Jane you have to thank. She's been taking care of you."

"So I gathered," Brett said, with the first show of any embarrassment for his circumstances as he looked around the room with its few but very feminine belongings. "Which reminds me, what happened to my clothes?"

Oliver grinned. "You were pretty wet and frozen when we got you back here last night. I stripped you down to your birthday suit. Your things are downstairs drying in the laundry room. But I'm sure Jane can find you something to wear until everything's dry." Oliver's reply received a nod. Then his eyes grew narrow and speculative. "Now it's my turn," he said smoothly.

Brett immediately heard the difference in his tone.

"How *did* you get here?"

"My mother owns a house out in the Hamptons. I drove down from Boston and took the ferry across the sound yesterday afternoon for an important dinner meeting last night at the yacht club, after which I'd hoped to spend the rest of the holidays with my son. I was trying to get back to my mother's when I had the accident."

Oliver frowned down at his boots. "Do you realize that the road from the yacht club is nowhere near where we found you?"

Brett quirked a brow. "No, I didn't. I'm not familiar with Montauk, and it's been years since I've been to the yacht club. I might point out that the weather conditions for driving were not ideal."

"There is that," Oliver conceded, gathering his things. "I take it your wife didn't accompany you to this... er...dinner?"

For a moment Brett was tempted to object to the line of questioning. But then he reasoned that, having already mentioned his son, it was a fair assumption that he was married.

"My wife died almost ten years ago," he stated without any emotion.

Since Oliver couldn't think of an adequate response, he didn't make one. He lifted a hand in a vague gesture and walked to the door. "Well...I've done all I can do. Jane will get you something to eat. I recommend bed rest and more sleep."

"Are you sure Miss Lindsay won't mind?"

Oliver stopped at the door. "Miss Lindsay is not used to having company. You've thrown a monkey wrench into her routine, and she's still figuring out what to do."

Brett was surprised by the information. Why would someone that attractive never have visitors beyond an outspoken but friendly doctor? Why did she only have a black Labrador retriever for companionship? And why was she out in Montauk all alone, to begin with?

"I don't want to make more work for her," Brett said sincerely. "You've both done more than enough for me, as it is."

Oliver chuckled. "Don't worry about it. Wait until you get my bill." With that he left the room.

Brett lay back and thought about the two people who'd come to his aid the night before. Oliver Seymour seemed to be very up-front and honest. And although he claimed mere friendship, Brett could detect a certain proprietary air toward Jane Lindsay. Protective. There was no question that Oliver thought a lot of her.

As for Jane herself... frankly, she was a puzzle, although a pretty one. Brett couldn't help feeling there was something very familiar about her, not only in her face but in her voice. Using the line "Haven't I seen you somewhere before?" would have been a very poor start to finding out. Brett was sure that Jane Lindsay would not respond to the obvious.

Other than the framed photo on the bureau, there was nothing in the room to tell him much about her. She read a great deal, as was evident from the filled bookcase. And it was not frivolous stuff, judging from the titles. Things on economy, nuclear energy, child welfare, the homeless.

Jane represented a woman probably not much past thirty who was intelligent and bright. He didn't know what she did for a living, but it allowed her to live in relative comfort in one of Long Island's oldest and wealthiest communities. She lived alone and seemed capable of taking care of herself with a minimum of things or people around her. For a woman who was so pretty, there was a curious lack of vanity about her. She seemed to favor clothes that were purely functional and that did nothing to enhance or emphasize what he guessed to be a comely body. She didn't wear jewelry or makeup or anything that would bring attention to her person. Her hair, a glorious rich strawberry blonde with sparkling highlights, would probably be considered unfashionably long, but he really liked its wildness.

Jane Lindsay had all the makings of a truly stunning woman, but either didn't know it or didn't care. Brett had known only one other woman who wasn't vastly concerned with her looks and whether or not men found her attractive. That had been his wife, Carolyn.

Brett's consideration of Jane quickly switched by way of comparison to one of his late wife. Carolyn could not be said to have been beautiful, but she'd always possessed a kind of pale delicate prettiness that always drew attention to herself because she appeared so helpless. In truth, she had been. Brett had known her all his life. Carolyn was an overprotected shy girl with not much to say for herself. She had no particular interests, and seemed inclined to do or say whatever was expected of her. It had led Brett to be protective of her when they were children, and a comfortable confidant and escort as a teenager.

Brett could hardly imagine Carolyn managing alone, and of course she'd never had to. Her father, a stern real estate magnate, ran her life the way he ran his business. He expected unquestioning obedience from her the same way he would one of his employees. But when Stanley Hastings had gone as far as to handpick even a husband for her, Carolyn refused to comply for the one and only time in her life. She'd run tearfully to the Chandler household, more specifically to Brett, pleading for him to do something.

He was only twenty-five at the time and still trying to establish a career as an aeronautical engineer rather than go into the family business. But his father died suddenly, ending the indecision. Brett had always loved Carolyn, but only as one loved a favorite younger sister. He'd never thought of marriage to her until her pleas for him to save her had once again brought out his protective instincts.

He'd known that Carolyn's father would not voice many objections to the union. Brett had acutely understood that with the joining of the two families and their real estate interests, Stanley Hastings, through his son-in-law, hoped to control it all someday. In that respect he was to find he'd greatly underestimated the character of both young people.

So they were married, and Brett had sidelined his interest in designing planes for the more practical goals of real estate and taking care of a wife. Brett was shortly to find that although Carolyn was sweet, trusted him beyond question and relied completely on his judgment, sweetness did not make for either great love or passion. He'd also hoped that motherhood eighteen months later would mature her and make her more self-reliant. But it had not. If anything, Carolyn seemed afraid of the infant Jonathan, as if the responsibility was too overwhelming.

Brett closed his eyes, feeling the sharp pain behind his lids. He didn't want to think of either love or passion. He particularly didn't want to think of Carolyn, with whom not even his patience and delicacy could spark more than obedient tolerance for the physical side of their relationship. While she was not put off by sex, it was obvious she could have lived the rest of her life without it. Brett had always seen it as his failure that he could not teach her the joy that was possible with their intimacy. Of course, she'd simply died too young to have experienced a lot of things.

Suddenly Jane Lindsay came back to mind, as he'd seen her that morning. He recalled her long shapely legs and firm high breasts with their prominent centers outlined beneath the sweater. She had not been coy or shy with him, an indication that she didn't resort to games or subterfuge with the opposite sex. But Brett couldn't help but wonder what it would take to shake her and get some show of reaction.

When Brett opened his eyes again, Jane was standing in the bedroom doorway, thoughtfully watching him. Then suddenly, for no other reason than the awareness that this woman was naturally, freshly attractive to him, Brett felt his body physically responding to her. It was completely unexpected and he shifted restlessly on the bed to gain control.

Brett noticed that except for a curling froth of hair over her forehead, she'd gained the upper hand on her thick hair by tying a rolled bandanna around it.

"Oliver tells me you've decided to stay," she said, her arms overburdened with clothes and a small tray of food.

Brett barely smiled. "No. Actually, I was going to ask you if you'd mind my company for one more night. Then I promise I'll be gone."

The sincere request flustered Jane and she was caught between being indifferent and softening toward him. Instead she suddenly became clumsy. The tray tilted precariously.

"Here, let me help you," Brett said, starting to rise from the bed. It was only when he saw Jane's gaze drop to his waist and widen that he remembered he had no clothes on. He quickly recovered and hastily sank back. The sudden movement jarred his whole body, reminding him of the injury to his head. "Damn! On second thought..."

"I'll forgive you for not being gallant," Jane quipped with a spark of humor, a sudden rosiness in her cheeks. She put the tray down on the night table next to the bed. "I brought you some coffee and made an omelet and some toast. I hope that's okay."

"*Anything* would be okay," Brett said, beginning to feel tired again. He tasted the coffee. Sighing dramatically he closed his eyes. "Ahh... ambrosia!"

Jane smiled to herself as she knelt to remove the pile of newspapers from the stool and replace them with the clothing she'd brought in. She sat back suddenly on her heels and lifted her head to find Brett staring at her. Jane found herself fascinated by his eyes and his habit of looking directly at a person as if to penetrate all the outer shells. She got quickly to her feet. She had no intention of letting him get *that* close.

Brett sensed her withdrawal and reached for the plate of food. "This looks wonderful," he complimented her as he lifted the fork. "I'll probably eat the plate as well."

Jane reluctantly admitted to herself that she liked the low resonant timbre of his deep voice. And she very much liked his sense of humor. It was something she'd only previously credited Oliver with having, although she thought at times that Oliver's was decidedly black. After she'd put away her stack of laundered clothing and checked to see if she'd gotten all the newspapers together, Jane could think of no other reason for staying and turned to the door.

Brett was reluctant to have her leave, wanting her company and a chance to learn more about her. His voice stopped her at the door. "Er... Can I possibly get another cup of coffee?" he asked. "The omelet was excellent. I'll have to remember the name of this place," he teased.

"Don't!" Jane said. "I'm sorry, but... I don't make a habit of coming to the aid of complete strangers." She picked up the tray without looking at him.

"I'm sorry," Brett said in a low voice. "That was a thoughtless thing to say, considering how much trouble I've put you through."

Once again she was surprised by his sincerity and his immediate consideration for her feelings. This man was very likable.

"Short of trying to commit suicide, I don't imagine that you chose to have an accident in my backyard. I just don't want you to..."

"Take too much for granted," Brett supplied, watching her. He'd been correct in his first impression of Jane Lindsay. She was a *very* careful woman.

"That's correct."

"I understand," Brett said. He hesitated. "But I do have two other favors to ask before I wear out my welcome. I'd appreciate it if you could phone my family and let them know I'm okay."

Jane felt ashamed of having been so contrary a moment ago. She nodded and wrote down the number as he recited it.

"And the second request?" she asked.

Brett's eyes held her gaze deliberately. "Will you come back later and keep me company?"

She just stared at him. In a million years she never would have guessed he'd ask such a thing of her. But the prospect was interesting, and Jane couldn't deny that. *Yes,* she was a little curious about him. *Yes,* it might be interesting to know a bit more.

"Yes," she said, making an odd movement of her head that was a half shake and half nod, as if she couldn't quite make up her mind.

Brett gave her a small smile but didn't say anything more.

"By the way," she added as she leaned against the door frame. "All of your clothes are dried and there on the stool. There's also a robe and towel. You may want a shower and shave later."

"Thanks," Brett responded. "Both will go a long ways toward making me feel human again. Whose bathrobe is it?"

Jane saw a look in his eyes. "It belongs to the man who owns this house," she said honestly.

"Then perhaps I shouldn't use it." He was fishing, and he knew it.

"Why?" Jane challenged him at once.

"I think it would make us both uncomfortable."

"*I'm* not the least uncomfortable," she said clearly. "*He* wouldn't care, and *you* shouldn't, unless you're allergic to cotton."

She was sorely tempted to slam the door behind her, but stopped. She was *not* going to let his false suspicions hang in the air. "It's only a warm bathrobe, Mr. Chandler. Don't try to draw conclusions from it. You'd be dead wrong."

They stared at each other until Jane closed the door between them.

Brett lifted a brow and a corner of his mouth in a wry smile and let out a low whistle through his teeth. "You've got spirit, Jane Lindsay," he mused to himself, liking that show of strength in her. But he was equally intrigued with the part of herself she was protecting so fiercely.

It was a full hour before Jane got back upstairs with the second cup of coffee. She'd made the call to the Hamptons and had not been surprised when a housekeeper answered and politely offered to bring Mrs. Chandler to the phone.

Until that moment Jane had not considered that Brett Chandler might be married, since he wore no ring and had not immediately asked to call a wife. Now Jane could only wonder what Mrs. Chandler's reaction was going to be upon hearing her husband had spent the night at the home of an unknown woman, no matter what the situation.

When a cultured airy voice finally answered, Jane was flustered into a simple opening that had no finesse but was to the point.

"Hello, Mrs. Chandler? I'm calling about your husband." Jane waited nervously. Then the voice laughed cheerfully.

"Heavens, I hope not. My husband's been dead for more than ten years!"

"Oh," Jane whispered, feeling foolish. "Then..."

"You must be referring to my son. Is he all right?" Mrs. Chandler anxiously asked.

"Yes, he is. He had a car accident last night in the storm. He suffered a gash on the head and a mild concussion, but he's fine."

"Are you a friend of his?" The voice hesitated.

Jane smiled. "No . . . I found him after it happened and a neighbor helped to get him to my house. I live in Montauk. Your son asked if I would call and assure you he's okay."

"Well, I am relieved to hear that. He left an important dinner party at the club and never made it home. I thought his family had finally driven him to run away." She laughed lightly.

Again Jane smiled. The man upstairs did not strike her as being irresponsible. She imagined that if he had problems he'd stand and face them.

"Has he seen a doctor yet?" Jane was asked.

"As a matter of fact, yes, but he isn't seriously hurt."

"That's good. What did you say your name was?"

"I'm sorry, I didn't. It's Jane Lindsay."

"Thank you so much, Miss Lindsay, for calling me. Do you have any idea when Brett can be moved?"

"Tomorrow. . . ."

"Fine. Tell him for me he's not to get into that car and drive himself. I'll send someone to pick him up in the afternoon. Where are you located?"

Jane supplied the information and hung up. Ruefully she concluded that Brett Alexander Chandler not only came from a family of means, but also that the easy humor must be hereditary. At once Jane put her curiosity in him into a proper perspective. There was no question about it; it couldn't possibly be pursued. The yacht and country club group put her most definitely beyond the pale.

With a funny sense of disappointment Jane went to refill his coffee cup. She was still inordinately curious as to whether there was a second Mrs. Chandler.

Chapter Three

There didn't seem to be any sound at all in the house. It was almost eight o'clock in the morning and Brett was used to rising earlier, but a persistent nagging headache had seduced him into an extra hour of languishing between Jane's warm sheets. He desperately wanted coffee, but more than that, he just wanted to get up and move around.

Halfway down the stairs the Labrador silently appeared below and stared up at Brett. The animal had never seemed more than distantly interested in his presence, and as Brett calmly descended, the dog watched his progress. Then Jones quietly turned and ambled back the way he'd come. Brett knew that Jane had to be somewhere close at hand, since the dog almost never left her side.

He sniffed the aroma of freshly brewed coffee and followed the scent. At the kitchen door he stopped to take in the view that greeted him. Jane was leaning forward on the counter, reading through a recipe book. Next to her stood a mug of coffee and a mixing bowl containing flour, milk and two broken eggs. She sighed and straightened from her provocative position to stand with a hand on one hip as she used an index finger to follow the written directions.

"I don't think I have any confectioner's sugar, Jones. Do you suppose it will matter?" Jane murmured to her companion.

Brett smiled and stepped into the kitchen. "I think it depends on what you want it for," he offered.

Jane swung her head around, to find Brett only a few feet behind her. All she could do was stare and feel her stomach muscles tighten.

"I'm sorry. I didn't mean to frighten you," Brett apologized with a smile as his eyes swept over her. At this range he could see how smooth her skin was, and how her cheeks seemed to always have a natural rosiness of their own. Her hair was tied back, the same as the day before with its wispy escaping soft tendrils.

Jane swallowed, feeling somewhat overwhelmed. In his unconscious state with his hair matted with snow and his skin pale and bruised from the accident, she could tell Brett Chandler was a well-built, good-looking man. Now he'd shaved and showered and dressed. The overall effect left Jane speechless and all her senses awakened . . . as if after a very long dormancy.

Brett's cheeks and jaw showed a firmly sculptured face with strong lines and character. His white formal shirt was open at the throat, sans bow tie, of course, and the formal black slacks just emphasized his lean body and the muscular length of his legs. When she realized she was staring, Jane lowered her gaze to the recipe book.

"No. You didn't frighten me. I just thought you were still asleep."

Brett turned to lean back against the edge of the counter next to her. "I think I've had enough sleep to last a month. I'm not usually such a slug, you know."

Jane looked at him earnestly. "I'm sure the last few days must have been very boring for you."

Brett's hazel eyes became dark gray as he looked right at her. "I wasn't bored at all. If I had to pick someone to come to my rescue again, it would still be you." His voice was low and caressing.

Jane gnawed the inside of her bottom lip, trying not to overreact to his words, although they did make her feel suddenly lighthearted. "And Oliver," she added.

Brett watched her and grinned slowly. "Okay, if you insist. Oliver, too."

He looked at the containers and jars around her. "What do you need confectioner's sugar for?" he asked, at the same time reaching for a clean mug from a rack over the sink and helping himself to coffee. "Are you making breakfast for us?"

"I was going to make a large puff pancake sprinkled with confectioner's sugar. But it's been a while and I forget some of the ingredients." Then she became impatient with herself for such fancifulness. "But maybe you'd prefer something else. Something simple like eggs or cereal...."

Brett lightly touched the hand that still rested on her hip. "Oh, no... you're not going to dangle a puff pancake before me and then substitute cereal. Let's have the pancake... even without the sugar," he said very naturally and removed his hand.

Brett moved away from the counter, determined not to do anything that she could misinterpret. He rather liked Jane Lindsay and he wanted her to be comfortable with him. Considering he would leave in a few hours, perhaps it was a foolish thought. But Brett didn't have a sense that their meeting should come to an end.

"Look, I'm probably in the way. Do you mind if I wander around and get my land legs back?"

Jane shook her head, tendrils of hair feathering around her face. "No, go ahead," she said with some relief. "I'll just finish here."

Brett smiled and left the kitchen.

Jane looked at the empty doorway, slowly relaxing again. In a way she was glad that when he was gone she'd stop being so damned nervous. On the other hand it had been rather different, having someone like him around. He was not someone who could be ignored, nor had she been able to do that since his arrival.

Jane turned back to the sink and absently set about finishing the batter for the pancake, but her mind now went back to the night before. Everything about it had been different and unusual. Much later, after she'd reported the conversation with his mother and brought the second cup of coffee, Jane had sensed the uniqueness of the situation. She'd threatened to sic Jones on him if he didn't stay put and get more rest. Jane had given him two more aspirins, and Brett had willingly gone back to sleep for the rest of the afternoon.

It had been nearly nine in the evening when her guest was awakened again. Oliver had called the hour before and declined the invitation to join her for dinner.

"What do you mean, you can't make it for dinner?" Jane had asked irrationally.

"I mean I'm not coming to dinner tonight. I mean I got invited for a couple of beers and a game of cards. Now, I know you're prettier, Jane . . . but you don't play poker."

"But . . . what about Mr. Chandler?"

"What about him?"

"What am I supposed to do with him the rest of the evening?" Jane asked with uncharacteristic panic in her voice.

Oliver laughed. "That's a loaded question. I don't think you'll have to do anything with him. I don't think he has the energy."

"What?" Jane asked, confused.

"Never mind. Look, just have a nice quiet dinner. And it will do you good to talk to someone else besides me and Jones."

"Oliver, this is not funny."

Oliver sighed. "Come on, take it easy. Don't do anything you don't want to do. Let him read a newspaper. Tell him Jones's life story...."

"Oliver..."

"Tell him *your* life story."

There was a sudden silence.

"Okay, not a good idea." Oliver sighed again. "You'll be okay. Just remember he'll be gone tomorrow. It's not like you to get so rattled over the presence of one injured man."

Jane shook her head. "You don't understand. And you're no help at all, Oliver Seymour," she muttered.

"I'm more help than you realize. I'll see you tomorrow." And he hung up.

So there she was, fixing another tray of food and taking it up to Brett Chandler for dinner. When she entered her room she noticed that he had donned the white terry-cloth robe, and wisely neither of them made mention of it or its owner.

"How are you feeling?" she asked.

"Much better." Brett sighed. "Dr. Seymour was right. Sleep helped a lot. What time is it?" he asked, using his hands to comb his springy hair into order.

"Not quite nine," Jane said, looking for a place to set down the bed tray. "Sit back in bed," she ordered him and set the tray across his lap.

"Mmm. You must have heard my stomach protesting from downstairs," Brett said wryly and looked up at her. "Aren't you going to eat?"

Jane shrugged, backing toward the door. "Yes, of course. My dinner is downstairs."

"Since I've been ordered to stay put, why don't you fix another plate and join me?" He observed her indecision and could see the excuses forming in her head. "I really would rather have your company. Please?"

That was the magic word, although she didn't smile, merely nodded. "All right. I'll be right back."

Brett grinned as he watched her leave, feeling as if he'd made some progress. Jane was back quickly, and sat in the Queen Anne chair with her food on a smaller tray. She realized this was much nicer than eating downstairs in the kitchen.

"Mr. Chandler, I spoke to Oliver, but he won't be coming to see you tonight. He doesn't think you need him anymore."

Brett nodded. "He's right. I don't." He tilted his head at Jane. "Considering all we've been through in twenty-four hours, I think first names are in order. Me Brett. You Jane." He was actually rewarded with a full smile that had him staring at her for a long second. She was more than just pretty when she smiled.

"Brett, then," she whispered.

There was a very comfortable silence as they ate. Jane stole furtive looks at him, but Brett was far less subtle and openly stared at her from time to time.

"So, tell me about yourself," Brett ventured casually. "What kind of work do you do?"

She analyzed and digested the question, looking down at her plate. "I'm a writer."

"What kind of writer?"

"Free-lance. I do articles, essays, commentaries. Sometimes I'm assigned topics to research and write about for specific publications."

Brett chewed thoughtfully. "Have I read anything by you?"

"If you read *Esquire, Insight, Business Week, Savvy . . .*"

"I do. But now I'll have to pay more attention to who writes what I read." They talked about what she did. He proved to be skilled at drawing Jane out of her tendency to reticence and she found herself answering his questions un-self-consciously.

When they'd both finished eating, Jane put everything onto one tray to take back to the kitchen. "I'd better take this stuff downstairs. I have to let Jones out for his run...."

"Will you come back?" he interrupted softly.

Jane didn't meet his gaze. "It is getting late, and I..."

"Am I keeping you from something?" he asked, but Jane could see he wasn't trying to be sarcastic. True, there was always a project to finish or one to start. Always something to edit or process. But she didn't have to do it tonight. She knew she'd never be able to concentrate.

"No, there's nothing, I guess. I mean, I do like to watch the late-night news and read the papers, but..."

"Good. So do I. If you have a TV up here we can watch it together." He was very comfortable with his suggestion, and it made Jane feel like he'd made himself right at home. But Jane wasn't used to sharing things, particularly a home, with anyone. She was not used to sharing herself.

"Well...there is a small one behind my chair. I usually watch the one in the study downstairs."

"We can set the smaller one on the bureau," Brett offered.

"Yes, I suppose we could," Jane murmured. "I'll be right back."

When she'd returned to the room it was eleven and time for the local news to come on. Jane put the set on the bureau where they could both easily view it. There was no talking while they watched, and Brett seemed totally absorbed in the coverage of the day's events.

Jane was always interested in how the local networks presented their individual programs. She knew it to be a highly competitive aspect of TV. After all, the news was essentially the same in terms of facts and information, but all the stations were constantly vying to present them to the public in a new way. It was interesting to see how creative the network programmers and directors could get with cold facts. Secondly, she watched with fascination the constant turnover of faces and personalities hired to report and anchor the news. Appearance and approach counted for a lot. It was up to the faces, the personalities, the quirky off-beat characters to convince an audience that what they did with the news was better than the other guys. It boiled down to images, charisma... and ratings. What made good journalism or good reporting, what made for news might be questionable. But on the air, everyone looked beautiful.

Halfway through the national news the commentator announced that a special report was waiting from the station's Washington correspondent. Jane froze. Then she quickly got up from her chair and crossed to the TV. "Let's see what the other station is doing," she said as she reached to turn the channel.

"Let's hear the special report first," Brett said from the bed, not understanding why she'd want to change networks.

Not being able to think of a plausible reason for the change, Jane reluctantly sat down again and clasped her hands together between her knees. After the commercial break the report came on.

Jane stared at the screen, focusing exclusively on the handsome face of the middle-aged reporter with his well-modulated professional voice. He knew exactly where to emphasize his words, where to let his intonation indicate skepticism, surprise, horror or amusement, while primarily remaining impartial to the content overall. It took skill, talent and experience to present an image the country could trust and this correspondent with his urbane delivery was the epitome of it.

Brett was watching with equal interest, recognizing the man on the screen as the one whose image was framed on

Jane's dresser. He had the same distinguished looks and persona that all of the older correspondents possessed. Brett's curiosity was piqued, but he said nothing until the program had ended.

By then Jane had regained her composure, but much of the loosening up Brett had encouraged during their dinner was gone.

"I thought he looked familiar. The correspondent is the man in the picture on your dresser. I noticed it this morning." Brett was watching her, but Jane wouldn't meet his inquiring gaze, busying herself instead with putting the set back behind her chair. "Are you related to Harry Lindsay?" he asked, quite smoothly. There was no reaction. None at all.

Slowly Jane stood to face him once more...aloofly. Brett regretted the distance. "No. It's just a coincidence that we have the same last name," she informed Brett quietly.

"Is that why you have a framed picture of him? Coincidence?"

Jane hesitated. She'd never had to explain before. It was only by chance that Brett Chandler had seen the picture.

"Sort of. I met Harry Lindsay on a senior class trip in high school with my journalism class. He was considered just about the best newsperson around and . . . my class was thrilled at the opportunity to meet him." Jane glanced briefly at the photo and shrugged with a small derisive smile. "It's nothing personal. He gave everyone in the class an autographed picture."

"You must have been very impressed by him. You framed your copy," he commented finally.

Jane swallowed, bending slightly to pick up the newspaper from the foot of the bed. "I was," she said, her face expressionless. "I still am." Jane stood up and took a deep breath. The subject of Harry Lindsay's picture was closed. "I'm going to say good night now...."

"Why don't I sleep on your sofa and give you back your bed?" Brett suggested, again moving swiftly to divert her attention.

Jane was slower switching emotional gears, but firmly shook her head at him. "It doesn't matter. I sometimes sleep downstairs if I'm working through the night on something. Besides, you can't sleep on the sofa. It's not really very comfortable."

"All the more reason why we should change places. Why should you be uncomfortable for my sake?"

"Because I'm probably in much better shape than you are," she said wryly with a small smile.

Brett carefully touched the bandaging at his temple. "I concede the point," he said dryly.

"Good night, then...."

"Wait a minute. Aren't you going to read the papers to me and then tuck me in for the night?"

Jane turned back to stare at him. "No, I will *not* tuck you in."

"Okay, okay. I'll settle for the sports, stock reports and the editorials ... in that order. Remember my delicate condition," Brett cautioned with mock innocence as Jane made to protest further.

To her own amusement, she finally gave in and settled back into her chair.

"It won't be necessary to start with 'Once upon a time...'" Brett advised her. "I have that part down cold."

Jane coughed rather than laugh, biting her lip to control the giveaway quivering of her chin. The newspaper crackled and rattled as she found the sports section.

"I don't suppose you have a teddy bear I can hold on to?" he asked.

"You're incorrigible," she stated firmly, ignoring his charming slow smile. "No, I do not have a teddy bear." But she was relaxed enough once again to entertain a wistful memory. "I never had one as a child. I always wanted one," she said.

"Do you realize what a deprived childhood you had?" he teased. But Jane's tight smile in response held little humor.

"We can't have everything, can we?" she said in a brittle tone, and promptly began reading from the football play-off scores.

Jane was halfway through the editorials when she looked up and saw Brett had his eyes closed. She watched him for a second as he lay quietly, before slowly folding the paper and standing.

"It was a boring editorial, anyway," she murmured, turning off the lamp and heading for the door. "Or maybe *I'm* the one who's boring," she finished as she closed the bedroom door.

The review of the previous night ended as Jane considered what else she needed for breakfast. She remembered she did have some grapefruit and set about sectioning one, and then fed the patiently waiting Jones.

Brett, in the meantime, had had his own review of the night before. He remembered clearly when Jane had gotten up to leave the room, because he had not been asleep as she'd thought. He had listened to her read the reports, enjoying the wonderful cadence of her voice. She read well and her delivery was adept, very professional.

He didn't want her to know he was still awake, because he was trying to assimilate all the information he'd learned about her in their short time together. He guessed that she'd done something else with her life before becoming a free-lance writer on Long Island. And he was still convinced he had seen her somewhere before.... Sooner or later it would come to him. It didn't make sense, either, that a woman with so few personal possessions would hold so dear a photograph of a television personality.

Brett noticed as he walked slowly around the small house that it was comfortably furnished with good furniture, charming pictures on the walls, baskets filled with dried flowers and magazines, a few hearty plants... but he didn't get a sense of Jane belonging to this place. There was really nothing that suggested her. In the living room there was no evidence that Christmas had just come and gone—only a small artificial tree on a pine table in front of the large window, undecorated. There were two items that might have been presents sitting beneath it, and if Brett had to guess, he would say they were both from Oliver. There was nothing personal to indicate that there were, in Jane Lindsay's life, friends or family with whom she could have shared the joy of the holidays.

On impulse Brett knelt and began to light a fire in the stone fireplace. It was evident that it had not been used at all since winter began. When he finally had a healthy blaze going, he thoughtfully continued his survey of Jane's house. He came to another small room, which she obviously used as a study or den.

On the desk was stationed an expensive IBM computer, hooked up to a printer. There were notebooks and reference materials, more books, papers and a haphazard stack of article reprints. Brett lifted the one on top and began to read the first paragraph. It was a piece on the place of women in male-dominated American corporations. There was her byline... N. Jane Lindsay.

The article underneath was a Viewpoint from the *Washington Post* on the difference between disciplining a child and child abuse. And yet another piece on the overdevelopment of midtown Manhattan. Brett raised his brows, very much impressed. The variety and complexity of her work reaffirmed his earlier assessment that Jane was a smart, aware woman. But it also made her more elusive, mysterious.... He couldn't be sure, for instance, what it would take to penetrate that hard invisible fortress she'd so carefully built around herself. Brett put down the articles and re-traced his steps to the kitchen.

Jane knew immediately that Brett was behind her. "Breakfast's about ready. I'm just waiting for the pan-cake," she added, brushing away the tendrils of hair around her face.

"It smells good in here." Brett sniffed the air.

"I'm only a fair cook," she said a bit nervously. She wasn't used to pleasing anyone's culinary tastes but her own. Oliver she didn't count, because he never seemed to mind what she put before him when he came to dinner.

Brett chuckled. "I'm at your mercy. I'm going to be the last person to complain, although you have been taking very good care of me so far."

Jane flushed at that and turned to remove the skillet from the range to transfer the large fluffy pancake to a plate. She had trouble getting the spatula under an edge.

"Here...let me do that," Brett said easily, taking the pan and utensil out of her hand.

Jane felt the warmth of his fingers on her own. "I'm not usually so clumsy," she said with irritation, but relin-quished her place to him. As she stepped away, Jones moved in, sitting down and looking up expectantly at Brett. It was clear that Jones was used to his mistress feeding him non-doggy treats.

"Sorry, boy," Brett murmured to the animal. Jones gave up and walked from the kitchen to lie in the hall. Brett lifted an amused brow at Jane. "I hope he didn't leave on my ac-count."

Jane smiled at him. "He will eat just about anything. Jones is spoiled rotten."

Brett laughed. "Including me, if you ordered him to. How did he come by a name like Jones?" he asked, care-fully sliding the pancake onto the waiting plate.

"It's just a name," she responded, searching in a cabinet for cinnamon and syrup. "I couldn't see calling him Duke or King or Fido." Again Brett laughed, and Jane found herself enjoying the sound. "Anyway, Jones had a good strong sound to it. Simple. Functional. Plain...like Jane," she ended flippantly.

Brett heard the sarcasm. "Now there I disagree with you. I always thought of Jane as a name with tradition and history. A lady's name. A name you can depend on, like Jane Eyre," he said, taking the cinnamon tin from her and shaking the spice over the pancake.

"Like Jane Doe," Jane retaliated. "I've never liked it much. It always seemed like a name you'd give someone when you don't know what else to call them and don't want to think about it."

Brett pursed his lips at her observation. He turned his head to follow her movements around the kitchen. "And what does the *N* stand for?"

"The...*N*?" she asked quietly.

"I saw it on one of your article reprints."

"It stands for Noel," Jane said in a small flat voice.

Brett was surprised. "Noel?" he questioned.

Jane grimaced, caught between being embarrassed and annoyed. "Isn't it awful?"

Brett shook his head. "Not at all. It's rather beautiful. Very unusual. Noel..." He breathed out the name, tilting his head at her. "I take it you were born on Christmas?"

"Christmas Eve." Her response was short and final. She hoped he would drop the discussion.

"You must have been the best Christmas present your parents could have hoped for. Still...I think I prefer Jane." Then he picked up plates and silverware and headed for the living room.

She greatly doubted that, and turned to say something on the subject when she realized where he was headed with their breakfast. "Wait a minute. There's no dining room. We'll have to eat in the kitchen."

"I thought eating on the coffee table in front of the fire would be nicer."

Jane frowned. "What fire?"

Brett hid a smile. "The one I started in the fireplace," and he left her standing there.

It had never occurred to Jane to try that, and now she wondered why it never had. Of course, after Brett Chandler left she would very likely go back to her more familiar routine. Somehow that conclusion did *not* give her back either her sense of safety or privacy. Her life had inadvertently been invaded and everything about it seemed changed. It was subtle and insidious.

Yet she'd managed very well on her own for the last three years without visitors, unexpected or otherwise. Carefully Jane carried the breakfast to the living room on a tray. At once she was startled by the comfortable warmth of the room and the cheerful glow the firelight cast. Brett had placed large pillows from the sofa on the floor at either end of the coffee table. He came to help her with the tray, setting it down in the middle of the table. On the one hand Jane was instantly charmed by the setting—it was cozy and bright—but on the other, the circumstances suddenly seemed too soft, too romantic and it made her uncomfortable. And Brett had become something else. Not just a stranger who'd been injured and who'd needed her help. Now he stood before her, a man in full possession of his senses and strength. Handsome, confident...and very male. The truth was, now Jane was afraid to be alone with him, afraid of getting to know him, of liking him.

Brett straightened from the table and faced her. His smile was tentative and Jane was alert to a difference surrounding them both. She watched as his jaw tensed and his gaze swept in a leisurely fashion over her features.

"I want to say something to you before we sit down...."
he began, and Jane instantly became nervous. She had no
idea what he was going to say, but she was sure that she
didn't want to hear it.

Jane began shaking her head and opened her mouth to
forestall him. Brett calmly laid a large hand against her
cheek. His eyes were serious. The light feel of his hand sent
an odd sensation spiraling through her. It was at once protective and caressing.

"There's very little I can say that can adequately express
my thanks to you, Jane. I'm very grateful for all you and
Dr. Seymour have done for me."

Jane self-consciously focused her eyes on his shirtfront.
She really didn't want him to be grateful, either.

"You've been very gracious, and much more attentive to
me than I deserve."

"I'm sure that's not true." Jane found her voice at last.

"In any case...thank you for being there," he finished
in a gravelly, sincere voice.

Jane swallowed, mesmerized by the look in his eyes,
trying very hard to know what he was thinking. She felt him
reach for her other hand and thought in some apprehension that he was going to kiss her. He was lifting her hand.
Gallantly he bent his head to briefly touch his lips to the
back of her hand. She studied the bent head. She hadn't
expected something so...simple. And for a perverse moment she wondered if he indeed thought of her as old-
fashioned. Victorian. Plain old Jane....

Brett saw a brief moment of sadness in her green eyes. He
wondered if he'd presumed too much. How arrogant, after
all, to think that in a few hours with her he could break
through the defenses of years.

Slowly Jane pulled her hand free, the skin warm and tingling from his touch. The silence was charged, but before

either could say anything more, there was a great knocking on the door that made Jane visibly jump.

"Th-that's probably Oliver," she said. Curiously, Jane wasn't sure if she was glad or disappointed at the interruption. She made a hasty retreat to the door to let in her neighbor.

The atmosphere changed immediately. Oliver and Brett greeted each other with easy male camaraderie. But Jane was still going over the insignificant encounter between Brett and herself while trying to maintain her usual cool and efficient exterior. Neither man seemed to notice her emotional struggle. Oliver invited himself to their breakfast. He voted to sit, however, on the sofa rather than lowering his bulk to the floor.

In due course Oliver removed the bandage from Brett's head wound. The abrasion was still red, but not nearly as bad as on the night of his accident. During the breakfast, conversation turned to Brett's family, and Jane listened with undisguised curiosity as Brett spoke freely about his mother and son. Jonathan was thirteen and mad for hockey. That led to a vigorous debate between Oliver and Brett on the merits and shortcomings of the two local teams. Brett talked of managing his mother's real estate interests. He briefly touched on a family conflict involving his father-in-law, and property left to Brett's son by his late wife.

"My wife would have been very sorry for the trouble her gift was creating," Brett explained with a small smile.

"But it's hardly her fault," Oliver commented.

"I agree. But you didn't know Carolyn. She would have found a way of convincing herself that it was. She was rather self-effacing that way," Brett said.

Carolyn, Jane thought. *His wife's name was Carolyn . . . and she had died.* While the conversation continued Jane was busy trying to visualize the kind of woman Brett Chandler had been married to. She must have been rich and from a very good family. Had she also been beautiful and smart, cheerful and outgoing...a fair match for her husband? Although curiously, Brett had just mentioned that his wife had been "self-effacing." And why had she died so young?

She looked at Brett as he good-naturedly talked with Oliver. *And there was a son named Jonathan....* She listened as he spoke with quiet enthusiasm and great love of his son, and in the pit of her stomach she felt an envy that hurt and made her think bleakly of her own family.

"...Yes, she's taken very good care of me," Brett was saying, bringing Jane out of her daydream.

Jane hastily came to her feet and began to stack the tray with their dirty dishes. "I'm sure if it had been me, you would have done the same thing," she said briskly.

Brett grinned rather wickedly at her. "For the most part. Some things I would have done a bit differently!"

Oliver chuckled silently, but Jane was only confused by Brett's double meaning and quickly escaped to the kitchen. There she took more time than was necessary to clean up and stack the dishwasher, listening absently to the murmuring and occasional outburst of deep male laughter from her living room. Even Jones had momentarily deserted her for the liveliness of the other room.

There was yet another knock on the door. Jane answered, and stared blankly at the stocky, middle-aged man of average height who stood before her. Politely he removed his hat, exposing a bald pate, and nodded a greeting.

"Morning, Miss. I'm here to pick up Mr. Chandler," he said with authority.

"Oh. Yes," Jane responded. "He's inside." She held the door open for him.

"No, thank you. If you don't mind I'll just wait out here. Whenever he's ready." He replaced the hat and walked away to climb behind the wheel of a 220S Mercedes sedan.

Jane closed the door, another jumble of feelings attacking her. Last night she could only think that today Brett would be gone. But now that today had arrived, she'd nearly forgotten that he would be going. She walked to the living room where both men now stood waiting.

"There's a driver waiting for you," Jane said to Brett. She was controlled again, unmoved. "He said he'd wait in the car."

"Yes, that's Charles Borden, my mother's grounds keeper."

Jane suddenly couldn't face him, couldn't be too close to him. He was leaving and she'd already begun the process of distancing herself...of being alone again. "I'll get your jacket." She turned toward the hall closet, not paying any attention to the words that he and Oliver were exchanging, or to Brett's brief gentle stroking of Jones's head as he walked to meet Jane by the door.

Oliver went into the kitchen to get more coffee. Brett shrugged into the black dinner jacket, pulling up the short inadequate collar against the biting cold weather. Jane wasted no time in opening the outer door onto the crisp day, and they both stepped through. The recessed entrance protected them from the wind and blocked the view from the waiting car.

Brett turned to face her once more. Jane hoped he wasn't going to thank her again.

"Would it be okay if I came back?" Brett asked seriously. He watched her face closely, trying to gauge her reaction. Two days wasn't nearly enough time to know a person. He was naturally curious about Jane Lindsay. He wanted to know more about her, what made her tick, why she had closed herself off from the mainstream of life. He wanted to know what she was afraid of.

There was a spark of pure surprise in her green eyes at his question before they became wary. She shrugged a shoulder lightly. "Why?" she asked reasonably. "It's pretty lonely out here. I like it. I can't imagine why you would."

He laughed soundlessly. "You won't give an inch, will you?"

"I give an inch . . . you'll want a yard," she said frankly. "People always want more than what they have or what's given to them. It's human nature, I suppose."

"And what more do you want?" he asked softly, not seeming to mind the frosty day as they stood confronting each other.

Jane wasn't going to be baited again, however. "I have everything I want. I can't think of a thing I'm missing," she said.

Brett's roaming eye continued to assess her and Jane met his gaze unflinchingly. She wondered what he was looking for, and began to be disconcerted by his steady, unwavering examination. Slowly a complacent smile curved one corner of his mouth.

"Then, Lady Jane, you're in for one hell of a surprise."

The next few seconds were so unexpected that Jane had no time to react. Brett's hand came from nowhere to tunnel under her thick hair and curve his still-warm hand to her neck. He wasn't surprised at the stiffness, but maintained his hold. The touch formed a bond that could not be taken lightly. For touching suggested a trust.

Slowly the hand drew her forward. There was a little resistance from her, so Brett bent forward to meet her instead, not giving her a chance to push him away. He pressed his slightly opened cool mouth to her own lips and with only the smallest pulling and pursing, encouraged a kiss in return. His lips were mobile, and the feel and mastery of his mouth made Jane move her own accordingly, adapting, fitting...shocked, but not uncooperative. The kiss was brief and soft, and Brett didn't attempt to press the advantage he held at that moment. He lifted his mouth and retreated before Jane could reject him.

Of course she could always slap him, but Jane had too much self-control to do something like that. The moment had been long enough for him to know her mouth felt wonderful, capable of full sensual response, and the knowledge sent a startling jolt of sexual tension straight to his loins.

Brett's hand released her neck and slid to her shoulder, which he squeezed gently. "See you," he whispered and quickly turned away to get into the back of the waiting car.

Jane stepped backward into her house and closed the door. She stood holding the doorknob tightly. His remark sounded awfully close to a promise. For a moment Jane was excited. But then she let the feelings of hope go. There was absolutely no reason in the world for Brett Chandler to return to Montauk, and she certainly wasn't going to hold her breath until he did.

Oliver was sitting in the kitchen reading the paper. "So...do you want him to come back?" Oliver asked, scanning the news headlines.

"Don't you know it's rude to eavesdrop? You're going to grow a wart on your nose," she said tonelessly, pacing up and down in the small space. Suddenly she thought that Oliver sometimes understood more about her than she wanted him to. Jane let out a tired sigh and leaned against the edge of the sink. "Besides, it has *never* mattered what I wanted."

Oliver peered at her over his half glasses, his gray eyes amused but filled with understanding. "You didn't answer my question," he reminded her softly.

Jane arched a brow, crossing her arms over her chest. "And I'm not going to," she said haughtily.

Chapter Four

There was no opportunity on the hour or so's trip to Southampton for Brett to dwell on the details of his adventure in Montauk. Each time he slipped into a private reverie about Jane Lindsay he was pulled back reluctantly by the tidbits of news and information from the driver. Charles Borden launched into a blow-by-blow outline of what to expect once they reached the Chandler estate. Brett, even as a youngster, had always been appreciative of the inside gossip he'd gotten from his family's retainers, which often kept him out of trouble with his parents. And as he grew older, he was also amused that if he really wanted to know what was going on, he only had to question the household staff.

Stanley Hastings, Brett's father-in-law, wanted to call another meeting with the other board members of Inland Estates as soon as possible. Stanley was still trying to persuade Brett to sign over the interest in the properties his daughter Carolyn, Brett's late wife, had left to his grandson. Since they had originally been Hastings properties, he was going to try to prove, no doubt, that blood ran thicker than water. Brett was relieved to hear that his mother had declared that business would have to wait until he had had a chance to fully recover from his accident.

But his mother, ever one for taking full advantage of her position in the family, had committed Brett to helping her host a New Year's Eve party the following evening. There he knew he would be expected to be charming and, knowing his mother, forced to play swain to an eligible and available lady or two. The only saving grace lay in the information from Charles that well over two hundred people had been invited, leading Brett to see the possibility of slipping away early with no one the wiser.

Brett loved his mother dearly. She was cheerful, irreverent and affectionate. But he had no intention of letting her pick and choose his companions. Besides, her idea of eligibility and his own were diametrically opposed.

Brett's thoughts switched rather easily once more to Jane, who was nothing like any of the women he had previously known or been involved with. Jane didn't have the bright packaging that immediately made other women attractive. But then Brett would guess that she wasn't the least bit concerned with impressing anyone. That was somewhat refreshing and added to her charm. In her own unpretentious way she was very ladylike. "Lady Jane" suited her perfectly. Brett was just about to pursue the idea further, when he was once again interrupted with the announcement that they had arrived in Southampton. Giving up the ghost—at least temporarily—with a frustrated sigh, Brett climbed from the car and walked up the brick pathway to the front door.

He stepped through into a bright, warm entranceway and stopped for a moment to try and figure out where everyone was. A pair of ice skates and battered hockey stick lay on the floor next to an antique mahogany hunter's table, and a helmet was in the porcelain fruit bowl on top of it. A six-foot-long scarf striped in Jonathan's school colors was wound around the alabaster throat of a bust on a pedestal, and a discarded sweatshirt lay in a heap on the floor. Brett quirked an amused brow at the scene, convinced that Jonathan truly had the undying devotion and love of his grandmother, since she'd never tolerate having her house so abused by another living soul.

He moved with complete familiarity through his childhood home, passing the living room where a huge Christmas tree dominated one corner. The family presents, all opened Christmas morning, had already been cleared away. Brett passed the den and rounded a corner into the spacious kitchen where a short plump woman was expertly constructing trays of canapés for the New Year's Eve feast.

"Hello, Maggie," Brett greeted her, reaching over her shoulder to help himself to several small rounds of pepperoni. By way of reply he received a smart rap on the knuckles.

"So you're back," she said, wiping her hands on an apron and lifting one tray to take it to a large commercial refrigerator.

"Did you miss me?" Brett asked, popping the snack into his mouth and leaning over the table to see what else he could pilfer.

"Not me, you scamp. But you nearly drove your mother to distraction," Maggie said, closing the refrigerator door.

"Where is Mother?"

"When she learned you were okay and not in any danger, she turned to driving *me* crazy! It's that party tomorrow night, you know."

"I know," Brett said and grinned in sympathy.

"I sent her to see about the flowers and balloons. I figured that should keep her busy for a couple of hours."

Brett chuckled. "Poor Mother. I wonder if she ever realizes who really runs the house."

"Your mother does, and don't you forget it, young man," Maggie admonished him with a wag of a short chubby finger.

Brett put up his hands in mock surrender, his hazel eyes twinkling mischievously at the older woman, who stood all of five feet three inches tall.

Her pale blue eyes looked over the tall handsome man, whom she'd known and helped raise since he was the age his own son now was. She shook her head over the wrinkled state of his tuxedo, his naturally shaggy hair, the awful red mark on his forehead and the few scratches on his cheek.

"I swear, if you're not the death of your mother, young Jonathan will be. First you in that devil car and then Jonathan playing hockey."

Brett was very quickly alert. "He hasn't hurt himself, has he? Is he all right?"

Maggie impatiently waved that aside. "Of course not. He's out and about with some of the local boys. He's as agile and quick as you were at that age. But you know your mother. She expects he'll come home one day with all his teeth out."

That got a deep rich laugh from Brett, and slowly Maggie let her own love and amusement show through the concern. "We're very happy it wasn't serious," she said softly.

"The Chandler clan are a sturdy bunch, Maggie my love. We're hard to get rid of," Brett said, kissing her quickly on the forehead before exiting the kitchen.

The thought of a fresh change of clothes became Brett's next priority, and he was halfway up the stairs when the door from the garage burst open and he heard his mother's voice. Brett came back down to meet his mother in the hallway. She entered from the kitchen with a box of silver and gold balloons, and behind her trailed a young delivery boy, struggling under the weight of a portable tank of helium gas.

"Now I have no idea where I'm going to put that ugly tank.... No, no! Don't lean it against that wall. Someone's likely to trip over it," Priscilla Chandler gently advised the teenager.

The older woman, still strikingly attractive at nearly sixty-five, stood considering as she mumbled and lamented to herself. Brett stood quietly watching by the stairwell. His mother had given up tinting her short wiry hair years ago in favor of its now natural platinum color. It was becomingly styled around her squarish face, accenting her strong cheekbones and jaw structure. Her gray eyes, now as always, were bright and expressive. Under her open sporty winter parka she wore a stylized jogging ensemble in pale pink, which had never seen a moment of real exercise.

"Well, couldn't you stay and inflate the balloons for me? I'm sure I have no idea how that thing is supposed to work," she said, pointing airily to the peeling gray tank.

"Sorry, ma'am," the young man said. "I'm only supposed to deliver it for you...."

"That's all right. I'll take care of it later," Brett announced, making his presence known at last.

"Oh, Brett. You're here," his mother said lightly, but her eyes quickly went over her son to ascertain for herself that he was okay.

"I'll take that," Brett said with a nod to the delivery boy, reaching into his pocket to hand him payment for his help.

Brett wheeled the tank into the den for the time being. Then he returned to his waiting parent.

"Hello, Mother," he said and bent to give her a kiss on her soft cheek.

Again she took a careful look at his face, at the angry cut and the scratches, in much the same way as the housekeeper had done. Priscilla Chandler sighed and shook her head. "Just like when you were a boy..." she said softly. "Are you sure you're all right?"

"I'm a little battered and bruised, but I survived. You worry too much."

"Mothers always worry. I'm convinced that's what we're for," she commented dryly, patting her son's cheek as he helped her out of her coat. "Why aren't you upstairs getting some rest? I should call Dr. Nelson to come have a look at you, just to be sure...."

"I don't need any more rest, and I've already seen a doctor."

Priscilla scoffed as Brett hung up the jacket in a small closet. Following him to the den, she sat on the loveseat in front of the fire. "How good a doctor can he be? He sent you out without any kind of dressing on that cut...probably never took you to get X rays...."

Brett laughed softly. "I think you would have approved of the way he handled me. I made it back, after all."

"Was he a head doctor? Sometimes I do believe you need to have yours examined."

"A retired pediatrician."

Brett's mother gave him an amused and skeptical glance. "And you're probably the biggest baby he's ever seen to."

"No doubt," Brett agreed and grinned.

"And what about this...this woman who said she found you?"

There was no inherent criticism in Priscilla Chandler's questions, Brett realized. Just understandable concern for his well-being. But the reference to Jane aroused a surprisingly strong and immediate need to champion her.

"Who was she?" his mother questioned further.

Brett shrugged lightly. He was also not inclined to say too much about Jane, when he'd barely had time to reflect on what he knew of her himself. And he was strangely reluctant to share her yet with anyone, even with his mother.

"She's a writer. She lives on one of those private cul-de-sacs on the northern pond before you get to Montauk Point. I took a chance at trying to get back here and made some wrong turns."

"I told you you should have just stayed the night at the club. Next time you'll pay attention to what I say," she said sagely.

"Yes, Mother," Brett responded dutifully. "And by the way, I appreciate your sidestepping Stanley for me."

Priscilla grimaced. "The man is impossible."

"Well, he didn't build his fortune by always being a nice guy."

"But what about the board? They do seem to be on his side."

"Legally the land belongs to Jonathan. As his parent and guardian I'm of the opinion that if it's to be developed it should be for a more humane purpose than expanding the family wealth."

"Yes, I know, Brett. And I think Carolyn would have liked the idea," she said smoothly. "Will you continue to try and table a decision at the next board meeting until some alternative plans can be developed?"

"I think so. I don't think there's any need for me to be at the next meeting, however," Brett said, standing to remove his wrinkled jacket. "That's why I spent so many years training a director. After Father's death it may well have been vital for me to head the business completely, but it's no longer necessary. Everything is in order and the company is stable. Eric Noble has managed an excellent team in the last five years. You can trust him to act in our best interest and not let Stanley railroad him into anything."

"Yes, that's true," his mother conceded. Her eyes followed Brett as he slowly walked to the door. "Does this mean that you're definitely going to Germany this spring?"

"Yes, it does. I thought you'd be proud that I've been invited to help design those new gliders."

"As a mother I would be *happier* if you'd stay on the ground and behind a desk instead of up in the air with planes that don't have engines."

Brett laughed, knowing his mother enjoyed complaining about his penchant for planes and their engineering design. Priscilla Chandler was *very* proud that her son was considered an expert aerodynamicist; he'd done work with some of the largest aerospace companies in the country as well as NASA. She'd been prouder still that he had willingly put his own career goals on hold for nearly fifteen years while he stepped into the family business after his father's death. Also while he took a wife, promising to protect and care for her. He was always coming to someone's rescue.

"Of course I'm proud of you, Brett Alexander, and your father would have been, too." With a deep sigh she also stood and joined her son at the door. "Now go on up and get out of those clothes. I'll have to see if Maggie and I can salvage them in time for the party tomorrow night."

Brett groaned. "Don't tell me it's formal. Are you going to parade another line of women before me?"

She gasped at him. "Brett! Would I dare to interfere in your personal life?"

"In a minute," he said easily, not the least bit fooled by his mother's show of indignation. He headed toward the stairs. She looked up at him once again with love and concern.

"Brett, it's just that...well...I realize that Carolyn was not the wife you would necessarily have chosen."

"Mother..."

"You've made many sacrifices for your family, more than was fair to expect. But I do want to see you settled some-day—*and* happy."

"Mother, I have been happy. I have you, I have Jonathan. And I have not led a widower's life in seclusion," he pointed out tactfully.

"I'm sure. But there should still be one special person for you."

Brett smiled gently at her. "Mother, I promise to inform you personally if I ever find her."

Brett had not really been interested in marriage since Carolyn's death. His emotional and physical needs over the years had been satisfied by a small selection of women whom he'd met primarily through acquaintances. When each affair was over, he and they had gone their separate ways. Only once had there been a persistent clinging on the woman's part, but Brett had not allowed her emotional tantrums to sway him.

It was also true that perhaps under different circumstances he would not have married Carolyn Hastings, but at least there'd been Jonathan before she'd gotten so ill and been advised against further pregnancies.

"I'll just change and be right back with this suit."

"Oh dear... I still have so much to do yet before tomorrow night," Mrs. Chandler murmured. She brightened suddenly. "Oh, Brett. *Will* you be a dear and play piano tomorrow before the dance band arrives?"

"I will not," Brett said promptly, not giving in to his mother's soft plea. "But Jonathan and I will blow up the balloons for you."

"Well, I suppose that will have to do," she said, sighed and turned to retrace her steps to the kitchen.

Brett had managed to make it to the upper landing when the front door opened, and closed again behind a tall young boy who added his gloves to the hockey helmet in the fruit bowl, then started up the stairs two at a time.

"I'm back, Nana!" he shouted in a voice already signaling a change to a deeper tone. Suddenly he looked up and spotted his father waiting patiently at the top. He doubled his energies to reach the top of the steps. "Dad!" he called out joyfully.

"Hi, big guy," Brett said warmly, placing an arm around his son's shoulder and hugging him to his side as Jonathan openly hugged him back.

His cheeks were an apple red from being outdoors. He pulled off his knit ski cap and a bush of dark blond hair was exposed. While he had most of his mother's fair coloring, he resembled his father a great deal in build, promising to attain a similar height.

"When did you get back?" Jonathan asked. They walked to the guest room Brett used when visiting. His own boyhood room had been given to Jonathan when the boy had come to live with his grandmother just after Carolyn died.

"Not too long ago. Charles came to pick me up."

"I wanted to come for the ride but Nana wouldn't let me. Did you really have an accident?" Jonathan asked as they entered the room and he immediately plopped down onto the bed.

Brett smiled at his son's youthful fascination for all the gory details. "Yes, I did."

"Were you unconscious?"

"Mmm-hmm," Brett responded, stepping out of his shoes and unbuttoning his shirt.

"But who found you?"

"A dog."

Jonathan's eyes were curious. "Really? A Saint Bernard?"

Brett laughed. "No. It was something a little bit smaller. A Labrador retriever."

"Boy, that sounds great."

Brett raised a brow. "What? Being unconscious, or being rescued?"

Jonathan blushed. "Not being unconscious, Dad. I mean the dog."

"Of course," his father said dryly.

Jonathan looked at his father and saw the reddened head wound. He shrugged. "It doesn't look too bad. Did it hurt a lot?"

Brett grinned and murmured wryly, "I had a thundering headache when I came to, but all in all it wasn't too bad. I'm really sorry I missed your hockey game yesterday. Who won?"

"We did," the boy answered absently. "The other guys were wimps."

Brett grinned at his son's use of words.

"Tell me more about the dog. Who did it belong to?"

Brett shook his head. He'd almost forgotten about the million and one questions his son was capable of. He shrugged negligently, trying to keep the information basic. "A female writer who lives out near the Point."

Jonathan was interested. "Oh yeah? What does she write?"

"Articles for magazines and newspapers."

"Is she famous?" the boy asked, watching his father.

"I don't think so, but her work is probably well-known in her field."

Jonathan thought for a moment. He picked up a small ornament from his father's night table and began to idly toss it up in the air. "What's her name?" he asked.

Brett quickly reached out, caught the airborne item, and returned it to the table with a gentle admonishing look at his son. "Lady J—Jane." Quickly he corrected himself. "Jane Lindsay."

Jonathan's eyes grew wide. "Wow, Dad! *You* met Jane Lindsay!"

Brett stopped and turned to look quizzically at his son's sudden exuberance. "You sound as though you may know her better than I do. Where did you hear the name Jane Lindsay before?"

"She wrote this neat fantasy about how all the kids in the world got together and formed their own government and then they ended wars forever. They decided not to have leaders, but to work together to make decisions."

Brett was intrigued. "And who gave the children this idea to form their own government?"

"Well, this girl from another world with green hair."

Brett raised an amused brow and glanced skeptically at his son. "Why is it all the really smart people who know how to save the world come from outer space?"

Jonathan thought for a moment and then shrugged. "Because they don't know anything about politics," he stated with simple logic. "It's a great book, Dad. You should read it sometime."

"Maybe I will. So you think a lot of this Jane Lindsay?"

"Sure! I wish I could have met her." Jonathan thought for another moment and then looked at his father. "Is she pretty?" he asked.

Brett realized that his son was indeed growing up and that he had obviously begun to notice agreeable differences in the opposite sex.

"Yes, she's very pretty." Brett sat down next to his son and began pulling on a pair of running shoes.

"Are you going to see her again?" Jonathan asked but Brett avoided giving a direct answer.

"Tell you what. Let me change clothes and I'll tell you everything over lunch. Afterward you and I are going to help your grandmother prepare for the party tomorrow night."

Jonathan didn't look enthusiastic at that idea, but was too polite to say so. "Doing what?" he asked cautiously.

"Inflating balloons," his father informed him and watched the gray eyes brighten considerably.

BRETT WAS VERY GLAD for his mother's sake that the party was such a success. He had done his part as host, greeting the arrivals, smiling, shaking hands, kissing cheeks, circulating among the guests. He was comfortable and familiar with the social rituals. He'd danced with his mother twice and had even grabbed Maggie in the hallway to dance for a few minutes.

Few people questioned him about the reddened injury near his forehead or the fading scratches on his cheek, and to those who did he flippantly explained them away as the work of an outraged lady friend. As he'd surmised, his mother had made an effort to introduce him to the daughter of one of her friends. Brett had been duly impressed with her beauty, stylishness and quick wit. But it all struck him as being too superficial and too practiced. He couldn't detect one single natural or vulnerable facet, and that made him unusually reserved toward her feminine overtures. Suddenly he was comparing her to the honest and simple appeal of Jane Lindsay. To his mother's hopeful, Brett was polite. But no more than that.

Jonathan had put in an appearance, passing his grandmother's inspection. He was well mannered and unobtrusive, partaking liberally of the many trays of food until his father had set him a limit. Jonathan had planned to stay up for midnight and the toasting in of the New Year, but by eleven-thirty had declared that grown-ups were weird and had quietly gone up to his own room.

Brett had watched him go, knowing that what preyed on his son's mind was having to go back to school in just a few more days. He had pleaded once again to be allowed to come back home from his prep school. But in an earlier conversation Brett had regretfully explained that the arrangement was necessary, at least for the remainder of the school year.

Jonathan had never liked boarding school, but Brett had always been concerned that it would be too much to expect his mother to care for the boy full-time. Brett himself was spending more and more time traveling for Grumman. It was not ideal for any of them, but it was the best he could do for the moment. Brett's traveling, meetings and conferences had made it necessary for Jonathan to stay with his grandmother when he was very young. Brett had been asked twice to teach at the engineering school of M.I.T. and now he was thinking seriously of accepting. He'd already done one semester as a guest lecturer and liked the Boston-Cambridge area well enough to have bought a house there, so that he and Jonathan could be together.

Twelve o'clock approached and the extra staff hired for the evening circulated with trays of noisemakers. The guests began to mill about the grandfather clock, getting ready for the countdown to midnight. Brett stood alone near the fireplace with a glass of champagne in one hand, his free hand in his pants pocket, pinning open the front of his tuxedo. The room was glittering and bright, filled with noise, laughter and music. The balloons, laboriously inflated by Jonathan and himself the night before, were clustered at the center of the ceiling waiting to be released. The men and women were outfitted in high fashion, evidence that they didn't lack money. But all Brett could think of was the quietness of the small house somewhere on Montauk.

He knew that Jane Lindsay would be home alone tonight. Jones would be there by her side. Perhaps Oliver Seymour would stop by with a bottle of champagne for a toast before heading home from his own evening's entertainment. Perhaps not. But Jane would have spent the evening by herself.

It bothered him. He didn't want to think that there was no one with whom she could reminisce over the triumphs or failures of the old year, or even plan dreams or resolutions for the new. He took a deep breath, and there was the image of her standing outside her door the day before, as he prepared to leave. He could see her eyes, large and thoughtful as she considered his request to come back. It had been a spontaneous question, not entertained at all until that instant. Suddenly Brett knew he couldn't let it end right there. He had no idea what he'd expected, but her cool appraisal of him and his request had shaken him, because he could see that Jane had not for a moment thought him sincere.

Brett had also not given any thought to kissing her until that moment in the cold. It had only been a light goodbye kiss. He hadn't done it as a matter of course, but because he wanted to find out how her mouth would feel under his. Her skin had the same sweet effervescent floral scent that had played on his senses for two days and two nights in her room. Brett could smell it still.

The countdown began and Brett suddenly pushed away from the mantel and made his way quietly to the den. He set down his glass, and sitting on the arm of the loveseat, reached over the desk for the phone. In a second he was dialing Jane Lindsay's number.

Brett didn't suppose for a moment that she wouldn't be home. Halfway through the third ring, she finally picked up her phone.

"Hello?" he heard the soft feminine voice reply. The tone was open, warm, completely free of caution.

"Hello." Brett, too, was caught off guard. He hadn't expected that hearing her voice would make a difference. It did. "Do you know who this is?" he asked softly, doing nothing to identify himself.

There was a barely audible intake of breath. "Ye-yes," was the whispered answer.

Brett smiled and relaxed. She could be surprised. *Score one for him.* "Good," his voice crooned through the line.

"Happy New Year, Lady Jane." He held the receiver a little longer. He didn't expect an answer and didn't wait for one. With a satisfied smile Brett hung up.

JANE SAT ON THE BLUFF just below the lighthouse, squinting against the bright sun and high winds rushing in from the sea. The day was not very cold.

Next to Jane the black Labrador sat peacefully, waiting to take his signals from the woman who was so deeply in thought. Jones, not having to deal with complex questions or answers about his life, lifted his face ecstatically into the wind.

The two were on the return trip from Montauk and Jane's weekly visit to pick up mail and packages, groceries and other personal items. It was the one day she allowed herself to walk along the main street of the town to observe its citizens going about their business. It was the one day she treated herself to lunch in town, the one day she allowed herself to stop by the Chamber of Commerce office to find out what was happening locally, although she rarely participated in local events, and to visit the library to spend time reading through current magazines and newspapers. It was the one day Jane allowed herself to blend in, however surreptitiously, with the rest of the world before retreating to the little cottage outside town. After three years of living here, she still knew no one beyond a shopkeeper or two, a serviceman here and there and the town librarian. But then no one knew who she was, either.

This one-day reprieve used to be enough to remind her that there were simple pleasures to enjoy, and it allowed her to live in relative contentment. But it *was* all relative to who she interacted with. The people from Montauk were straightforward and easy enough to read. But as Jane attempted to recapture the equilibrium of being alone, Brett Chandler was proving to be much harder to dismiss.

She'd never realized until after he'd gone just how quiet the small house got at night, or just how strange it was not to hear another human voice for hours on end. Jane had become too accustomed to addressing Jones, whose repartee was decidedly limited, or Oliver, who spent little time with her. She had not heard so much laughter, or been so tempted to it herself as in the two days she'd spent in Brett Chandler's company. It had been a strange feeling, but it had been good.

Jane hadn't believed him when he'd asked if he could come back. And she didn't believe the kiss he'd given her expressed any genuine feeling, seeing it only as the tactic of a sophisticated and polished man used to bestowing favors. But what Jane also couldn't believe was the shock of realizing that she had wanted to respond. For a heady instant she had wanted to know the full aggressive pressure of his mouth. Instead the kiss had been humble...and very gentle. Did she want Brett Chandler to come back? She had no idea. Jane only knew that his unexpected appearance to begin with, and his departure, had changed something around her.

Slowly she got up from the hard cold surface. It was nearly three-thirty and the sun was dropping lower in the sky. In another thirty minutes it would be completely gone. That was another thing Jane disliked about winter, she thought disagreeably as she pulled her coat about her. The days were too short and the nights much too long when they were spent alone.

She and Jones didn't often drive all the way out to the Point, where the lighthouse stood. The Point gave one the sense of having gone as far as one could go, but sooner or later you had to turn around and go back the way you came in order to reach any other destination. It was almost a blunt reminder that one could only run so far from life. Sooner or later you had to return to it.

Jane gathered up her stack of mail. There had been three checks for recently published articles, an advance and a contract for a book proposal she'd submitted in October. There were more reprints, and a request for her to speak to a women's group that had been passed along by one of her editors, but she knew she'd decline. And there was the anonymous letter, informing her that Jimmy Cochoran, a man who had once promised that her life wasn't going to be worth a dime if he ever got his hands on her, had been released from the state prison after having served time for second-degree manslaughter charges.

Quickly Jane climbed back up the cliff and headed for her car, Jones trotting several feet ahead of her. She didn't want to think anymore about Brett Chandler. There wasn't any hope there. And she didn't want to think about Jimmy Cochoran's release. There might not be much future there, either. Then the subject of men led her to probably the most influential man in her life. Harry Dean Lindsay, renowned national TV personality, respected political correspondent and reporter from the nation's capital, friend of politicians, diplomats and presidents. Her father.

She recalled Brett asking her if there was a relationship between them, and remembered feeling her stomach flutter and tense as she'd answered no. Harry Lindsay was not about to jeopardize his reputation and career by acknowledging an illegitimate daughter.

Angrily Jane put the car into gear and headed down the narrow Montauk road to her house. Everything used to be so simple. It was rather fortuitous that with the appearance of Brett Chandler her life had been turned upside down again, confusing her, threatening her, making her angry. She couldn't find her balance anymore, and reflected dismally that she wasn't sure she ever would again.

Jane was old enough now that thoughts of her father didn't hurt so much. She'd never really known him. It had taken years of probing her mother to find out about him. For example, Jane had guessed that her conception had been used as a threat held up to Harry Dean Lindsay by a naive but very ambitious young woman, who'd thought that he would own up to his responsibility and marry the pretty young researcher from his news staff he'd gotten pregnant. Instead, Harry had had Margaret Latham transferred to an out-of-the-way affiliate station in Philadelphia.

Transferred, alone and pregnant, Jane's mother had been forced to acknowledge she'd greatly misjudged both her value to Harry Lindsay and his sense of fairness. Margaret Latham had made a basic error of judgment and now was left to raise her child alone and have her ignorant of her parentage. Her own maternal instincts had been somewhat less than motherly, and the growing little girl had lived with a perpetual sense of not being wanted.

Jane had been nearly twelve when her mother told her who her father was, explaining why her last name was Lindsay and her mother's was not. Until she was fifteen, Jane would watch TV and read about the handsome correspondent with the charming smile who was her father, alternately adoring him and hating him for never wanting her. She had also taken it into her head that her mother was deliberately keeping her from her father.

Jane remembered both her anger at her mother and her blind devotion for a man she'd never met or spoken to. Years later she conceded that it was to her mother's credit that she'd prevaricated about what kind of man Harry Lindsay really was. But Jane also wondered if it wouldn't have been better to tell her outright that her father wanted nothing to do with her, rather than have her go through the humiliating and devastating experience of finding out for herself.

By the time she was seventeen she'd already decided that she wanted to be a journalist. Fortunately she was aided by an early recognized ability to write, as well as a natural curiosity for the facts and truth that made her work thoughtful. In high school, Jane's senior class made a four-day trip to Washington, D.C. to meet with top reporters at the *Washington Post* and the press corps from the White House and Capitol Hill. Harry Lindsay was one of the speakers arranged to meet with the group.

Margaret Latham, neither overly demonstrative nor given to dispensing motherly advice, nonetheless sent off her daughter with the hope that the trip might be everything she wanted it to be. She didn't caution against overinflated expectations, since she herself had ignored such warnings when she wasn't much older than Jane. Awkwardly she had told her daughter that she loved her, the first and only time Jane was ever to hear those words spoken to her by either parent. The three simple words would later be repeated like a refrain in Jane's mind and heart. She would find that the words were often freely spoken but rarely seriously meant.

Jane's class had arranged to meet with Harry Lindsay on the set and take a tour of the newsroom. Her face had been overly flushed with excitement, her hands damp and sticky like a child's. The students asked their questions and joked with the accommodating man sitting casually on the edge of his TV desk and basking in the admiration of the impressionable group.

Jane could not utter a single word. For the full forty-five minutes of the interview she'd sat mesmerized, staring at him. It seemed like the culmination of endless fantasizing and daydreaming to finally be here to introduce herself, to see his eyes light up with pride and joy at seeing his own daughter at last. Harry Lindsay amicably autographed pictures of himself for the students and one by one they trooped off after the tour guide to see the studio. Jane was the last one to reach him. She'd planned it that way so that they could have the moment privately together. Then she was standing right in front of him, surprised that he wasn't much taller than her own five feet six inches, but not caring. There was a complacent smile on his full mouth.

"And your name?" he asked, head bent over the glossy image of himself.

Jane still found it hard to speak. The pause was so long that Harry raised his head to cast a glance at the slender young female. He quickly took in the wavy reddish-blond hair hanging loosely down her back, the wide bright green eyes. Suddenly he was very alert, and his recognition was both instantaneous and frightening. It was then that Jane had spoken.

"I—I'm Noel Jane Lindsay," she stuttered in a wispy voice.

What happened next was so surreal, so intense in its emotional impact that the rest of the trip to Washington was completely and forever wiped from her memory. Jane had watched not surprise but horror and cold outrage transform her father's features. The early warmth and amused regard in his eyes for the young audience was now an icy stare, pinning Jane in place, commanding her not to say the words or ask the questions that would establish their relationship.

Harry Lindsay could see much of himself in the startled girl. Her green eyes and shape of her brow were his. The wavy hair, thick and shiny was Margaret's. She had to be about seventeen or eighteen and was guilelessly open and trusting.

"Noel Jane Lindsay. That's an unusual first name," he commented, beginning to write on the bottom of the black and white photo.

Jane could only blink at him. This wasn't the way it was supposed to go. She couldn't possibly tell this cold distant man she was his daughter. "I—I was born Christmas Eve," she whispered, watching for any sign of feeling, any reaction at all. "Isn't it strange, our last names are the same." Her little laugh had been nervous.

He looked down at her as he put his pen away. He slowly handed her the photo and she absently reached out to take it. Harry Lindsay very pointedly held her hopeful gaze.

"But it *is* just a coincidence, isn't it?" He smiled most charmingly and stood straight. "Enjoy the rest of your stay in Washington." Then Jane was staring at his receding form.

She recalled that her eyes had filled with tears and that she'd stumbled blindly through the studio corridors until she found a ladies' room. There she'd been instantly, violently sick to her stomach. It had been an hour before she could pull herself together. She'd gone back to her hotel room alone, and couldn't be persuaded to leave it again until the class was on the way home.

She had become a journalist, a reporter, determined to be every bit as good as Harry Lindsay. She'd been hired by a local network in New York and had been diligent and persistent. She was quick and witty on the air, hyper with energy and personality. She worked hard, as well. Pushing, sidestepping the rules. Getting good stories—but one summer night, paying the price.

It was election year and she was covering a campaign. It was boring, routine. A lot of men in navy-blue suits paying lip service to promises they'd never keep. Jane and her Minicam crew had followed up on a carelessly tossed out communication that there was some sort of confrontation at a local campaign headquarters. Jane had pursued it, walking into an emotional argument between a campaign worker and a young man named Jimmy Cochoran, who'd lost his job because of political favors granted by the local candidate.

No one expected anything to come of it. He'd yell and scream and curse, be escorted from the building, and probably just vote for the opposition. But Jimmy had pulled a gun. His eyes were desperate and very angry.

Jane began taping the incident, moving closer to the small group of people trying to persuade the young man to calm down before someone got hurt. Her adrenaline pumping furiously, Jane had moved her mike back and forth between the members of the group, even as they yelled for her to back off and get out of the way, but she'd held her ground, moving closer and closer to get this firsthand story.

And then there had been the clear click of a light switch, white light blinding the young man as the camera suddenly ran. Jimmy had flinched . . . and the gun had gone off. The young campaign worker was hit and slumped to the floor, Jimmy Cochoran staring in disbelief at the downed man, then up to Jane as she held the microphone toward him. And then the threats had been yelled at her, accusing her, telling Jane it was her fault. And she'd believed him. She could hear them still, especially in her dreams.

Fifteen seconds. Not a lot of time. But time enough for unexpected violence. Time enough for worlds to shatter and lives to change or end. Fifteen seconds that would be crucial to three people's lives.

Jane pulled the car into its garage and got out to gather her numerous bundles. She entered the darkened house, once more acutely aware of the choices she'd made. She'd backed off totally from her father, her career . . . the past. Yet somehow it was catching up to her, still unresolved. Coming back to haunt her.

Again Brett's image, his laughter and wonderfully resonant deep voice entered Jane's mind. She didn't want to think of him with any kind of hopefulness. She didn't know if she had the strength to hope and be disappointed again.

Oliver *had* been with her New Year's Eve. When the phone rang at a minute to twelve Jane had no doubt that it was a wrong number, dialed by some inebriated party goer.

There had been all the merriment in the background, but when she'd heard the voice her heart had thundered in her chest, her hands had gripped the receiver tightly. Of course she'd known who it was. His softly uttered "Happy New Year, Lady Jane" had caused her knees to weaken with the utter sweetness and simplicity of it being said specifically to her. Brett had hung up before she could reply.

"Who was it?" Oliver had asked curiously behind her, pouring them both champagne for the midnight toast.

Jane had taken quick gulps of air to calm herself. "It...it was a...a wrong number," she'd lied.

Weeks later Jane knew she'd been right to do that. February had begun and nothing had changed. She hadn't stopped thinking of Brett, but she reasoned that in time she would. She'd become very good at overcoming disillusionment. And then February 16 the package came, so she would never know if the contents had been intended as a belated valentine. The gesture nevertheless had nearly been her undoing.

Silent tears of complete disbelief had rolled down Jane's cheek as she unwrapped the tissue paper, then gently clutched the soft stuffed teddy bear to her chest.

Chapter Five

It had been a good day. She felt at peace. Jane knew that for her it was an occasional feeling, and she was going to enjoy it to the fullest. She and Jones were on the way back to the house and the cold sharp wind had flushed her cheeks with becoming color. Her hair was a wild curtain of firelight behind her. She was feeling young, exhilarated and carefree. The dog trotted about her, never getting too far away but sniffing out the bushes and shrubs for interesting scents, slowly working his way back toward the house.

Jane had finished two very important articles and felt the pressure of deadlines lift from her shoulders. She and Jones had had a good romp along the beach together. She'd even treated herself to a new sweater from a cute little boutique in town.

There were predictions of winds and heavy rains later on, but so far even the weather had cooperated. It was sunny and extraordinarily clear with cloudless pristine blue skies. The temperature had struggled to forty degrees, unusual for the end of February, but Jane nevertheless felt very hopeful that spring was close at hand.

Her only wistful thought was that there was no one to share the moment with. She didn't often wish that, but every now and then she would have liked to turn to someone at her side, smile and express her thoughts and ideas, or ask a speculative question and debate the answer. None of this ever happened, however, and with a contented sigh, Jane supposed that it wasn't so bad most of the time. She refused to believe that her good spirits might in any way be connected to the postcard she'd received from Brett Chandler two days ago, the second in as many weeks.

The first bore a picture of Montauk taken from one of the terraces of Guerney's Inn, a well-known resort on the southern shore. Written diagonally in a masculine looping handwriting was, "Having a good time, but wish I was there." Jane had read the card repeatedly, assigning a different meaning to the message on each occasion. The words were too standard and corny to be taken seriously. She had known a moment of pleasure, but in the end Jane had decided Brett was being sarcastic at her expense and had thrown the card into the cold ashes of the fireplace.

Since Jane had not expected the first card, she was equally unprepared for the second. That one showed Boston harbor with several old schooners and fishing trawlers. The message on this one had been, "I bet my chowder is better than your chowder." Her mouth twitched into a grin, slowly spreading into a smile as she shook her head in wonder. As with the first card, she read it over and over, both delighted and suspicious. The cards were friendly and lighthearted. But what struck Jane most of all was that Brett Chandler had remembered her. And, of course, there had been the teddy bear. Even now it sat on her bed pillows, a testimony to what was becoming the paradox of Brett Chandler. So far he stood in stark contrast to the men she'd known before.

Oliver, who'd joined Jane for breakfast just the morning before, had spotted the card on her kitchen table and openly read it. He'd laughed at the message, commenting, "That could prove to be an interesting contest. I wonder how he plans to conduct it?"

"He's only teasing, Oliver," Jane had patiently explained.

But nonetheless, Oliver's remark had prompted Jane to retrieve the first card from the fireplace. She'd gently wiped away the gray ashes and straightened out a bent corner, sorry that she'd reacted so childishly. After all, she'd lived on the Point for three years and had never received what could be called a personal piece of mail before. She pinned both cards with decorative magnets to the door of her refrigerator.

Nonetheless, she had steadfastly refused to give credence to the request Brett had made about coming back. So when Jane walked the last twenty feet or so to the house, she came to an abrupt halt at the sight of the sleek parked sports car. The sudden painful thud of her heart against her chest wall couldn't disguise the unbidden rush of excitement, a covert expression of delight in what was proving, after all, to be Brett's sincerity. Jane knew that their brief encounter had been interesting, though insignificant. All the same, he had sent the cards and the teddy bear, and he was somewhere nearby right now. Mixed with all of Jane's excitement and curiosity, an enormous fear was building. She also couldn't help but wonder what he might want from her.

Slowly she walked to the corner of the garage and saw that the front door of the house was partially open. Suddenly the door was pulled open, Jones came bounding out, and Brett stepped out behind him. Jones barked once as he circled her. But her eyes were riveted on Brett.

He, too, spotted her. The long silent moment of confrontation as they stared openly at each other was filled with surprise, caution, shyness—and gladness, although the latter was held tightly in control.

It was obvious to Jane that Brett had fully recovered from his mishap. As a matter of fact, it was hard for her to believe that the tall lean man before her, his short leather aviator jacket open to the winter elements, had ever known an ill moment at all. Brett appeared very fit and vigorous, and most decidedly male and handsome.

Jones stood between the two silent adults, looking from one to the other. Jane absently put out a hand to the animal and he came to her to be petted before wandering off on his own. The wind was tousling Jane's hair. Brett liked the way she didn't seem to care that every strand wasn't in perfect order, the way she stood so fresh and natural without a speck of makeup and not needing any. And he found her more attractive than ever.

Jane lifted one shoulder in a slight shrug. "He...he's very proud of himself. He thinks he found you again."

Brett's hazel eyes roamed her face carefully, even as a corner of his mouth formed a half smile. He was trying to gauge her reaction to seeing him, but other than that her cheeks were rosy and she was gazing steadily at him, Jane gave nothing away. For his part, Brett was instantly glad he'd come.

"He did. There was no answer when I knocked but I was able to walk right in. Your door was unlocked," he said with a small frown of disapproval. "I was looking for you inside."

"I took Jones down to the beach for a run. We weren't gone very long. Anyway, I almost never lock the doors. I never have visitors."

"There are two kinds of visitors. The invited kind and the uninvited kind. It's the second you have to watch out for." Brett lectured her smoothly.

"Like you?" Jane asked evenly. He'd already put her on the defensive, so that she did not see his criticism as concern.

Brett raised his brows. His jaw tensed, but then he gave her a self-deprecating nod. "Touché," he murmured tightly.

Jane became embarrassed at having fenced with him. "Why were you looking for me?" she asked.

He should have remembered her wariness, should have reasoned that she'd want to know why. He hadn't been all that sure of the reason himself, except that she seemed to be constantly on his mind. He wanted to find out if it was just curiosity. "I did ask if I could come back."

Jane shook her head. "I never said yes."

Brett tilted his head and wickedly narrowed his eyes at her. "Ahh...but you never said no."

Jane felt herself blushing, and bit her lip in uncertainty. "Touché," was her own reply, and slowly they began to smile at each other.

Brett lowered his gaze to the movement of her lips, suddenly remembering the feel of her soft mouth against his.

"Why don't you come inside?" Jane suggested. "I'll put some coffee on."

Now Brett smiled fully at her. "That would be nice. Thank you."

Jane walked around him, feeling her insides react to his presence, and continued calmly into the house. "I'll be right in," Brett said, opening his car door.

She already had the coffee maker going and was setting out cups when Brett let himself in, Jones with him. Jane could hear him speaking to the dog in a low voice as Jones sniffed curiously around him. She noted with a surprised smile how easily Brett made himself fit in. He wasn't any less comfortable conversing with the animal than she was. And Jones was much more responsive toward Brett than he was to Oliver.

Brett entered the kitchen. Jane turned just as he swept his long fingers through his windblown hair and got a quick glimpse of the healed wound on his forehead.

"Sit down. Coffee's almost ready," she said. Once again she was starting to feel awkward and shy in his presence, again feeling her space changing and shrinking because of the man making himself at home there. When there was nothing else to fiddle with at the sink, Jane poured the coffee and brought the mugs to the table, sliding into the seat opposite Brett.

"Before I forget...I have something for you. A gift," Brett said as he retrieved a brown paper bag from the floor.

Jane's eyes widened. "A...gift?" she asked blankly. She put her elbows on either side of her steaming cup and pressed her fingers lightly to her cheeks. "I really wish you hadn't. It's not necessary...."

"Wait until you see what it is first and then decide," he responded lightly. Brett put the bag on the table and gently pushed it toward her.

She couldn't help the slightly suspicious look in her eyes as she glanced warily at Brett, but his hazel eyes were mysterious. Jane opened the bag and gingerly reached in, withdrew a box and stared at it. It took her a long second to understand and then she smiled in genuine amusement at Brett. He in turn sat and thoroughly enjoyed another of Jane's instant unguarded moments.

"Confectioner's sugar?" she asked.

Brett shrugged and took a sip of his coffee. "I understand it's a must with a puff pancake. I'm hoping that you'll prove it to me sometime soon," he said smoothly. He was both surprised and amused when he saw the blush on her face. "Go on. There's something else in there." He nodded toward the bag.

Once again she reached in and this time withdrew a Maxwell House coffee can, taped at one end. "It's awfully heavy." And then inspiration brightened her eyes. "It's a fruitcake!"

Brett nodded. "An old family recipe. Mother won't give it to anyone, but she's very generous with samples."

"But...your mother knows nothing about me."

Brett arched a brow. "No...but I do."

Jane slowly shook her head in wonder. She had never met anyone like Brett Chandler. He really was thoughtful. And he had obviously learned enough about her to realize that a fruitcake was not going to offend her sensibilities about accepting a gift from a stranger.

"I hope you like fruitcake," he remarked. "There's a thousand calories in each slice, but that never stopped me."

Jane laughed lightly. "It shouldn't." She glanced briefly at him through her lashes. "This was...was very thoughtful of you."

"Happy February 21," Brett said with an airy wave of his hand.

Jane tilted her head. "What's February 21?"

Brett shrugged. "The day before February 22."

Jane laughed.

Brett's smile suddenly softened. "And it's the day I came back to see you. I wanted you to remember that especially."

Jane stared at him, seeing a caressing light in his eyes and hastily hid her confusion behind a quick sip of coffee. "While we're at it, I want you to know I got the postcard. I mean, I got both of them. And...and the package you sent. With the teddy bear...." Her voice faded awkwardly.

"I know," Brett answered, nodding toward the refrigerator where the two cards were attached to the door. Slowly he reached across the table to still the nervous movement of her hands. Her green eyes rose to his face, and again he could clearly see Jane's vulnerability. Brett smiled gently. "And you're very welcome." He gave her fingers a brief squeeze and released them. "Sometimes a teddy bear is good to hold on to. I thought it was a bit more cuddly than Jones."

"Do you think I need something...cuddly?" Jane asked quietly, staring down at the table.

Brett hesitated. He was very careful how he answered. Cuddling was one of the things he suspected Jane lacked in her life. The teddy bear was merely symbolic.

"Teddy bears are standard childhood equipment. If you never had one before, then it's about time you did."

"Jones is very good company, thank you. I won't let you hurt his feelings by trying to replace him with a teddy bear," Jane said lightly.

"I wouldn't dream of it," Brett responded quickly. "But we can all use as many friends as we can get."

Jane bit her lip once more. She didn't think Brett meant anything significant by his words, but it brought into focus the very limited number of people she could call friends. As a matter of fact, they could be counted on one hand, she thought in irony. Jones included. Jane lifted her eyes thoughtfully to Brett's handsome face, seeing the healthy tanned look of his skin and his thick hair streaked with quicksilver threads. She bet he had a wide circle of friends. He was the kind that would.

She didn't ask him about the phone call on New Year's Eve. It was less tangible a thing than the stuffed animal or postcards, and the sense of disembodiment in their voices, the few words spoken still cloaked the call in magic and mystery. Jane preferred to keep it that way. Whimsically she thought for a moment that if she believed in fairy tales, Brett Chandler would be an ideal candidate for a knight in shining armor.

"You didn't come all the way back to Montauk just to see me, did you?" she had to ask. The doubt was there, but so was an effervescent hope.

"Oh, but I did." Brett grinned seductively at her. "You have me intrigued, Jane Lindsay." The voice was low and smooth.

"Intrigued? That's an interesting word."

"I want to know more about you."

"There isn't so much to know," Jane responded, feeling her defenses coming back into play. She would have liked not to be so careful with Brett, but they were treading on very private ground. "I'm a free-lance writer and I live on Montauk."

Brett nodded. "And you're a very good writer. I know that now."

"How would you know that?" she asked, eyeing him cautiously.

"I looked you up and then tracked down some of your work. Your writing is very thoughtful. I like your way of raising questions that need asking, even when it's not clear what the answer should be."

Jane was very surprised at his assessment. But it also made her uneasy that Brett had gone to such lengths to find out about her.

"Jonathan agrees with me," Brett went on. He took a sip of coffee, looking at her over the rim of the cup. "Apparently you wrote a . . . er . . . 'neat,' I think he called it, book about children who save the world."

"Oh . . ." Jane smiled softly. "He means *Colorblind*." She shrugged. "It was just a fantasy idea I had . . . ."

"Obviously a very good one. It's a hit with Jonathan and his friends."

"What else did you find out?" she asked quietly.

Brett could hear the tightening in her voice. He wondered what she was afraid he would find out. Yes, he knew about the shooting three years ago. He had gone through a few more papers than just the ones he'd mentioned. He'd had a friend who was a lawyer dig out the court proceedings and the newspaper accounts. It was clear to Brett that the incident had in no way been Jane's fault. It had been a simple case of bad timing, compounded by the angst of a young man angry enough to do something foolish. And yes, someone had died . . . but it might easily have happened without Jane being there. It might just as easily have been Jane.

The newspaper account said that the young man, a Jimmy Cochoran, had shouted threats at the stunned female reporter, promising revenge and holding her responsible for the death of the campaign worker. But Brett didn't believe that revenge would ever come to pass. He was convinced, however, that much more than the shooting held Jane a prisoner of her past. Now he suspected that her isolation was just a way of running from whatever it was. His search had also led him to another Jane Lindsay. Now it was clear why she'd seemed so familiar when they'd first met, but the person he'd found was the opposite of the woman he was coming to know.

"I found out that Jane Lindsay was once Johanna Lynn, popular superstar news reporter in television."

Jane's hands gripped the mug until her knuckles were nearly white. She was angry. Brett had no right to dredge up her past.

Brett could see her withdrawal. He'd touched on something she was very sensitive about, but he wasn't going to retreat now.

"Go on," Jane ordered bluntly, staring at her hands.

"When I first saw you I thought I'd seen you before. You worked for a local network for six years before quitting to devote yourself to writing." Brett's eyes roamed over the woman in front of him. There had been nothing about the Jane Lindsay aka Johanna Lynn of television fame that had attracted him. This new Jane, who had stopped and started her life all over again, Brett knew he could like a great deal. He liked her staunch independence and confidence, her quiet dignity and self-possession. These were qualities that made her strong and capable. She possessed a sense of humor, though it was rather wry. She was very shy with her real feelings, and very careful around men. Someone had hurt her or misused her trust and love. She wasn't going to give either again easily.

"I found an old picture of you in a magazine." He paused. "Why did you let them change your hair?"

It was not the question Jane thought he would ask. He was not going to strip away the layers of who she was. She shrugged lightly.

"The station director thought that my hair was too curly and unmanageable. They cut it, straightened it, styled it. That's show biz," she said dryly. "If they don't like you the way you are, they make you into what they want you to be."

Brett shook his head regretfully, remembering the photo of the pretty but too thin reporter with the obvious stage makeup and the high fashion ensembles. It was almost ridiculous that the person in the picture and Jane were one and the same.

"It must have been a very lucrative career. Why did you give it up?"

Nervously Jane got up from the table and momentarily busied herself with rinsing out her mug. "Fame and fortune aren't everything. The pace was killing and there was no opportunity to do stories in depth." She didn't add that the competition was often fierce and ugly, her personal life shallow and lonely because she was a threat to some men and an easy target to others. And the rewards did not begin to fill the void in her life that had left her with a sense of not belonging anywhere and not being loved by anyone.

"What about your family?"

Jane swung from the sink. Her eyes were filled with a sadness and pain that held Brett spellbound for a moment. He'd touched another nerve.

"I have no family." Jane said. "This is my home."

"Why Montauk Point?" Brett challenged at once. "Why this far out on Long Island, all alone?"

"Because that's how I wanted it." Jane's voice was strained. "Look...don't try to analyze me, Brett. You don't know me well enough. I live here by choice. Period."

Brett got up slowly to face her, aware that she was agitated. "Are you running from something? Someone?"

"No! I...of course not," Jane ended impatiently. "I just want to...to be left alone. I didn't ask you to come back." The words were out quickly, but she regretted them at once. Jane bit down on her bottom lip. She tilted back her head as Brett advanced toward her. There were only a few inches between them. For an irrelevant moment Jane remembered Brett lying in her arms the night she found him in the snow; remembered the premonition that because of him everything would change. It was happening already.

"Did it ever occur to you that I might come back because I really wanted to see you again?" he asked quietly, his gaze holding her attention. "Couldn't you believe that I might find you attractive and want to know you better? Didn't the thought pass through your mind that maybe...just maybe, something could develop between us?"

His honesty left her totally vulnerable and unprepared. She had never allowed herself to indulge in daydreams.

"No. It...it never did," she said softly.

"Well, it's true," Brett answered, taking another step closer.

Half of her wanted to deny his presence, the other half wondered what he would do next. Brett lifted a hand and cautiously laid it along her cheek.

"Look...you're right. We don't know each other, do we? Perhaps this is happening too fast, or maybe I'm pushing you too hard. I'll slow down, Jane. But I won't stop," he said with a curious growling note in his deep voice. The determination sent waves of anticipation through her.

"Why?" she asked in heartbreaking bewilderment.

Brett arched a brow. "Don't you ever ask anything but why?"

"I'm a writer and writers are nosy."

"Well, I'm nosy, too. About you." Brett tipped his head thoughtfully to one side and let his thumb caress the smoothness of her cheek. "Does that frighten you?" he inquired very softly.

Jane hesitated. Too many people had used her frailties against her. But she let her green eyes reflect the tug-of-war going on inside. Slowly she nodded.

Brett began to smile at her. "My mother and son will vouch for my character. I'm kind to small children and kitty cats, I always remember birthdays, and I rarely lose my temper." The smile became a curious sensual lift of the corners of his mouth. "I want to get to know you better... quickly. But I'll settle for just being friends for a while." For a moment Brett's eyes grew serious and he let his gaze wander over her features. His thumb moved to the corner of her mouth. "I like you, Jane. I won't ask any more questions about your past, but don't ask me not to be interested. I'll even leave right now if that's what you want. But I'm hoping that it's not."

All of Jane's sense told her she might be better off not believing Brett Chandler. But there was something deep inside her that warmed completely to his words. At least he had not deceived her in any way. And if the truth were known, *yes*... she was terribly, achingly attracted to him. That hadn't happened in years.

As though Brett could understand her ambivalence, he came closer still, so that he could see her reactions clearly. He'd made the decision that actions spoke louder than words, and he was going to kiss her. He wanted to touch and taste her. Slowly he lowered his head toward Jane and her eyes transferred their attention to his mouth, watching in fascination as his lips began to part purposefully. Even that small motion sent a twisting cord of sudden need and curiosity through her. Jane held her breath until she felt his mouth gently cover her own. And then she let it out in a rush as Brett's lips coaxed her, moved teasingly against her own in small rubbing movements.

He hadn't taken full possession yet, as if waiting for Jane to decide whether or not she wanted this. Then with a slight tremulous parting of her own lips she inadvertently encouraged Brett to add pressure.

Jane felt Brett's tongue tantalizingly light over her lips. His hand was still against her cheek, and he let it slide downward until his thumb could touch her bottom lip. His lips gently pressed and pulled, easing her mouth open even more.

They touched nowhere else. The kiss, sensual but tentative, allowed Jane the time she needed to trust Brett more. In a corner of her mind, however, was the thought that if this was how friendships were conducted, they were already in deep trouble. She could feel the pleasure beginning to escalate. When her body swayed toward Brett she quickly twisted her mouth free and turned around to lean her hips against the sink, needing the support to steady her suddenly weak knees. She closed her eyes and drew her bottom lip between her teeth, still feeling the pressure of his mouth.

"Do you?" Brett asked behind her, so close that Jane could feel his warm breath on the back of her head.

"Do I what?"

His fingers began to stroke and feel the curly weight of her hair. He could smell the sweet perfume of her hair, just as he'd remembered from December. "Do you want me to leave?"

Jane knew that to answer was to make a commitment. She let out a sigh. Sensibly she guessed it was only a matter of time before she had to open up her world to other people. Sooner or later she would have to take another risk.

"It's snowing again," she said absently. The heavy flakes outside the window created a dervish of movement in the wind. It was hard to believe it had ever been sunny earlier in the day.

"So it is." Brett's tone was equally absentminded, but he wasn't interested in the snow. "Jane?" he asked again, prompting an answer from her.

"I don't know," she said and her voice quavered. "My life here has been comfortable. Uneventful." Slowly Jane turned to face him, her green eyes weary and honest. "I...I don't know if I'm ready to change that, Brett. There are so many things in my life...in my past that you know nothing about." She shook her head. She didn't know if she could make him understand. She had given up expecting happiness, love or a family. It was an accomplishment to just get from one day to the next.

Brett was merely watching her now, but he said nothing.

"You know," Jane began again, carefully avoiding eye contact. "You can probably choose from a long list of available women who wouldn't be nearly as...as difficult as I am."

"I don't find you difficult at all. And you will learn that I am nothing if not persistent when I want something."

It was like a warning and Jane took it to heart. They stood staring at each other, still tentative, but neither denying the mutual attraction.

Footsteps stomping outside the door suddenly jolted them back to their surroundings.

"That's probably Oliver," Jane said, thankful for the interruption. She moved around Brett and headed for the door. When Jane opened it, Oliver found himself facing an unexpected welcoming committee, Jane, looking somewhat flushed, Jones—and Brett Chandler.

"Well!" Oliver said boisterously and put out a hand to Brett. "I thought I recognized the car outside."

With a lot of chatter, the hellos continued all the way into the living room. With the addition of Oliver, the atmosphere and tension between Brett and Jane was dispelled. Brett, for his part, was disappointed by the interruption and although very glad to see the doctor again, would have liked time alone with Jane even more.

Oliver very eagerly suggested the three of them have dinner together. He had brought a bottle of wine and a large sack filled with fresh clams.

"Where did you get them?" Brett asked.

"Down near the marina. I was out cod fishing this afternoon and got them coming in. Thought Jane here would have mercy and feed a hungry man if I supplied the fixings."

"You're full of baloney, Oliver." Jane took the smelly sack and the wine from the big man. "You just don't want to clean and shuck them yourself."

Oliver laughed. "Every word of it's true!"

"Why don't we do chowder?" Brett suggested, knowing full well that Jane would remember his postcard.

Jane headed for the kitchen and the two men trailed behind her. But the space, while barely adequate for two people, was impossible with three. Jane solved the problem by quickly assigning specific chores to the two men, seating them at the table. Before long the small room was a beehive of motion, laughter and talk.

Jane could see that the two men genuinely liked each other. Oliver inquired about Brett's recovery after leaving Montauk and the state of his car. Their voices became a comfortable background of sound to Jane's own tumbled inner thoughts.

She liked Brett Alexander Chandler, but didn't fool herself into thinking that anything between them could grow and endure. Their backgrounds precluded that. Brett was from a family of good breeding and long lineage. He was not going to get involved with someone whose beginnings were questionable. But it might be exciting for a while to explore her interest in and attraction to him. It had been so long since she'd been able even to remotely trust the motives of a man.

Jane brought her attention back to the conversation taking place behind her.

"There's only Grumman at Bethpage," Oliver was stating.

"Yes, I know. They're doing some testing tomorrow and I have to be there."

"I didn't realize you worked for Grumman," Oliver said.

"I don't, exactly. I'm what they call an expert consultant. I free-lance for them on a per project basis. I'm an aerodynamicist. My specialty is wing design. Whenever they're developing a new plane, I'm called in. The X15 was one of my first jobs. Right now Grumman is trying to compete with Germany on the development of a new glider that's more streamlined and lightweight than the ones that are used now in aerodynamic competition."

"You're an engineer?" Jane asked.

"Sometimes," Brett admitted. "When I'm not running Inland Estates for the family. When I get tired of fighting with developers and the Environmental Protection Agency, I go stick my head in the clouds."

An hour or so passed very quickly until the chowder was done and ready to be eaten. Again Brett lighted the logs in the fireplace. The chowder was served with crusty chunks of French bread, a salad and Oliver's wine, and the meal was laid out on the coffee table. The conversation was light and unimportant, a good deal of it spent discussing the merits of Long Island clam chowder, which Brett admitted was tasty but couldn't hold a candle to Boston's. Jane, a smile of contentment curving her mouth, let Oliver and Brett argue it out. She was just enjoying the company and the sudden sense of well-being. It had been a while since she'd felt this comfortable, this normal in the company of men.

It was Oliver stirring and standing to stretch his great body that alerted Jane to the fact that it was late. Not once during the entire afternoon or evening had Brett mentioned where he'd stay the night. She could hear the commotions of the late winter storm outside and had a clear vision of Brett's accident in his car back in December. But this was different from that night. *They* were different, and there was a mutual curiosity and expectation that begged to be explored.

Jane slowly stood and the three of them carried the dinner things to the kitchen. Still the question hadn't been asked.

"Well...I'd better get going before I get snowed in," Oliver said, opening the closet door and reaching for his sheepskin coat. "Jane doesn't have the room to put two of us up for the night!" he joked.

Quickly Jane and Brett exchanged sheepish glances.

"I thought of driving into Bridgehampton. My mother's away, but the housekeeper is there," Brett said.

Oliver shrugged into his coat. "That's silly. Why drive on a night like this when you don't have to? Remember what happened the last time! You might as well stay."

When Jane and Brett exchanged looks this time, she slowly began to blush.

"I...think it would be best if you stayed," she said in a thin voice, her eyes communicating unconsciously with him.

"I could leave," Brett insisted quietly. Oliver pretended not to notice.

Jane's heart raced but she made the decision firm. "Rescuing you is getting to be a habit. I could set Jones to guarding you again, you know."

Brett flashed her a wide smile. "Jones is a marshmallow and you know it." Nonetheless his eyes grew warm...and pleased.

"Well, children," Oliver began in an expansive tone, "I will leave you two to your own resources."

Jane shot him a quelling look, but Oliver only chuckled and turned to Brett.

"It was good to see you, Brett. I'm glad my doctoring didn't leave you with an unsightly scar."

Brett grinned at him. "I'm not that vain. But I thank you, and my mother thanks you."

The two men communicated on a level that went unnoticed by Jane. "Don't be a stranger," Oliver said.

Brett pursed his lips. "I don't plan to be."

Oliver nodded, and with a brief wave of his hand closed the door and was gone, leaving Jane and Brett standing in the hall. Brett looked over his shoulder to find her watching him openly.

"More wine?" he suggested.

"Yes, please," Jane responded, and together they slowly returned to the living room. She sat in one corner of the sofa and Brett in the other. He poured them both more wine and passed her a glass.

"Thank you for letting me stay again."

She took a delicate sip from the long-stemmed glass. "I didn't have the heart to make you struggle through a storm tonight."

Brett leaned back into the cushions, let out a deep complacent sigh and stared thoughtfully into the flames.

It was very quiet for a long time, but not uncomfortable. Jane sipped her wine and watched Brett. It was rather nice having him here like this. It surprised her that she could be so specific, but he did seem to possess those qualities that she would most want in a man, but had honestly never thought to find. Certainly not among the class of men she'd known in New York City. Everything and everyone there had been so fast. Too often she had found herself the sacrificial lamb, simply because she herself wanted so badly to be wanted and loved.

Jane continued to let her mind wander quietly in the warm dimness of the room. Brett's eyes were closed and he held his wineglass with the base resting on his stomach. She loved the peacefulness. There were no attempts at bright conversation or efforts to impress. There was no coyness, no games-playing, no need to pretend. She could be comfortably herself without being judged.

"What time do you have to be in Bethpage?" Jane asked.

Brett sighed. "Nine in the morning. I'll be up and gone very early, so I'll try not to awaken you."

Jane shrugged, looking into the bright flames. "It doesn't matter. I'm always up early myself."

"Can't sleep at night?" he guessed after a second.

"Sometimes…" she admitted reluctantly, recalling those occasional bad dreams.

Brett turned his head slowly to look at her. "That's what the teddy bear is for. Don't tell me he's falling down on the job?" His voice was like warm soothing honey; it flowed around Jane and was sweet and concerned. She laughed lightly, her eyes sparkling.

"I don't want to wear him out," she admitted wryly.

Slowly he reached out to capture one of her hands. It was very slender, the fingers delicately tapered. He'd perceived her as being so strong and independent that the feminine softness of her hand surprised Brett. Absently he rubbed his thumb on her skin, savoring the texture, aware that she made no move to withdraw the hand. Brett then laced his fingers through Jane's and slowly, their eyes watching each other carefully, their hands closed together. Hers was cool and lost in his larger warm clasp. Jane liked the protective feeling.

"Jane. I have to ask you a question," Brett said in a hoarse voice. When he felt her loosen her fingers to pull away he squeezed gently, applying just enough pressure to object.

"Brett, I . . ."

"Just one. I promise."

Jane gnawed her lip, knowing that it could be one of hundreds of questions that she wasn't prepared to answer. But she nodded. "All right."

"Tell me about the man who owns this house."

The question made Jane blink in confusion. She had granted him one question—and once again it wasn't the one she thought he'd ask.

"Norman Rosen?" she asked, still bewildered.

"Is that his name?"

Jane made a vague gesture with her free hand. "Norman used to be program director at my network. I think he's now vice-president of the news division." She didn't know all that much about him. Just that he and his wife had come unasked to her assistance when she'd truly had nowhere else to go three years ago.

"I'd just quit my position at the station. I was renting an outrageously expensive apartment in Manhattan and my lease was up. I didn't really want to stay...." Jane hesitated, not wanting to go into details about the shooting, the threats, the trial . . . the nightmares. "Norman and his wife gave me the keys to the house and a road map to Montauk. They told me I could stay as long as I wanted. It's a vacation house they haven't used since their kids left home. I was looking for a quiet place to work. This was it."

Brett shifted slightly, resting their joined hands on his thigh, moving slowly and unobtrusively so as not to make her nervous. "What if this hadn't happened for you? What would you have done then?"

Jane frowned. "I...I don't really know. I had considered Boston. I'd been asked to do a writer in residence program at Radcliffe, but...I turned it down."

"Why?"

"I really didn't think I knew enough about anything to conduct classes. It seemed presumptuous when I knew I had so much still to learn myself."

Brett let her finish. He didn't think she was aware that her fingers were convulsively clutching his.

"Then there's no one who has a prior claim? No one waiting in the wings I'll have to challenge to a duel?"

Jane felt a bubble of laughter, hysteria probably, suddenly well up within her. That meant that someone would have to know her well enough, care enough. "No, there's no one," she answered.

"Good," he said simply.

Brett continued to hold her hand, the simple touch connecting them harmlessly so that a gap was bridged. It made Jane feel safe. She suddenly felt there was a possibility that they could really get to know each other. Be friends, as he'd suggested.

"Why didn't you become an engineer full-time?" she asked.

He grinned at the question, pleased by her interest. "I had to take over my father's position with Inland Estates when he died. I couldn't manage the business and design planes, so...I gave up planes."

"That must have been disappointing," Jane offered.

Brett shrugged, again absently rubbing his thumb over her hand. "Disappointing, but not hard. I couldn't see turning the business over to strangers. My father knew I wanted to be an engineer, but no one expected him to die so suddenly, either.

"Then I got married and there was no time to think of what might have been."

Jane hesitated before asking her next question. "How did your wife feel about your decision?"

Brett became thoughtful and quiet, reliving in his mind those early years when his life had not really been his own. There had never been a question of Carolyn's understanding. She had always just let things happen around her. Brett acknowledged that he had not exactly been unhappy, but certainly there had been times when he'd felt something was missing—the sharing of deep feelings and love.

"I don't think Carolyn felt one way or another. She let me do whatever I thought best."

Jane could not detect any particular emotion when Brett mentioned his wife's name. Perhaps ten years was enough time for his hurt to have healed. She sighed and leaned her head so that one cheek rested against the back of the sofa. She knew that Brett was right. Sometimes you simply do what you have to do without questioning. But there was always a "what if?" Jane lived with that if things had gone differently might have significantly changed her whole life. At least Brett had his family.

"When I was a kid I wanted to be just like my uncle," Brett began reminiscing in a soft drawl. "He'd been a pilot in the Korean war. I was always imitating him."

Jane smiled. "Were you one of those little boys who pretended he was Superman and wore a bath towel as a cape?"

Brett laughed. He shifted on the sofa, moving closer to Jane. "No. But I did fashion a pair of wings out of cardboard once and thought of jumping off the garage to fly. I suppose it's just as well my mother discovered my plan and I lived to tell the tale. Once I hitched a ride to the local airport and stowed away on a courier plane. They didn't find me until we'd reached Chicago. The pilot let me ride in the cockpit with him when they sent me back to New York."

"You certainly were creative," Jane said dryly.

"Little boys are," Brett agreed. "I stuck to making paper airplanes after that. Some of them were very intricate. That's how I got involved with designing plane wings." There was a small pause and then he spoke again in a very low voice. "And who influenced your decision to be a journalist? Besides Harry Lindsay, that is?"

Jane nearly jumped at the mention of her father's name. She couldn't admit to the relationship, or rather the lack of one. She didn't want Brett to think less of her the way others had because she couldn't claim a father. She couldn't tell him how awful it was not to be wanted.

"No one, I guess. I've always liked to write...."

Brett smiled gently at her and interrupted. "Were you one of those dreamy teenagers who kept diaries and journals and recorded every thought and feeling?"

She blushed. "Yes, I guess I was." Perhaps she'd secretly believed that if her father could ever see what she'd accomplished, how much she'd inherited from him, there would be some basis for a relationship.

"I got into TV by accident. But I don't think I ever really wanted to go in front of the cameras."

"Then why did you?" Brett asked. He sat up slowly and turned so that he was facing Jane.

"I don't know," she said with a kind of bewilderment that showed she'd never thought about it before. "I was in the right place at the right time when the station wanted to hire more women."

"You know...there are people who would envy you."

She shook her head. "There's no reason to. I didn't like it very much, but I was a good reporter. I learned a lot during those years about what makes a good story."

Brett stretched an arm along the back of the sofa so that his hand could touch her hair and one shoulder. "I for one am glad you quit."

Jane turned her head and stared at him. "Why?"

Brett's eyes were soft and dark and took their time examining her face. "I didn't like what they were doing to your hair."

She felt as if she could sink right into his eyes. Their gazes locked together and communicated. Again Jane knew a kind of breathy anticipation that made her heart begin to race.

"It...it's probably too long. One of these days I'll cut it," she murmured.

"As long as you don't take off too much...." Brett slowly let his hand slip under the heavy weight of Jane's hair. His fingers slid through the silken strands, lightly touching her scalp and she quivered gently at the tingling sensation his touch evoked. Brett curved his free hand around her waist and Jane felt herself being pulled toward him. She was too fascinated to object, and too curious to stop....

Her body turned easily until their mouths touched and pressed. But Brett wasn't going to be satisfied this time with light kisses and teasing. His appetite had been whetted and he had a strong feeling that Jane felt the same way. She might be tentative, but she was not completely unwilling.

Brett's mouth opened masterfully over hers and took instant possession in a determined but nonetheless gentle way. He rubbed and coaxed and manipulated until their mouths were fused, then his tongue tantalizingly began to stroke against Jane's lips, seeking entry. He heard the quivering intake of her breath, felt the small tremor that shook her body.

Her hands were restless, first twisting together in her lap and then reaching to hold onto his forearms. Jane felt his persistence and as if hypnotized, she slowly opened her lips to let his tongue plunge deeply inside to explore the sweet recesses. A sound bubbled up inside, a moan that Jane didn't dare express. But her tentativeness slipped away and she became responsive, meeting both the sensual twisting of

Brett's wide mouth over her own and the seductive thrust of his tongue. She began to melt against him.

There was such a natural acceptance on Jane's part that Brett was amazed. He would not have been surprised if she had shown a reluctance to let him hold her, but he was very glad that she didn't. As Jane allowed him to take charge, but responded according to her own needs, Brett could sense a distinct difference between her and every woman he'd ever known before.

With Carolyn, Brett had known he'd always be more of a caretaker than husband. She had never expressed desire, passion, even love, but rather a kind of desperate gratefulness that had been poignantly sad and frustrating. With the few women he'd known afterward Brett had always sensed that their attraction and response to him had been based on whatever presence or power they imagined he held, and not in the mutual satisfaction they might have shared together, whether physically or emotionally.

Jane's response was so honest that it made him feel humble. She didn't ask or expect anything of him. She was only concerned that she herself not be made to do anything she was not ready for, anything that could compromise her feelings. Brett knew he didn't want to hurt or frighten her. He couldn't move too fast. He was starting to care very much both about the person she was and what had made her who she was. He'd only thought of it in passing once or twice since December, but that framed photo on her bureau of Harry Lindsay suddenly came to mind. Brett wanted to know what place that smiling image held in Jane's life, and he was sure there was one much deeper than she'd admit to right now.

For her part, Jane had imagined that Brett's interest in her was physical. She was used to that. That was how men related to women in her experience, limited though it was. She didn't hold that against him because Jane also believed that

Brett was more sensitive and aware of her than most other men had ever been. She just wasn't sure how far she could trust her own feelings. It was just that now with their mouths moving so pleasurably together, the feel of the fire, the warmth of Brett, the gentleness of his hands did something new to her. And it *did* frighten her. She wanted to hold onto him for a little while and just melt completely into her senses. The barriers in her mind began to come down, following the inclinations of her body. He moved his hand and tenderly caressed the side of her face, and his mouth grew more demanding, the kiss deeper, headier... his tongue delightfully more aggressive.

But Jane knew that she would be unable to separate her senses from the workings of her heart. If she gave in to her feelings now, her desires and long-forgotten needs, she would also give in and care about this man. She suddenly wanted to. And if she gave in, it would not just be a little bit, but the whole of her would be consumed and she would be lost.

A liquid fire was starting a flaming course through her body. Her stomach knotted and there was a gnawing growing tension in the core of her that needed to be assuaged. For an instant she pressed closer to Brett, but when he would have pulled her into his arms and across his half-reclining body, Jane abruptly pulled away.

Both of them struggled with the moment. There was surprise and desire in their eyes, and there was no mistaking what they were feeling. Again Brett observed that startling vulnerability in Jane—and he could see her slowly gaining control over it. She was fighting everything that was happening between them. Nonetheless he reached out and brushed over her moist mouth with the padded surface of his thumb. Brett was surprised when she too extended her hand and touched his cheek and jaw.

Jane sighed and sat up, removing herself both physically and emotionally from the moment they'd shared.

"I have to let Jones out for a run. I'd appreciate it if you'd let him back in before you go to bed...."

Brett sat up and looked at her, trying not to lose the warmth of those last few seconds.

"There's fresh linen in the chest behind you for the sofa bed...."

"Jane..." Brett started slowly, the hoarseness in his tone reaching out for her attention.

The drawling, caressing tone rasped along her spine, but Jane squeezed her eyes closed and turned away sharply toward the front door, where Jones was already waiting for his mistress. She quickly let the dog out and closed the door again, but didn't turn around.

"I'll set up the coffee maker for the morning, and you know the shower is upstairs...."

"Jane, listen to me!" Brett said urgently, moving to stand behind her at the door. She stopped talking and quietly stood waiting. "You don't have to be afraid of me," Brett said clearly in a calm voice.

"Why would I be afraid of you?" The question was spoken in a whisper.

Brett took a step closer. "Afraid, perhaps, that I won't take you seriously...that I might hurt you. Or disappoint you," he guessed.

She turned around now, her back pressed against the outer door, her green eyes wide and direct. Brett was surprised to actually catch a glimpse of hurt and sadness, and to see moisture turn her eyes a deep sea green...stormy and deep.

"You're protecting yourself. You're here with no friends, no family, and you're not going to let anyone get too close to you, are you?"

Her chin rose stubbornly, quivering for a second. "I don't need anyone."

"Don't you?" Brett asked quizzically. He reached out to touch her hair, but Jane twisted her head to one side. "You don't need anyone to talk with, share with? Someone to praise you and encourage you and who understands?" Brett let his hand press the wall next to her head and he leaned toward her. "Then you are most unusual, Lady Jane," he whispered against her temple. "The woman I kissed and just held was not telling me that, at all."

Slowly she turned her head to stare at him. "You're very good, Brett Chandler. You're experienced and sophisticated, but I won't be just another conquest for you."

Brett frowned, his jaw working tensely. "I hadn't thought to conquer you. I thought what just happened was mutual. Something we both shared and wanted. I want to explore this...this feeling I seem to be developing for you. Why can't you trust me?"

"What feeling is that? Curiosity?" Jane challenged.

Brett watched the myriad emotions that changed her expression from one second to the next. "Yes," he admitted. "And also caring."

Jane shook her head to deny his assertion, sending her hair flying about her face. "I'm not like Carolyn. I'm not a princess or a damsel in distress. I don't need to be rescued. I'm too old to believe in fairy tales and too smart to believe in happy endings." Her voice quivered in her throat.

"What do you believe in?" Brett asked.

"*Myself.*"

"That's rather selfish," Brett said firmly.

"It's safe," Jane shot back.

"And what about love?" Brett asked, his hazel eyes watching her mouth that was responsive and soft and giving, but hadn't been kissed or explored nearly enough.

Jane's shoulders slumped and she blinked away the tears that had gathered in her eyes.

"I don't know," she said in a tired, weak tone. "I don't know anything at all about it."

It certainly wasn't the response he'd expected, and Brett didn't have a suitable comment. So when Jane eased past him and slowly started up the stairs, Brett simply let her go.

Chapter Six

The world was quiet and still...peaceful, and yet Brett lay awake restless, thinking about the woman upstairs...and about love.

Brett had always imagined that he knew what love was. He'd come from a loving home with parents who'd demonstrated it by being there when he needed them. He had in return tried to be a good son, someone they'd be proud of. He'd shown his love for Carolyn by his willingness to care for her and in his understanding that she would never be the wife and companion he would have hoped for. Love was expressed in the joy and delight he took in his son Jonathan, in watching him grow and develop into his own person. Sometimes love was thinking of others much more than of oneself. When you got right down to it, it was pretty easy to love someone.

Brett shifted on the sofa bed, his feet once more poking the sheets loose from their anchorage beneath the mattress. These foldout beds were not made for his long frame. His mind tried to assimilate Jane's parting confession. Why wouldn't she know what love was? Was she saying that she had never been in love, or loved anyone? Or that no one had ever loved her? Was she saying that she didn't understand what loving was all about?

For the first time the lack of concrete information about Jane began to frustrate Brett. It made her very existence seem almost arbitrary and inconsequential. But she *had* to begin from somewhere.

Brett sighed, his brow furrowed in thought, and swept a hand restlessly through his hair. He fought for understanding, for some key that would unlock the mystery that was Jane Lindsay. One thing Brett knew for certain; he wanted to know all about her. And he wanted her. He wanted slowly to open her protective shell and touch the Jane Lindsay that hid beneath. He wanted her to respond to him and not to her past. He wanted to—what . . . love her?

Perhaps it was too early, but it was the first time the thought of loving anyone had occurred to Brett since Carolyn. Or had Jane inadvertently been correct in suggesting he was only playing at gallantry? And even if he was sincere about caring, was it to be as superficial as his relationship to his first wife? *No.* If he went the distance, this time it would only be for love. It would only be for someone he *wanted* to spend his life with.

But what was love? Perhaps he didn't know what love was either, Brett thought in confusion as he lay with his hands clasped behind his head, staring at the ceiling beams. He wondered, however, if it was possible that he and Jane could teach each other. The other thought that kept coming back to him, particularly since his return, was that Jane had a conspicuous lack of family members to be connected to. But he remembered he had one vital clue to follow up, and he had every intention of doing so.

The unanswered questions that buzzed around his head began to exhaust him, and slowly Brett found himself settling into an uneasy sleep. His dreams were a confused mixture of Jonathan at three years of age crying for his mommy. There was also Carolyn, her face and features impossible to see clearly or in detail. There was his mother taking him by the arm, determined to introduce him to a room filled with beautiful women. He didn't want any of these women; he wanted to go to his son, who stood smiling happily at a young woman with red-gold hair....

Brett jumped and opened his eyes. He found himself staring into the dark liquid eyes of Jones. The dog was sitting quietly, but Brett knew that something was wrong. The house was still very quiet. But he sat up on the side of the bed, throwing the blanket aside. With a whine from the front of his throat, Jones turned and headed toward the stairs. Brett, wearing nothing more than his Jockey shorts, didn't hesitate to follow as the animal climbed to the second floor.

Brett walked into Jane's room immediately behind Jones, taking no time to consider whether it might be inappropriate to enter unannounced in the middle of the night. There was enough light for Brett easily to make out the four-poster bed, to find the slender form of Jane beneath the covers, her legs drawn up as she lay on her side. She was crying very softly into her pillow.

Brett stopped at the foot of the bed and listened in heart-wrenching surprise to her poignant lament. A quiet, private anguish seemed to be easing its way out of her. He realized that Jane was still asleep and moved quietly around the side of the bed so as not to startle her. Jones stood at Brett's side, as if expecting him to make his mistress better. Brett recognized the animal's amazing insight and gently ruffled the fur on his neck.

"Good boy," Brett whispered, then cautiously seated himself on the side of the mattress facing Jane. Something rolled against his back, and when he reached behind him it was to find the teddy bear he'd sent her. Brett placed it on the night table.

Brett lowered the covering that she'd tucked under her chin. She wore a sweater similar to the one she'd worn in

December, shapeless and hiding much of her body. Brett began to brush the hair from her face. Her cheeks were wet with tears. Gently he used his fingers to wipe away the tears, his heart contracting once again at finding her like this. He knew Jane to be so strong and independent that it made him instantly angry that anything or anyone was capable of doing this to her.

"Jane. Jane, wake up...." His words were low and soft.

Jane twisted her head on the pillow and moaned deep in her throat. Almost at once she stopped crying.

"Jane...come on, sweetheart. Open your eyes." The endearment was uttered very naturally. Jane moaned again. Then her lashes fluttered and her eyes opened. The green depths were awash in moisture, but she focused on Brett.

"Brett?" she questioned in a soft, confused voice.

"Yes, it's me. Are you all right?" he asked with deep concern, using his large warm hand to sweep her hair back from her face.

"Y-yes. Yes, I—I just had a dream." The confession made her fully aware that something had happened while she was asleep to cause him to come to her. She realized that she must have been crying again and hastily wiped the tears away, sniffling to clear her nose.

"I'm fine. I..."

Brett could see she was trying to gain control, as was her way. He stood and lifted the covers, moving easily to slide into the bed next to her. Suddenly Jane was wide awake and gasped at his near nakedness.

"What...are you doing?"

"Giving you something more substantial to hold onto until you go back to sleep. Move over."

Automatically Jane did as she was told, but continued to protest. "Look, I'm all right. Really."

"You had a bad dream and it upset you," Brett said with smooth authority, settling himself in the bed. At once Jane could feel a wonderful comforting warmth from his body.

"I appreciate your concern, but I'm not a child. I'll be fine. I'll probably go back to sleep in a few minutes...."

"Or you'll lie here in the dark and think about it for the next hour or more. Trust me. You'll settle down much quicker if you feel safe."

She was intrigued by what he was saying. "How do you know that?" she asked.

"Years of experience with a small boy who made night-time visits after bad dreams. Jonathan used to tell me it was safer in my bed, because I was bigger than the monsters," Brett informed her with a straight face. He turned his head to look at her in the dark. Oddly, Jane found herself relaxing. The temptation to smile was very strong. He really was good at doing that to her.

"Besides..." Brett began again, readjusting the covers over them both and getting comfortable, "...you were right about the sofa bed downstairs being uncomfortable." He lifted the arm nearest Jane, and it was a second or two before she realized that he intended her to lie against him.

Jane's heart began to thud in her chest. Unexpectedly a well of fresh tears rose into her throat and threatened to choke her with overwhelming feeling. "This... isn't necessary, Brett. I've had nightmares before and I've survived."

"I know. But isn't it much better when there's someone who understands, Lady Jane? Even just a friend?"

Jane lay biting her lip in indecision. But she was thinking of their proximity and how dangerous it was. She was so aware of his raw masculinity, his strength, and much too conscious of her own weakness and need of the moment. But if he held her, if all he did was hold her for a little while, she would consider it a rare gift indeed.

Slowly Jane moved under the raised arm, and even more slowly lowered her head onto his shoulder. But she tried not to let any other part of her come into contact with him. She would have been more comfortable if her hand could have rested on his chest, or her thigh lain against his . . . but she didn't dare. And Brett didn't force her, although his arm settling around her back caused her to roll more toward him. For a very long time Jane lay stiffly until the strain of it caused her body to relax and go limp. The cotton fabric of his shorts rubbed against her hand, and the rest of him was so bare and firmly male. The subtle manly scent of him she found reassuring.

Brett turned his head so that his nose was snuggled into the hair at her temple, and closed his eyes as he enjoyed the sweet smell. There was a sudden ache deep inside him, and he experienced a gentle fulfillment at being able to hold her this close. There was something deeper and more substantial happening here with Jane than instant sexual gratification would have provided. This felt very right—the way he'd felt when he'd momentarily opened his eyes in December and found concerned and curious green eyes watching him carefully.

Jane was feeling that this was too good to be true. She would survive the dream, as she'd said to Brett, but she was more afraid of the nightmare she'd endure if he turned out to be a dream, as well.

For many minutes they lay quietly together, both of them deep in their own discoveries and enlightenments, aware of what they'd been missing in their lives. As their bodies touched in this innocent way, both of them felt deeply vulnerable, wanting so much more.

Brett absently rubbed his hard jaw against her head. He had no real idea as yet where this budding relationship was going to go. He only knew that from this moment, right now with Jane in his arms, there was no turning back. He had no

You may already have won the

MILLION DOLLAR GRAND PRIZE!

SWEEPSTAKES RULES & REGULATIONS. NO PURCHASE NECESSARY.

Harlequin Reader Service®   Sweepstakes Entry Form

This is your **unique** Sweepstakes Entry Number: 4A 159698

This could be your lucky day! If you have the winning number, you could be the Grand Prize Winner. To be eligible, *affix Sweepstakes Entry Sticker here!*

If you would like a chance to win the $35,000.00 prize, the $10,000.00 prize, or one of the many $5,000.00, $1,000.00, $500.00, or $5.00 prizes ... plus the Cadillac and the Vacation of a Lifetime, *affix Cash and Bonus Prize Sticker here!*

To receive free books and gifts with no obligation to buy, as explained in the advertisement, *affix the Free Books and Gifts Sticker here!*

154 CIH NBG8

Please enter me in the sweepstakes and tell me if I've won the $1,000,000.00 Grand Prize! Also tell me if I've won any other cash prize, or the car, or the vacation prize. And ship me the free books and gifts I've requested with the sticker above. Entering the sweepstakes costs me nothing and places me under no obligation to buy! (If you do not wish to receive free books and gifts, do not affix the FREE BOOKS and GIFTS sticker.)

YOUR NAME   PLEASE PRINT

ADDRESS   APT. #

CITY   STATE   ZIP

Offer limited to one per household and not valid for current American Romance subscribers.

PRINTED IN U.S.A.

If order card is missing, write to: Harlequin Reader Service, 901 Fuhrmann Blvd., P.O. Box 1867, Buffalo, NY 14269-1867.

DETACH ALONG DOTTED LINE

DETACH ALONG DOTTED LINE

BUSINESS REPLY MAIL
FIRST CLASS   PERMIT NO. 717   BUFFALO, NY

POSTAGE WILL BE PAID BY ADDRESSEE

HARLEQUIN READER SERVICE®
MILLION DOLLAR SWEEPSTAKES
901 Fuhrmann Blvd.
P.O. Box 1867
Buffalo, NY 14240-9952

NO POSTAGE
NECESSARY
IF MAILED
IN THE
UNITED STATES

idea what horrors she was hiding from in her dreams and her past, but he would try to be there if she needed him. In a still-undefined way he needed her, too.

Jane felt the movement of Brett's jaw as a very personal kind of caress. He was continually surprising her, and even now in a situation fraught with latent sexuality and the possibilities of explosive passion, she simply felt safe with him.

More moments of silence passed—more moments, during which all sense of strangeness between them magically disappeared. Even Jones must have sensed the difference, since he finally settled down on the floor by the bed and with a gentle snort went to sleep. Jane began to feel a seductive drowsiness steal over her again and unconsciously wiggled herself into a more comfortable position next to Brett. He rubbed his hand up and down her back, feeling the light cotton of her sweater under his hand, but now also having a distinct sense of the feminine curves of Jane's body.

"Are you comfortable?" Brett's voice broke the velvet silence surrounding them.

"Yes..." came her hesitant reply. But she bit her lip, thinking something more should be said, some explanation or excuse for her crying in her sleep. "Brett, I..."

He moved so that they faced each other. The wiry hair on his broad chest brushed against her cheek. Instantly her stomach muscles curled at the blatant maleness of him. He leaned over and pressed a quick firm, provocative kiss across her mouth, then pulled back.

"Shh...just go to sleep. We'll talk about it some other time."

Jane nodded, giving in to his wisdom and now trusting it more than she realized. She even allowed her hand to lie tentatively against his chest before she went back to sleep. Brett listened for Jane's even breathing and felt her body relaxing into him, then he, too, succumbed.

It was still dark when Jane was startled into full awareness. She lay for a moment in confusion. She was alone and
everything about her was completely quiet. Jane turned and
reached out a hand—to empty space. But she knew she
hadn't imagined Brett's presence with her earlier in the
night.

Her stomach twisted with a queasy suspicion that she
might have been wrong about him, after all. His show of
tenderness hours before and her susceptibility to it now
made Jane feel rather compromised and foolish. With a
tremulous sigh of disappointment she threw the covering
aside and climbed out of bed. Feeling suddenly very dispir-
ited she made no attempt to don robe or slippers, but
mindlessly headed for the stairs to the first floor.

Jones was nowhere in sight; that instantly made her nervous. Softly she called the animal's name, but got no response. Then Jane noticed that the sofa bed had been put to
rights and that the light was on in the kitchen. When she
walked in she found freshly brewed coffee on the counter
and an already used mug. Jane went back into the hall. Obviously Brett had gotten up and left for his long ride to
Bethpage, but she couldn't help feeling hurt that he hadn't
said goodbye; he hadn't even left a note.

Suddenly the door opened and Brett appeared, having
used his shoulder to gain entry. Jones swept around his legs
and ambled over to greet a completely stunned Jane. She
stared at Brett, his arms loaded with cut lengths of firewood.

"What are you doing up?" he inquired easily. "Was I
making too much noise outside?" He managed to bend with
his heavy burden and retrieve a dropped log.

Jane stood there, feeling such relief at finding that he
hadn't just left her that it was hard to breathe normally. Her
heart pounded crazily against her rib cage.

Brett walked past her to the hearth and, kneeling, began to place the logs one by one in a wire basket on the floor.

"You were out of firewood, and I wanted to make sure there was some handy before I left...."

His back was to her, so Brett couldn't see the heart-stopping look on her face that made her eyes wide and very bright, or her childish stance, one foot on top of the other.

"If you're not sure how to get a fire started, have Oliver do it." With assurance and authority Brett gave his list of instructions. Then he stood, dusting his hands together, and turned to face Jane.

He stopped and stared at the ethereal image she made, standing there like Botticelli's Venus. He recalled her softness in the night against him. Her full breasts were also boldly prominent through her shirt, and Brett remembered the sensual pressure of them, as well. Jane seemed wholly unaware of the effect her scantily clad body was having on him. She was so beautiful that Brett had an instant urge to crush her to him and make love with her.

Jane was thinking the same thing. How extraordinarily virile and handsome he was in his black turtleneck sweater and dark trousers. She suddenly wanted to know the full power and strength of Brett against her. He slowly began to walk toward her, began to smile and with familiarity ran his hand through her hair, holding it away from her face.

"How did you sleep?" he asked in a caressing tone.

Jane met his gaze openly. Her features were now serene and lovely to see. Her blush was not from embarrassment, but from what she was feeling deep inside that was so new and breathtaking.

"Very well...thanks to you," she added sincerely.

Brett's heart turned over at her honesty. "It was my pleasure."

"It's still a long way to Bethpage. I suppose you'll have to leave soon," Jane said calmly.

Brett's hazel eyes regarded her for a long moment. "I should."

Jane nodded. "Will you do me one more favor before you leave?"

Brett nodded in affirmation. Jane walked gracefully around him to her den, disappeared into the dark for a few moments, then reappeared. She extended an envelope to Brett, which he accepted with a questioning look.

"These are for Jonathan. I thought he might enjoy them."

"May I?" Brett asked, lifting the envelope flap. He examined the contents and raised his brows. "You realize this will put him forever in your debt."

Jane smiled and shrugged. "Not at all. It's just that I don't know a thing about hockey and it seemed a shame to waste the passes. Maybe you could take him...."

"How did you come by the tickets?"

"I did a piece on the wives of hockey players. The tickets were part of the thank-you I received from the management office. You don't have to tell Jonathan they're from me."

Brett continued to look at her and smile gently. He put the envelope into his pocket and stepped closer, looking down into her eyes. But she was regarding him now with a kind of shy uncertainty.

"Brett..." she began. "About last night..."

Brett cupped her chin in one hand, raising her head, the action silencing her. "You don't have to explain to me. I understand." His thumb brushed gently over her mouth. "Now I have a favor to ask, too...."

She caught her breath. "Yes?"

"I want to kiss you before I go."

Jane smiled. "That's not a question."

"Isn't it?" he murmured, already beginning to slide his arms around her and draw her against himself. With enormous satisfaction Brett's lips slowly claimed hers, gaining entry at once to her warm mouth. His tongue began a flirtatious dance around her own. There was no shyness, no hesitancy on Jane's part, it was as if she had been waiting for this, too.

His arms tightened and Jane willingly leaned into him. One hand pressed intimately against her lower back so that there was no mistaking the distinct male outline of him. His fingers pressed and kneaded the flesh of her bottom through the cotton fabric. It was bold and suggestive, but more sensuous than erotic. Jane began to know a gnawing ache within her. His other hand slid under her hair to her neck and held it so that her mouth was fixed to his. He ravaged it hungrily, his tongue burrowing deeper and deeper with a passion that made Jane dizzy. She began to feel senseless, mindless, giddy with need, and pressed herself into his arms, not caring that his roaming hand was perilously close to finding her naked beneath the sweater.

Jane could hear their hurried breathing and sense the urgency their embrace was creating. Then she began to feel Brett easing up on the embrace. His mouth grew gentler, more seductive, until he finally raised his lips and their breathing mingled.

Brett took a deep breath, then held her face framed, tilted up to him. Jane watched his nostrils flare and his jaw tense and was totally mesmerized by his obvious holding back of his own desire. He was not rushing her into anything.

"You understand that I'll be back, don't you?" he asked in a gravelly voice.

Jane nodded, her eyes bright.

Brett kissed her on the nose. "Good. I'm glad we finally got that one out of the way." He released her a bit more. "Are you going to be able to get back to sleep?" he asked seriously.

"I'm sure I will."

"Don't forget...there's always Teddy. We're going to have to come up with a name for him...." He smiled, reluctantly letting her go and walking to the closet for his jacket. Jane hugged herself, following him slowly. Brett zipped up the aviation jacket halfway and turned back to her. When he bent to kiss her again she met him freely. Then he turned to Jones and stooped to pet him.

"Take good care of our Lady, Jones," he said, and Jane thought her heart would stop. *Our Lady...*

He opened the door and stepped out into the pearly haze of dawn. For a long silent moment they simply stared at each other. He turned her gently by the shoulder, patted her even more gently on the rear, and she automatically stepped back inside, away from the door. Brett closed it slowly behind her.

Jane stood perfectly still. She listened for the slamming of the car door, the sound of the engine starting, and the crunching of tire wheels on snow as he pulled away. Feeling suddenly empty and extraordinarily lonely, but also excited and hopeful, Jane climbed the stairs.

As she crept back into bed Jane couldn't help thinking that perhaps she'd paid her penance. Perhaps her soul had been purged of guilt, remorse and disappointment. She'd never asked for more out of life than to be wanted, and to be a part of it. Love was a gift, and Jane began to feel that it was possible that she would one day receive it for herself. Even if it wasn't Brett, she was willing to take a chance again.

He had taken so many liberties with his charm and sense of humor. But Jane readily acknowledged with a rich deep yawn as she settled back into peaceful sleep, what he'd given in return had been priceless.

BRETT DROVE AROUND the scattering of small cottages twice before he found the one belonging to Dr. Oliver Seymour.

Brett had no qualms about waking up the older man at such an early hour. For the moment Oliver was the only other person available who could tell him what he needed to know about Jane Lindsay.

Brett no longer even felt presumptuous about inquiring into Jane's life. He reasoned that if he knew more about her past, what had left her so withdrawn and careful, he'd know what *not* to do in the future—even though it seemed maybe a little premature to be talking about the future, when the present was still so tenuous.

Brett pulled his car onto the narrow shoulder of the road and walked the short distance to Oliver's door, then rang the bell twice. While he waited, he looked casually around the property. He quickly became aware that although none of the windows in Jane's house allowed for any view down the road to Oliver's house, from the side of his property a good part of Jane's house could be seen. Brett was still speculating on the strange coincidence of Oliver having that particular view when the door was yanked open by the man himself, as he uttered an array of colorful words to describe his feelings about being awakened at dawn. When Oliver realized who it was he stopped abruptly, scratched his beard-covered jaw and with a disagreeable grunt, waved Brett into the house.

Sleepy and yawning, Oliver led the way into the kitchen, which offered a wonderful view of Lake Montauk.

"The coffee will have to be instant. I wasn't expecting visitors," Oliver grumbled. He eyed the younger man, who was moving slowly about the kitchen deep in thought.

Brett turned to leaf through a paperback novel that lay on the table. Oliver watched him carefully although he sensed that Jane was the reason for this nocturnal visit. Oliver had no intention of divulging bits and pieces of Jane's personal life, and he knew and understood a lot of it. Besides, it really wasn't his place to do that. If Jane wanted Brett

Chandler to know things about herself, she would tell Brett of her own accord. Jane had enough emotional garbage to deal with, and he didn't know Brett well enough to help him possibly be the cause of any more.

However, he was pretty sure Brett wouldn't do anything to hurt Jane. She was a very smart young woman, but she was woefully ignorant in matters of the heart. Certainly not from want of trying in the past, but due to some very poor choices and unexpected rejection.

"I can assure you the book isn't all that interesting," Oliver commented dryly, squinting at Brett.

Brett's expression was earnest as he considered the doctor. "How long has Jane been estranged from her father?"

Oliver raised his brows. "Jane's father?" he asked blankly.

"Yes. Harry Dean Lindsay," Brett said pointedly, letting Oliver know decisively that *he* knew this information to be true.

"What makes you think Harry Lindsay is Jane's father?" Oliver asked with the right amount of incredulity in his voice. He wasn't a poker player for nothing and could bluff better than most.

Brett grimaced impatiently. "Give me a break, Oliver. She has an autographed, carefully framed photo of a well-known journalist displayed on her dresser, and you expect me to believe it's sheer coincidence that they have the same last name?"

Oliver continued to watch Brett blandly, although it was already apparent to him that Brett was not easily bluffed, either.

Brett arched a brow. "Should I even bother to mention the fact that she resembles him markedly when she smiles?"

Oliver winced, sighing deeply. Not just anyone would notice a detail like a smile.

"Why do you want to know?" Oliver asked gruffly.

After a long moment of considering the question, Brett relaxed into his seat. "I'm interested in the lady, Oliver. I suspect you've realized that. And you know as well as I do that Jane plays it pretty close to the chest. There must be reasons why she's skittish and lives all alone." Brett let that sink in while Oliver frowned deeply. "I know about the shooting three years ago...."

Oliver glanced up sharply.

"I don't believe any of it was her fault, but it shook her up pretty badly, enough to make her quit a very impressive career and run from New York City. But that's not all of it. That's not enough to explain why Jane is so...so..." Brett tilted his head and frowned. "Vulnerable. You know what I'm talking about, Oliver. You probably understand what motivates her better than anyone."

Oliver shrugged. "Supposing I do?"

Brett stopped. It suddenly occurred to him that maybe he'd read Oliver all wrong. Maybe the other man wouldn't be sympathetic to his wanting to know Jane. Maybe in a single-minded attempt to protect her, Oliver wouldn't care how he felt. Brett took a drink of coffee and set the cup down abruptly. His eyes pinned Oliver.

"Look...I *like* her. I want to like her more. Do I make myself clear?"

For a long second Oliver eyed Brett, but he was satisfied with what he detected in the younger man. He drained his cup and stood to make more coffee.

"Perfectly," Oliver answered finally, pouring the water and sitting down again. "Jane's been 'estranged,' as you call it, forever."

"Forever? What does that mean?" Brett asked, confused.

Oliver made vague gestures with his hand, struggling for an explanation. "It means Jane hasn't seen or spoken to her father since she was in high school."

Brett digested this. He stared at the half-empty cup, twisting it back and forth on the table by the handle. "Do you know why?" he asked softly.

Oliver shifted in his chair. "Yes, I do. But I don't think I can tell you, Brett."

"Why?"

"Because I think it should come from Jane."

Brett understood and respected that. "What about the rest of her family? Mother, brothers and sisters?" He looked up with eyes that were dark and questioning. "Husbands or children?"

Oliver was shaking his head. "Jane's an only child. There wasn't and isn't a husband, and there are no children. Her mother lives in California. She's married now to a screenwriter. They keep in touch, more or less, but she's not anxious for anyone to know she has a daughter who's thirty-four years old. It would cramp her style," Oliver added dryly. "Jane's been pretty much on her own since she started college."

Brett shook his head slowly. "I don't think I understand this. It doesn't sound like much of a family."

"I'm sorry, Brett. That's all I can say. It's Jane's life and her affair. You'll have to find out the rest from her."

Brett sighed in frustration and swept a hand through his hair.

"I will tell you this. She's had a rough time of it, and she's been badly hurt. I'd rather not see it happen to her again."

"I don't have any intention of hurting her," Brett said a bit impatiently.

"You can only do that now if she gives you the power to. Has she?" Oliver knew Brett would understand exactly what he meant.

"I don't think so. At least not yet."

"Then don't play her false, Brett. Don't make this a quick and dirty little affair. She deserves better than that. And if

Jane doesn't mean any more to you than that, then walk away now while there's no damage done."

Brett remembered warmly the curious but gentle night he'd just passed with Jane that had meant more to him than Oliver could understand. "I think it's too late to just walk away."

"Fine," Oliver said, standing and gulping down the rest of his coffee. "Then just let things happen. Be patient and follow your instincts. Trust them."

Brett got to his feet and slowly followed Oliver back to the hallway.

"On the other hand, don't be too soft with her. I give her a hard time myself occasionally, but believe me, it's out of concern and regard for her happiness. I'm what you might call a self-appointed fairy godfather." Oliver laughed lightly, but Brett thought seriously about that.

"Does she need one?"

"She did. But the time will come one day soon when I can hand over my magic wand," Oliver said flippantly.

Oliver opened the door to a cold February morning. He yawned again.

"Well, I hate to be rude, but it's still the middle of the night. Get the hell out of here, so I can get back to sleep."

Brett laughed, stepping outside, "I'll probably see you again soon."

Oliver frowned. "Oh no, you won't. If you have the sense I think you do, you'll come to see Jane and leave me out of it."

Oliver shut the door sharply, leaving Brett chuckling softly to himself.

JANE CONSIDERED the problems of Inland Estates and decided that the solution was very simple. The court case was not earth-shattering, and only because it involved two fairly prominent Long Island families did it rate press coverage at all. Only peripherally was it mentioned that a decision couldn't be made by either family, since the land legally belonged to a thirteen-year-old child, who probably didn't have the vaguest idea of what all the fuss was about.

After reading the latest update, Jane sighed and put the paper aside. She was slightly impatient with being so absorbed in the happenings of Brett's family, but it was precisely because it *was* his family that she was so fascinated. Well, the truth was, *he* was fascinating. Jane turned to the computer screen in her studio and tried to concentrate on the article she was developing. But her mind refused to cooperate and kept returning to Brett, as it was wont to do these days.

She stared at the screen, then got up to wander to a nearby window. Jones had comfortably settled his large body just outside the studio door, his eyes following the restless movements of his mistress. She'd been getting up and down from the P.C. all day, unable to work and unable to do much else besides sigh and daydream.

It was the last day of February, only a week since Brett's serendipitous appearance. But the night spent lying in his arms had stayed with Jane and each moment, each magic second of it was relived... and savored... over and over again. Magic was the perfect word to describe the feeling.

Jane watched the new subtle signs of spring. She'd never noticed the changes before, never particularly looked for them. But so much time spent at the window, expecting to see a sports car coming down the lane had alerted Jane to the happenings in the rest of the world. The benefit was a new awareness, a new urge to be out in the sunshine. The disadvantage was a lack of willingness to be alone hour after hour, churning out article after article.

Jane wanted to figure out what Brett was up to. Why did he bother to come back to Montauk when she gave him so little encouragement? He said he wanted to get to know her, that he liked her. But Jane only knew she was desperately afraid to believe him. She would hate it if Brett turned out to be selfish and insensitive, like other men she'd known.

She pushed her hands carelessly through her hair, tangling her fingers in the rich locks. She really *had* to do something about her hair. Not having cut or styled it for three years was making it difficult to manage, except that Brett seemed to like it just the way it was. Jane closed her eyes and leaned her forehead against the ice-cold windowpane. "Why are you doing this to me?" she whispered plaintively. "Why did you have to come and change everything?"

But what had Brett changed, after all? He had demonstrated merely with his presence how isolated and lonely her life was. He had shown a genuine sense of humor and charm that in all fairness wasn't even remotely like men she'd known. It was very real. He had shown such a gentleness, such a thoughtfulness for her just as she was, that Jane felt she must not be so terrible a person, even worthy of respect. Brett had also returned to see her, and the happenings of a week ago now had left her shaken. For Jane realized how easy it would be to become involved with Brett Chandler in a way that could destroy her.

Jane flounced away from the window and paced the room. Of course, maybe they could just be friends. Though he had kissed her rather passionately the last time, and she had enjoyed and probably encouraged it, he'd made no particular move to make love to her. But she'd never had a "friend" like Brett and suspected that given an opening, friendship was not all he had in mind. Jane resolutely decided she wasn't going to fall victim to another man's charisma again and risk being used and hurt.

"Come on, Jones. Let's go for a walk," Jane suggested, stepping over the dog and heading with determination for the door. The dog lifted his head to watch her. His senses told him this was not the weekly trip into town for packages, or the run on the beach that he loved. But the idea of a trip outdoors nonetheless sparked his interest and Jones got up spryly to trot to Jane.

She was flipping her hair out of the collar of her jacket when the phone started ringing. Impatiently Jane ignored it. She didn't want to talk to anyone. She just wanted to get out of the house, away from the P.C. Away from her fantasies....

Jane closed the door firmly, but could still hear the faint ringing of the telephone. Suddenly she picked up her feet and started running. She headed down Old Westlake Drive and out to the main road known as Montauk Highway, although it had only one lane in each direction and hardly constituted a highway. She ran until she was out of breath and panting and overheated from the exertion. Then she slowed to a pensive walk along the side of the road. Jones, delighted with this turn of events, explored to his heart's content. But Jane had not managed to shake her vague discontent, nor her thoughts of Brett. They vacillated back and forth until she didn't know if she hoped he'd return again, or hoped that he wouldn't.

Jane had no idea how long she walked or where, since she changed direction several times. At last she found herself on the outskirts of town and thought of stopping somewhere for coffee or cocoa, though she knew she'd have to leave Jones outside. With a tired sigh Jane turned around and headed back toward the road leading out of town and to her own house.

It was just beginning to get dark when she reached the turnoff in the road and in a final sprint of energy started running again back to the house. Her leg muscles protested, but gritting her teeth she kept going. Suddenly behind Jane there was a honking of a car horn and the narrow beam of headlights. She stood still to let the car pass, but found it stopping next to her. Jane watched in weak surprise when the car door opened and Brett unfolded his long body from the low seat. Leaning an arm on the car door he frowned at her. Jane was breathing hard, and although it was cold, there were beads of perspiration on her forehead.

"What are you doing out here?" Brett questioned.

Jane felt dumb. How could she possibly tell him she'd been trying to wipe thoughts of him from her mind? "I...I just went for...a walk," she said, still fighting for air.

Brett leaned closer. "Why were you running?"

"I...I thought it might be...good exercise," she lied. She was just too tired to be angry that it was all his fault that she was out here in the freezing cold.

Brett's eyes swept over her quickly and his frown now expressed concern and puzzlement. "You're sweating. You're not dressed properly for jogging in this weather..." He turned to pull forward the driver's seat and then whistled for Jones. The dog appeared and readily hopped into the back of the car. Brett put the seat back and turned to Jane. "Come on. We have to get you out of those clothes before you catch a chill..." And taking her hand he led her around to the passenger side. Without any more conversation Brett drove the distance to her house. He let the dog out and then came to help Jane, but she ignored his outstretched hand.

"I can manage," she said stubbornly, climbing awkwardly out of the car. She ached all over, but somehow made it to the house, Brett right behind her.

"I tried calling you," he said as Jane eased her way out of the jacket.

"I was only out for a short while...."

Brett looked at his watch. "At least two hours. And it's twenty-nine degrees outside." He took her jacket and his and hung them up. He turned to realize that it was pretty cold inside the house, as well. "Why is it always so cold in here?'' he asked and immediately headed for the living room and the fireplace. He knelt to begin a fire.

''It doesn't matter.'' Jane shrugged it off, nonetheless flexing her cold fingers. ''It's just me here.''

Brett looked over his shoulder at her in confusion. ''So you don't deserve to be warm just because you're here alone?'' he asked.

The question made Jane angry, first of all because he was right, and secondly because his incredulousness made her feel foolish. ''I don't mind being a little cold,'' she muttered as a chill wracked her body and she trembled. And then she sneezed. She glanced sheepishly at Brett, who gave her an I-told-you-so look as he walked slowly toward her.

''I want you to go upstairs and get out of those things, Jane. Take a warm shower and put on dry clothes.'' His voice was calm and reasonable, but again she felt her anger rising.

That was exactly what Oliver would have told her to do. She didn't want Brett to treat her as Oliver did. When she didn't move, Brett slowly reached out a hand to touch her damp cheek, then rested it against her hair.

''You're going to risk getting sick if you don't,'' he told her gently, but Jane stood her ground. ''Do you want me to come and help you?'' There was a soft suggestion to the question that dissipated her chagrin and made her feel very helpless standing there so stubbornly before him. From deep inside a part of her wanted to say yes.

Jane slowly shook her head. ''No, thank you.''

Brett smiled. ''Fine. While you're doing that I'll make some hot chocolate.'' Behind him, Jones, having stationed himself by his food dish, let out a low soft bark. Brett chuckled silently. ''And I'll feed Jones,'' he said, turning toward the kitchen.

Jane stood for a moment longer, knowing that all her resolve, all her pent-up desire to keep her distance and maintain control had just gone out the window. She didn't seem to have the strength to fight her own feelings and was very close to giving up.

It took all of twenty minutes for Jane to do as she was told. She came down the stairs slowly, her legs threatening to collapse under her. She peeked into the kitchen, to find Brett busily concocting something at the counter with Jones, an avid audience, planted next to him. Brett turned to face her. He smiled slowly and in his hazel eyes was approval of her two-piece velour pant and sweater set. She had twisted her hair into a loose Gibson knot, with dozens of tendrils still damp from her shower. Brett turned back to the counter.

"I see you don't feed yourself very often, either. There's not much in your cupboards." Jane opened her mouth to speak, but he interrupted. "I know, I know. It's just you here alone and why bother." He lifted the tray from the counter. "Let's go into the living room." Jane had no choice but to follow. Carefully she lowered herself to the sofa and sighed in relief.

Dinner was simple and filling, but even Jane had to acknowledge it lacked something. She asked about the Grumman tests, and Brett told her that all had gone well. Then he told her about the planned trip to Germany and the designs he was busy preparing for the building of a prototype glider. Jane glanced surreptitiously at him from time to time, wondering at his busy involved life and his persistence in seeing her. Why did he go to so much trouble?

Brett waited through Jane's silence, and she would have been appalled at how accurately he was now reading her mind. He grinned at her wickedly. "Before you ask me what I'm doing here, let me say I thought to take you to dinner."

"Dinner…" she repeated blankly, trying to remember the last time she'd had dinner out with anyone. She couldn't.

Brett lifted a brow. "Yes, dinner. As in getting dressed up and going out and letting someone else, preferably someone with talent, cook and serve you a meal. You may find it strange, I realize, but there's a whole segment of the population that actually considers it a fun thing to do from time to time."

He was gently teasing her. She lifted her chin haughtily. "I know that. I also know that it's considered good form to ask first."

Brett's expression was wry. "That's true, but I did try to call you first." He looked down at the empty soup crocks and half-eaten toast. "This isn't what I had in mind, exactly." Then he seemed to roll from his seat to stoop in front of Jane. He lifted one of her legs, and, resting her bare foot on his thigh, began to massage her calf muscles.

"Ohh . . . that hurts!" she moaned in protest.

"I know it does," Brett replied, continuing with his strong fingers on her tender flesh. "But believe me, it will be ten times worse in the morning. Why didn't you wear sweatpants and top if you were going to jog?"

Jane bit her lip against the ache in her legs. "I wasn't jogging. I . . . was just sort of running," she said lamely.

"I see," Brett said, but his expression showed otherwise. "The next time you decide to just sort of run, warm up first. Do some stretches to loosen your muscles. And when you finish, cool down the same way . . . slowly." He switched to the other leg, and Jane willingly let him lift it. She began to soften and feel warm at his sure touch. She looked at his bent head with its gray and black texture. She was so tempted to stroke it in affection.

"That should help a little. Tomorrow you'll be sore, but you won't feel like an invalid." He shook his head as his eyes roamed over her. He was still squatting on his heels. "I think you need someone to look after you," he said softly.

Jane let the comment sink in; she didn't agree or disagree, but the thought of someone actually caring for her, of Brett caring for her, was very appealing. "Did you take care of your wife?" The question was a soft inquiry.

Brett's jaw tensed, but his eyes were still open and discerning. "I tried to. Sometimes I think I wasn't very good at it."

They were mesmerized, looking into each other's eyes, each other's hearts and souls.

"Why did she die?" Jane blurted out in a whisper.

Brett's gaze finally dropped to her feet. She had small, narrow feet. They were warm and rosy. Carolyn's had been cold all the time. "She got sick about a year after Jonathan was born and became very weak. Leukemia. She'd never been particularly strong, and she never could build up a resistance even with treatment." He looked at her again, his voice calm, his eyes soft, but for Jane and not for the memory of Carolyn. Ten years was a long time to feel guilt and remorse. "She died when Jonathan was just three."

Jane looked away from those intense gray eyes. "Did you...love her very much?" She didn't know why she asked that. The question was out before Jane realized she had no right to put it. But again, Brett didn't seem to find it presumptuous.

If anything, Brett found it very telling that Jane would ask about his love for another woman. Was she simply curious? Or was there an element of jealousy? "Not as much as I should have. I married Carolyn because she needed me to."

Jane frowned at his response but didn't think it wise to pursue it. He had been surprisingly honest with her and some things, after all, were private.

"Come on," Brett said, standing. He took hold of Jane's hands and gently pulled her to her feet. Her knees cracked. "I'm going to help you upstairs to bed."

Jane scoffed. "I can walk!" Brett was already bending to put an arm under her legs to swing her clear of the floor. With a gasp, she anchored her arms around Brett's neck.

"Stop protesting. Enjoy the ride," Brett ordered, and then marched off toward the stairs.

Jane was silent. She recognized that she was very glad not to have to climb the stairs. She felt somewhat like a princess, very protected and pampered. She loved every minute of it.

Brett carried her easily, thoroughly enjoying the feminine feel of her body. Jane's eyes were riveted to his profile, to the lean male lines of his face, the still visible evidence of his accident in December. She looked at *him*, who was coming to mean so much to her.

Brett deposited her on the bed and pulled up the covers. He knew she was thinking the same thing he was. Last week they were together in this bed.

"I'll even tuck you in, although I recall I didn't rate such treatment," he reminded her gently, and watched her blush.

"You were teasing me," Jane offered. But Brett only smiled at her. Again there was a long moment of silence. Jane looked directly into his hazel eyes. "Are you . . . going to stay the night?" she asked in a low voice.

Brett was very careful not to let his surprise show. It was the first real indication he'd received from Jane that she might want him to continue seeing her. He had adjusted to the need to go slowly with her. Now Jane was taking the initiative. He'd really only thought to take her to dinner. He wanted to get her away from the house and to see her in another setting. Then he had to fly out of Montauk airport back to Massachusetts. *God knows,* Brett thought, *I want to stay with her....* He also realized now that he wasn't going to. *No,* better to back off right now and have an option later. Better to have her *want* him to return.

"Is that an invitation?" Brett asked in a hoarse voice.

Jane hadn't thought of it that way, realizing too late the implications. Her face showed a number of conflicting emotions, all of which pleased Brett, and all of which made him smile broadly at her.

He shook his head. "Sooner or later I'm going to have to go home to change clothes, read my mail, pay my housekeeper. Of course, you could come and visit with me...."

"No, I couldn't do that."

"Why not?"

Jane thought. *Why not, indeed?* "I...I just couldn't."

"Well, maybe not right now. Some other time, for sure. You'll like Boston."

Jane was watching him as he talked, making note of his easy manner and his sincerity. She thought suddenly of all the times she'd tried to thwart his attempts to pry too deeply beneath the surface of her life and how often she'd said no. She compared those times to his willingness to accept that, even as he gently coaxed her into sometimes saying yes. Jane couldn't believe his patience, and she wasn't sure she even deserved it.

Brett frowned at her continued stare. "What's the matter? Is something growing out of my ear?"

Jane grimaced prettily. "I...don't understand you," she whispered in a soft, confused voice.

Brett smiled from his hazel eyes with both tenderness and confidence. He'd come to know a lot about Jane. But she often gave much of herself away in a kind of sweet naiveté. Her comment indicated to Brett that Jane was starting to see him as different and apart from other men, hopefully she would begin to respond to him that way. Brett gently stroked her cheek. He had no problems, no hesitancy in touching her. He wanted her to get used to being touched by him.

"You will...soon," he promised easily. "Right now it's only important that you trust me. I'm making a date right now for next weekend," Brett said, reaching for the teddy bear and tucking it next to her under the covers. "The *whole* weekend," he emphasized pointedly, and Jane merely nodded. "We'll play it by ear."

Brett bent forward and gave her a chaste kiss on the forehead. She had expected one more like the bone-shattering one they'd exchanged a week before. But Brett stood up then, leaving her disappointed.

"I'll see that Jones gets his run, and then let him back in." He walked to the door and turned once more to look longingly at her snuggled in the bed. "See you at the end of the week," he reminded her once more.

The sound of his movements downstairs was so comforting and made her feel so safe that Jane was asleep before he left the house.

Chapter Seven

Jane wasn't listening to a word Oliver was saying. He droned on about how unfair she was being in refusing to leave Montauk when Brett invited her to visit in Boston. Perhaps Oliver was right; but she wasn't going to change her mind.

"Oliver, please!" Jane admonished with a soft groan at his continued harangue. It was true that Brett had willingly spent the last three weekends with her. He'd arrive on a Friday evening, once early on a Saturday morning, and they'd have two full days of being together. For the most part they did simple things, none of which Jane had ever done before in her life, and all of which she'd enjoyed a lot. Brett had kept his word and had not pried any further into her past, even when she knew he wanted to. But Jane didn't want her past to interfere with the present.

They had gotten past the first awkward question of sleeping arrangements. Brett readily took the sofa bed, never complaining about how uncomfortable it was, and never suggesting that they'd be more comfortable in her bed. They both knew that intimacy between them could develop swiftly, but there was an unspoken sense that it wasn't time yet.

Brett teased Jane about her questionable culinary skills, and Jane found herself setting out to prove he was wrong.

For Brett it had been a simple challenge that he hoped would stimulate and add to their time together. Jane rose admirably to the occasion. They'd fallen into a habit of Saturday lunch, and later dinner, and then a Sunday brunch before Brett left again. Sometimes Jane would prepare the meal by herself. Sometimes Brett would lend a hand. There would be a lot of easy conversation and laughter. Somewhere along the way they became entirely comfortable with each other, like friends, as Brett had predicted. It worked very well, except for the moments when they'd meet each other's gaze and recognize a deeper need....

Oliver was sitting at the table, continuing his dissertation on poor Brett and how he didn't envy the man. Jane gritted her teeth and put her attention now to a nut bread she was pouring into a loaf pan. She didn't want to confront the cold hard truth of Oliver's words. She was giving Brett a hard time. Not deliberately and, she hoped, not even selfishly. But her whole world had changed in the last month as her relationship with Brett evolved and grew. He had gently coaxed her into much of it, Jane realizing that he was continually extending her boundaries to include other places and people. Jane, however, had simply not been willing to go so far as to accept Brett's invitation to visit with him in Boston, or even to spend a day in Bridgehampton with his mother. She'd resolutely refused even to consider Bridgehampton, somehow having gotten it into her head that Priscilla Chandler would object to her. Boston held appeal because she wanted to be with Brett, but she also realized after two weeks in his company that if she ever left Montauk Point, she'd never want to return and live there all alone again. Once she opened the door to the outside world she'd be drawn back into it.

Jane turned impatiently from the counter. "Oliver, did it ever occur to you that what goes on between Brett and me is none of your business?"

"No," Oliver replied with a shrug. He wasn't a bit concerned that he had aroused Jane's ire. "Since you've seen fit to tell me at least a dozen times that there is nothing going on between you and Brett, it doesn't matter, does it?"

Jane stared at him and flounced around to place the loaf pan in the oven. "Don't you have anything better to do than to sit there being impossible!"

Oliver raised his brows, a wounded expression on his face. "I thought I was invited for lunch?"

"*That* may have been a mistake!"

Oliver chuckled. "It's not my fault Brett didn't make it today. Why waste a perfectly good lunch?" The minute the words were said, Oliver knew he'd scratched more than the surface of Jane's irritation.

Jane's face fell dejectedly and her eyes reflected her confusion. She reasoned that she had no right to react this way, just because Brett had not arrived for the weekend. He did have a life and family and obligations that didn't include her. She was more upset by the realization that she'd come to look forward to his visits and was disappointed now that he wasn't here. The relationship was the one she wanted—except that Jane had stopped wanting only that weeks ago.

She looked out her kitchen window onto a day that had spring written all over it. It was the kind of day Brett would have suggested they spend outdoors. It wouldn't have mattered to Jane what they did...they would have been together. She couldn't pinpoint when she'd realized, with a painful unerring certainty that she was in love with Brett Chandler. It really could have happened almost anytime since she'd cradled his injured body in her arms last December, but most certainly it had been strengthened the night he'd come to comfort her after that bad dream. It had grown each time she'd opened the door at the start of a weekend to find him smiling a hello. And it had settled in for the duration. Jane experienced it each time she had to wave goodbye when he left Montauk Point.

Her love was startling enough, of course, but it was not the only thing or Brett the only person that was changing her way of life. There had been the phone call from Norman Rosen, the man in whose summer house Jane was making her home. He and his wife were moving to California and they wanted to sell the Montauk house. She'd always known the cottage arrangement was temporary, but had never actually given thought to where she would move next. Jane recalled mentioning it to Oliver. He had responded, mumbling, "Yes, I know."

"How would you have known that?" she'd asked.

"You never indicated that this was a permanent situation, Jane. Wasn't it reasonable to assume that sooner or later you'd have to leave?"

Then there had been the evening on the late news when the network announced a substitute for Harry Lindsay, who was on a special assignment. Two weeks later the network admitted that Harry Lindsay had been hospitalized with a virus and pneumonia. Jane had suspected it was a ruse, but there wasn't a thing she could do about finding out what the real problem was. She couldn't very well call either the bureau in Washington or the hospital. She couldn't very well say that she was family...his daughter...and demand an answer. Who would believe her, and what would she do with the information, in any case?

Jane recalled that old maxim that trouble came in threes. The third one was a small news item that Jimmy Cochoran, recently released from prison after serving time for the accidental death of a political campaign worker, was once more in trouble with the law. A full recounting of the earlier incident involving Jane was given, along with her name and the statement that she was known to be in residence somewhere on Long Island. With a sense of fatality Jane knew her world was shrinking. There was never again going to be a place of safety from her past. Sooner or later she was going to have to come to grips with it.

"I think it's about time you forget about the past," Oliver interjected, doing a pretty good job of reading her mind. "You're a young woman and still have your whole life before you. Brett could be a part of it if you—"

"That…doesn't concern you, Oliver," Jane said bluntly to the older man. Why was everything so complicated? Why couldn't her life be the way it used to be? *God, no!* She couldn't go back to what used to be, and that was precisely the problem. She knew she didn't want to.

Oliver stood up and approached Jane slowly. Her eyes wore a haunted look as she sought Oliver's kindly gaze and felt his compassion.

"Of course it concerns me. *You* concern me, Janie girl. Brett Chandler's a good man. But I don't need to defend him to you. I think you realize it, too," Oliver lectured gently, very much as a father imparting fatherly wisdom. "So what's the problem?"

What, indeed, was the problem? Perhaps that she was enjoying herself and looked forward to each new week of the strange platonic relationship with Brett. He always arrived with a bag of props and surprises and she never knew what to expect from him. The very first weekend Brett had arrived on a Friday evening. They'd spent several quiet hours having dinner before the fire, filling each other in on their busy week, together taking Jones out for a long leisurely stroll in the cold night along the country road.

Jane had mentioned an idea she had for the use of the land that was being disputed between his family and Stanley Hastings. She'd said she wanted to write an article; would he mind? Brett had said he didn't and had even added some information that had not been available in the local reporting of the court case. Back at the house he had handed her a wrapped bundle of clothes. It was from Jonathan.

"He felt badly that he couldn't send you a nicer thank-you for the hockey tickets, but he'd already used up his allowance."

But Jonathan had sent a lovely thank-you letter from school. Jonathan had gone on to tell her all about his current school activities . . . the science project he got an *A* on, and the extra composition he had to write for English because he'd fallen asleep during an exam. He talked about his roommate who was okay, but didn't like hockey and didn't know how to play chess very well. Jane had smiled during her reading of the note, a sweet smile of pleasure at sharing part of Jonathan's escapades. She realized how very lucky Brett was to have such a son.

Now Jane unwrapped the soft gray fabric to discover sweatpants and top, and a blue sweatband with the name PUMA stitched on the front. Confused, Jane turned her eyes to Brett, who was grinning mischievously at her.

"I suppose you can explain this?"

"Sure. I told Jonathan that what you needed was a good jogging outfit and he volunteered to let you have one of his. It's gotten a little small for him in the last year."

Jane gingerly held up the offending garment. "And what am I supposed to do with this?"

"Jog, of course!" Brett answered. And he'd been very serious.

At seven o'clock the next morning he woke her, shouting up the stairwell. Reluctantly Jane had gotten up. Even more reluctantly she'd dressed in the outfit, surprised to find that it was only a little too big for her. She grumbled a lot about the absurdity of jostling her body in the cold at that hour of the morning, but she went along with everything Brett did, never questioning her willingness to do so.

Brett inspected Jane carefully from head to toe, making her put on a windbreaker over the outfit. He turned her around and gathered her thick hair into a ponytail, using a rubber band to secure it. Then he positioned the headband. Jane told him she wasn't going to work up enough sweat to need one, to which Brett had responded with a laugh, saying, "That's what *you* think!"

Then after ten minutes of showing Jane how to warm up, they started off down the road, Jones alongside. Jane got tired quickly, but Brett wouldn't let her stop to rest. Instead he told her to concentrate on breathing, and magically, just when she thought she was going to collapse, Jane found a rhythm and stride to keep going. Brett adjusted his pace to suit her, and encouraged her every step of the way.

Back at the cottage, they'd both showered and Jane had made the puff pancake again for breakfast, this time complete with confectioner's sugar. They'd jogged again the next morning, and the next weekend as well, and soon Jane was doing it during the week with Jones, enjoying both the exhilaration and a sense of physical and mental well-being.

What quickly became her favorite event, however, was brunch on Sundays. Jane had gotten used to a fire being lighted when Brett was there, and the two of them having all their meals in front of it. Jane loved the times they'd both stretch out on the floor, sections of the Sunday papers scattered about as they read the news to each other, offering comments or exchanging viewpoints. Never had Jane felt more alive, more grounded and important than in those relaxed simple hours with Brett.

Once he'd persuaded Jane to have dinner at a very casual eatery in the town of Montauk called WAVES, and as she'd sat watching the people around her, observing the interesting rituals of dating, of men and women being together, Jane realized how much she'd been missing. The dress code and the mood of the evening was very informal. But seeing the other women suddenly made Jane feel as though she'd been living for ten years in the backwoods, out of touch. She felt very self-conscious with her long loose hair and comfortable, but unstylish dark slacks and bulky sweater. Nervously she'd fingered her hair, only to have Brett reach out to take her hand and hold it within his firm warm grasp. He'd smiled and winked at her across the table with a look that Jane had come to recognize as meaning, *I like you just the way you are*.

All the same, early the next week, before she could change her mind, Jane drove to a popular hair salon in town and had them cut away three years of her life. She had said nothing about how she wanted her hair to be styled. She just wanted something different done. Then she sat holding her breath and refusing to look into the mirror as the fat locks were snipped off and fell heavily to the floor around her.

But when it was done, Jane couldn't believe what she saw. She couldn't believe that the young woman with the proud chin and long slender neck, with softly prominent cheekbones was really her. The look was much more than she could have hoped for. Jane felt so free of the heavy wavy locks, but wondered what Brett would think of the new style, since he'd always seemed fond of her long hair. When he finally stepped into the doorway the following Friday evening, his hazel eyes swept slowly but thoroughly over her changed appearance. He was so quiet, so thoughtful and intense in his perusal of her that Jane thought he didn't like it.

What Brett saw only strengthened the way he felt about Jane. The new style emphasized all Jane's strong physical points. Her hair had been cut to just shoulder length, and now the remaining wavy ends were looser and much more feathery. There was a natural off-center part that allowed her hair to frame her face and neck in a seductive manner. Jane had always seemed very pretty to Brett, but now she was even prettier. For a number of weeks he had been very physically restrained around her, but suddenly this small physical change, allowing him a glimpse of the full beauty she possessed, made Brett feel restless, desperate to close the safe distance they'd so far maintained between them.

"Don't . . . you like it?" Jane had questioned him.

Brett's eyes had held a look, a tender expression Jane couldn't interpret. "Yes. I like it very much," he had replied.

There had been times when he'd wanted to hold and kiss her, to try to coax her into more intimacy, if not to the point of consummation then at least close enough to satisfy the physical tension that was growing between them. Yet he was still careful not to rush her, still aware that Jane needed her sense of being in control. But the effort sometimes showed, and they were both very aware of it. So . . . was there a problem?

Jane sighed now and shook her head at Oliver in confusion. "The problem is me, I suppose," she whispered, and then looked at Oliver's concerned expression. "Oh, Oliver. I . . . I don't know what to do anymore." Jane's hair bounced against her neck and cheeks. Her eyes pleaded for understanding and patience from her stalwart friend. "I thought we could just be friends. . . ."

Oliver bit his tongue; he felt like telling Jane dryly that that had been a foolish hope right from the start.

"And now, Brett has been . . . more than I ever expected," Jane admitted, almost embarrassed to say it. "I want more, Oliver. And I guess I sort of know I won't get it."

Oliver shook his head sadly. He could easily guess what "more" it was Jane was asking for. He reached out a hand to stroke her hair, to comfort her. But Oliver was not one given to that kind of demonstration and he let his hand drop heavily to his side. "How do you know that? Have you suddenly developed clairvoyant powers and you've read Brett's mind? How do you know what he intends?"

"But..."

"There *is* no but, Jane. Haven't you figured out yet that this *friendship* is just possibly a prelude to something deeper? Why would the man keep coming back week after week if he didn't *like* you! Have you ever heard of anyone going back and forth between Bethpage and Bridgehampton by way of Montauk?"

Jane knew Oliver was only trying to help her make sense of her confusion. But didn't he understand? She'd taken more risks with Brett than with anyone else in more than three years. She was flying high, soaring, but she was doing it with a safety net—for as long as Brett only dealt with her here on Montauk, she'd never have to confront him with her past. She still believed that if Brett knew the real story of her parentage he'd see that any real relationship between them was impossible. What existed between them now had progressed much further than she'd imagined, and Jane was not sure she was willing to settle for just a momentary happiness.

It wasn't fair. It wasn't her fault that her mother had been manipulative and her father had refused to allow himself to be used. It wasn't her fault that she had parents who never should have been parents. She was here and she was real. *What about her?* But she couldn't have it both ways. It was impossible. She couldn't want Brett, yet keep him at arm's length at the same time. But instead of addressing the matter directly, she'd let it hang in the air over them like a rain cloud about to burst. It had come very close to doing so the last time Brett had come to Montauk.

Brett had stayed late into that Sunday afternoon, quite simply because he didn't want to leave. They had managed to stretch out the day, strolling along the sandy dunes of the southern beach. They listened to the rushing surf, screeching sea gulls and the wind. Silently each thought about Brett's upcoming trip to Germany, what the separation could mean . . . and his return. Brett looked into her eyes.

"Let's go back to the house," he'd suggested in a low, oddly thick voice, and Jane had mutely agreed, knowing full well what he was thinking and feeling. Once they were inside, a funny kind of tension had begun to build. He helped her out of her parka, then gently began to brush the sand out of her bright hair as she watched his face. His hands suddenly grew still and he wove his fingers into her hair. He bent his head and kissed her. Not at all like friends, but rather like a lover who was making his desire perfectly clear. The touch of their mouths and tongues had sparked an instant desire that rocked through them both. Brett kissed her with more purpose, more hunger as he rubbed his lips back and forth across Jane's willing mouth. The kiss, both tender and very urgent seemed to set the stage for the crossing of another barrier—one Jane wanted, but wasn't sure she was ready for.

Instead Brett had broken the kiss and reverently pressed his lips to her forehead. Jane could feel the taut control of his body against her own.

"Jane . . . come with me to Germany," Brett had asked.

Her eyes closed tightly, she shook her head. "I . . . I can't, Brett."

He sighed impatiently. "Why?"

"I . . . just can't. I have things to do here. You'll be busy anyway and my passport's not in order. . . ."

"Your passport?" he repeated blankly, pulling back to stare at her with a frown. "I'm asking you to come with me because I don't want to leave you and you think your passport is a consideration?"

"No, it's just that—" Jane tried to explain, then stopped because she really couldn't.

"You're afraid. Afraid to trust me...or even yourself." He felt defeated and closed his eyes wearily. "Jane... Jane..." he kept repeating softly as he cupped her face and looked at her. "I like coming to see you. I like the feeling of home that I get just being with you. I *want* you near me. And we belong together. I thought you were beginning to see that."

Jane looked at him sadly. "It's not that easy, Brett. If you think about it, you'll agree with me."

Slowly he released her and moved away. "It's very easy, Lady Jane. You either *want* to come or you don't. No excuses."

Jane merely looked at him helplessly, and when she didn't answer, Brett sighed and kissed her gently on her cheek. "All right. We'll do it your way. For now," he said mysteriously.

So it shouldn't have been a surprise when Brett didn't show up as expected this morning in Montauk. There was no way for her to express her disappointment. She hadn't expected to fall in love with Brett Chandler, but she'd always known there was nowhere for their relationship to go. Perhaps Brett had finally realized that, too. She felt herself slowly sinking into her own misery and sense of loss.

"Jane..." Oliver said softly. She turned to look bleakly at him. "I think you're making a big mistake."

Tears threatened as emotion snaked its way into her chest and throat and seemed to squeeze tightly. "It won't be the—"

Jones suddenly got up from the floor with a half-lazy bark from his throat and went to the door. Then there was a discreet double knock, and Jane drew her breath in sharply. It was the way Brett always knocked when he arrived; Jane stood rooted.

Oliver took one look at her stiff features and went to answer, opening the door with only a little of the trepidation

Jane had displayed in the kitchen, and with much more relief. He recognized that Jane was engaging in an emotional struggle, the format of which had been set when she was still a child. Did she deserve happiness? Was she really wanted? So Oliver was just as happy that Brett was here after all to take charge of the situation. And judging by the thunderous expression on his handsome face when the door swung open, that was exactly what Brett intended to do.

Brett stepped through the doorway, searching the older man's face for an idea of how things were. He detected empathy, exasperation and some amusement.

"I want to see Jane," Brett said in a tone that brooked no argument and didn't ask permission. Oliver jerked a beefy thumb over his shoulder.

"She's in the kitchen."

Before the words were completely spoken, Brett had sidestepped Oliver to walk toward the kitchen, absently stroking Jones's head in passing. He noticed that there was a peaceful fire on the living-room hearth. It was in front of the fire that they'd spent a great deal of time in the last month, talking and relaxing together.

He stopped abruptly in the kitchen doorway. Jane was braced against the counter. Her eyes involuntarily widened at the sight of Brett's stern features. She'd never seen him angry before, and couldn't understand why he was angry with her now. He had the option of just walking away and never seeing her again. But since he was here, his presence overwhelmed Jane with a flood of love for him that frightened her. Love for his honesty, his energy and patience. Love for the freedom he'd given her, even if it wasn't yet fully realized. She had come to need Brett too much and the peace he offered...the wonderful sense of belonging...when she had nothing to offer in return. And if her hands hadn't been gripping the counter edge so hard, Jane was certain she would have propelled herself forward and into Brett's arms, begging him to hold her and love her a little, too.

Brett was struggling to remember his mission, his determination to get Jane to open up to him. Right now she looked so bewildered, he wanted to reassure her that everything was going to be okay. Brett had promised himself not to push her, but he wanted her so badly, wanted to feel much closer to her than permitted by the boundaries she had established and he had agreed to. Seeing Jane now, Brett was even willing to continue with that charade—if only he might know Jane felt something for him other than as a friend. He thought of the time they'd spent together, companionable easy time. But he both wanted and needed more from her now.

His eyes softened as he took in the brightness of her own, her hair tumbled about her shoulders. The new style took away much of the raw vulnerability that had been there before, and replaced it with an alluring feminine sexiness that played havoc with his senses. Brett wanted to run his fingers through the scented silkiness of it, anchor his fingers there and urge her slender body against him. He wanted to wrap himself around her softness, her strength, her stubborn pride, and hold on forever.

Neither noticed Oliver standing in the hall, watching in curiosity as Jane and Brett silently faced each other. Assessing the dynamics of their meeting, he decided that his presence was not needed. With a further sigh of relief, Oliver retrieved his jacket from the closet.

"Sorry I can't stay for lunch, Jane, but—" he began, only to be interrupted by Jane talking to Brett.

"I didn't expect to see you," she said, her calm tone suggesting it wouldn't have mattered one way or the other. She turned to remove the fragrant bread from the oven.

Brett's eyes grew dark and cold. He recognized all the old defenses Jane was used to employing. "I had a flat in the middle of the highway," he stated.

"Maybe some other time," Oliver said over their voices. He was ignored.

"We have to talk," Brett said to her.

"Don't trouble yourselves. I'll see myself out," Oliver added, sidling toward the door.

Jones, sensing some tension, stood confused in the hall looking from Oliver to Jane in the kitchen to the male human he knew his mistress liked. Jones whined softly at no one in particular, but no one noticed.

Jane took a deep breath and stood tall. "You're right, of course. It's time we settled a few things." She raised her chin and slowly advanced toward Brett, to walk ahead of him into the living room.

"Have a good weekend!" Oliver said heartily, stepping outside and closing the door behind him. Shaking his head at the strange mating habits of the current generation, he began to chuckle. As he started for home, it turned into a full-blown laugh.

Neither Brett nor Jane paid any attention to the departing doctor. Nor did they notice the dog who, still sensing something amiss, slunk to a position behind his pacing mistress and settled down on the carpet to wait.

"Jane, I..." Brett began, but Jane put up her hands to stop him.

"Just a moment, Brett. I think I can save us both a lot of time and energy if I speak first." Then Jane took a deep breath, absently combed her fingers through her hair, pacing all the while.

Brett had not expected Jane to have anything to say, and was surprised by her approach.

"First of all, I think we both know this isn't going to work. I think it's probably for the best if we don't see each other again," Jane said quickly. She couldn't believe what she was doing, but Jane knew she had to cut off all ties to this man she loved.

"Do you?" Brett asked rather harshly, his tone of voice daunting her even more.

Jane wouldn't look directly at Brett, afraid that if she did her face and especially her eyes would surely give her away. "Y-yes. Our lives are vastly different, Brett. I . . . I'm settled here in Montauk, and I'm content to stay here," she lied. "Really, I am!"

Some of his anxiety dissipated as Brett watched this valiant but foolish display of pride. He crossed his arms over his chest in a gesture of challenge.

When he didn't say anything Jane felt compelled to continue talking. "It's such a terrible drive out here, and I feel so bad about all the time you've wasted and—"

"Have you enjoyed my visits with you?" Brett interrupted.

Jane stopped pacing. "That's not the point."

"Have you?"

"Well, yes. But . . ."

"Go on," Brett ordered.

Jane became slightly flustered. "Anyway, the point I was making was . . . was . . ." She kept her back to Brett. "We're just not right for each other. You're a very . . . very . . ."

"Very what?" Brett prompted.

Jane whipped around to confront him. "You're sophisticated and worldly and probably absolutely brilliant and should be with someone with a . . . a similar background."

Slowly Brett took a few steps toward her. "What kind of background is that?" he asked with intense curiosity, arching his brows as he speculated on her coming answer.

"You know what I mean, Brett. You're from a very notable family. You have a reputation and standing to uphold. Besides . . . I can't offer you anything."

Brett sighed. "Jane, there is nothing notable about my family. We simply have a fair amount of money and a well-established family business. We have no particular standing in the community other than what the gossip columns proclaim, and my mother's weekly attendance at a local game of bridge."

"This isn't funny, Brett," Jane said with wounded anger in her voice.

"You're right, it isn't! But it also doesn't make much sense!" he returned roundly.

Now it was Jane's turn to cross her arms over her chest. They glared at each other. "I told you I was going to be difficult!"

"And I told you I can be very persistent. I don't give up easily."

"You mean you don't know *when* to give up!" Jane shot back.

Brett arched a brow at her again. "What is it you're trying to say, Jane?" he asked in calm puzzlement.

Jane stared. Hadn't she made herself perfectly clear? Didn't he see it was impossible for them to continue like this? "We can't see each other anymore." Her voice cracked on the last words.

"Is that what you want?" he asked. His caressing tone was unexpected, and Jane actually hesitated.

"I think it's best."

"You didn't answer my question. Are you telling me you don't want to see me again?"

Jane's chin quivered and her eyes were fleetingly plaintive. If it had been any other person, Brett would never have noticed. He was very much aware of Jane's habits and what made her tick. He had not spent so many hours and weeks with Jane without learning what made her smile and laugh, what surprised and delighted her... what she wanted and didn't want.

Her eyes now seemed almost glazed as she continued to stare unblinkingly at Brett. "Y-yes." The response was very soft.

Brett took a deep breath and uncrossed his arms. He stepped right in front of her, but her eyes were focused on his white knit sweater.

"You're not a very good liar. That was an interesting little recital, and my reaction to it, Jane, is that it's a bunch of hogwash!" Jane's eyes widened and rose quickly to meet the glint in his own. Brett lifted his hands to her upper arms, holding Jane firmly. "It was noble, rather creative, and completely misguided."

"Brett..."

"You're not a shy person. If you didn't want to see me, I have no doubt you would have said so from the very beginning." Brett let his hazel eyes look at her with tender regard. "And I was reasonably sure by your kisses that you weren't repulsed by me, either...." Jane blushed deeply and started to speak. Brett shushed her by pursing his lips in a silent motion. "You've had your say. Now it's my turn."

He raised his hands to gently cup her face, and the very touch of him made Jane ache. Her eyes filled with tears. She couldn't believe he wasn't angry with her. She couldn't believe he hadn't walked out the door.

"I only have one question to ask you. Just one. Have I been wrong about the feelings that exist now between us?"

Jane swallowed hard. She should have known he wasn't going to ask a predictable question. So she wasn't going to lie to him again. What was the point? The one thing she would allow herself now was the truth of her own feelings. She would just have to deal with the consequences later.

Between his hands Brett could feel Jane shake her head. His jaw tensed with relief. "Then the way I see it, Jane, very little else matters," he whispered, bending his head until his lips pressed upon her own. He was reassuring her for the moment, and slowly lifted his head to stare earnestly into her green eyes.

"Lady, not one moment of my time with you has been wasted. Other than my family there is no one else I look forward to seeing more. Jonathan can't believe I actually know you. He holds you rather in awe. Mother's delighted. She wants to know who you are...."

"Have you told her?" Jane asked anxiously.

Brett brushed her cheek with his fingers. "Not yet. If I did, she'd want to meet you. I haven't been able to convince you you should," he reminded Jane.

Jane sighed, shaking her head slowly. "Brett...I'm not right for you...."

"What does that mean?" he urged.

"It means..." Jane looked up at him and Brett's heart melted at the helpless look of uncertainty in her eyes. "It means you should be interested in a woman like...like Carolyn," she improvised.

Brett shook his head. "I don't want to be interested in a woman like Carolyn. I had Carolyn, and I tried to make the best of it. She was everything you seem to feel is right in a woman. But she didn't have even a fraction of your strength or intuition. She didn't have your sense of humor or awareness. She wasn't interested in, didn't take part in anything beyond her own world. You have a lot of guts, Jane. I don't believe you will let anything defeat you," Brett said with a curious note of significance. "Carolyn was terrified of life itself. She was pretty, and very sweet and gentle. You aren't anything like Carolyn, but I wish I'd known you sooner.

"As to what you have to offer, there's only been one thing I ever wanted and that was just you. Heart, body and soul. And your trust."

As he spoke with such tenderness, Jane felt her control give way. Tears rolled down her cheek and under Brett's thumb, to be wiped away. Without another word he drew

Jane into his arms and simply held her as she held him. This was exactly what she'd always imagined love would be like. A kind of gentle acceptance and tender touching, combined with the wondrous excitement in her heart. She knew Brett couldn't love her, but he was giving her what she'd always wanted, nonetheless.

Now Brett was stroking her back, making her pliant, molding her to the length of him. She turned her face so that her cheek lay against Brett's chest. For a very long time Jane enjoyed merely being in his arms this way.

Jane felt Brett bend his head so that his lips could kiss her hair and then her neck. His action elicited a very weak moan and a sigh of contentment. His hands stroked a shoulder, moved to her chin and lifted her face. His lips grazed her cheek as he found his way to her mouth. Brett's possession was immediate and startlingly erotic. Jane didn't hesitate to express her own feelings, and willingly let Brett's tongue gain entry to her mouth. His arms tightened around her; now Jane could feel the firm length of him quickly changing. Her breath caught at the hard outline that made his desire evident.

Brett's mouth played sensuously with her lips, alternately teasing with little nips and pulls, then capturing hers to rub and gently suck, drawing her tongue to him. She met his embrace with her own growing need. The kiss was intoxicating, but Brett slowly broke contact. His gaze was drowsy and seductive, his smile gentle.

"I had no intention of leaving for Germany without letting you know how I felt, Jane, and setting the record straight. Because when I come back everything between us will be different." He kissed her briefly, then forced her to look at him. A muscle twitched in his jaw. "I also feel very strongly that we've been just friends long enough. Yes?"

Slowly a smile changed her face, brightening it. "Yes," she agreed.

Brett's eyes darkened with desire. He took hold of her hand and headed for the stairwell. Jane only knew a second's uncertainty as they climbed the stairs to her room. She was still fearful that Brett might be disappointed in her. But at the foot of her bed Brett once more took Jane into his arms, and his kiss quickly convinced her that she had nothing to fear from this moment. His mouth, continuing to tease, let Jane know he was capable of keeping the tension level high. Her sweater was removed and discarded and her blouse slowly unbuttoned before either of them heard Jones's plaintive whine from the doorway. Jane glanced at him and saw the animal's confusion. He didn't want to leave her, but sensed something new between his two favorite humans that he couldn't be part of. Jane walked the dog out of the room and into the hall. She stooped to pet him and rubbed his neck and head with affection.

"Everything is okay, boy. Go downstairs. Go on," Jane instructed softly. Slowly Jones obeyed. Jane turned to meet Brett's warm gaze upon her as he stood bare-chested by the bed. Slowly she stood and came back to him, closing the door on the world. Her eyes were bright, conveying a message of trust that made Brett's heart constrict. He held out his arms and Jane walked right into them, their lips meeting in joyous reunion.

The only interruption was to remove their clothing. Seeing him stand before her now, beautifully formed and toned, magnificently bare, made her wonder how many other women had fallen in love with this man, whom she found perfect in every way.

Brett had never understood why Jane chose to wear oversize shirts and sweaters that hid her beauty and did her no justice at all. He placed his hands now on her hips and slowly ran them up the silky smoothness of her skin, squeezing her waist and feeling her quiver under his hands. They came to rest beneath her breasts so that he could feel the full weight of them and the rapid beating of her heart. His gaze sought hers as his thumb gently tested the turgid pink nipples with their rosy aureoles. There was a combination of shy enjoyment and uncertainty in Jane's eyes as she allowed Brett this new intimacy, and he knew instinctively that she hadn't been with another man in a long time. Brett had no doubt that this moment was going to be significant, a treasure for himself. He wanted to give Jane the same feeling.

Brett used his hands on the side of her body to bring Jane toward him. The meeting of their naked bodies seemed to open a floodgate to the pent-up need between them. His mouth was demanding.

"Brett?" Jane questioned limply against his mouth, and the contact with his body was bold and hard. He put an arm around her waist and turned Jane toward the bed. Pulling back the covers he guided her under them, quickly joining her and reaching to pull her into his arms. Gooseflesh rose on Jane's body, and she shivered. Her breathing was hurried and nervous, but Brett smiled into her eyes and used his large warm hands and warmer body to soothe away her sudden apprehension.

Jane let herself sway toward Brett, inadvertently wiggling and rubbing herself against him to get closer. She loved the feel of his hairy legs and chest, so distinctly masculine. She loved the flexing under her own searching hands of his strong back and arm muscles.

"You are incredibly soft and beautiful," Brett groaned, capturing her mouth and letting his passion have full rein. Gently he rolled Jane onto her back and lay half on top of her while his mouth and hands demonstrated his feelings and need for her.

She had never felt so free, so abandoned before. It frightened her to realize that she was giving herself completely to Brett after three long years of no emotional attachment to anyone. She held nothing back, meeting and answering his demands. But he didn't rush her as somehow she'd thought he would. Brett proceeded in a slow methodical way until Jane's skin was so sensitized and her need so great, her body so weak and ready that she thought she would die. Urgently she whispered Brett's name, the sound muffled by his neck.

"Yes, sweetheart..." came back his hoarse response.

Brett shifted his body to lie completely on her. Jane drew in a sharp breath of pure pleasure as his weight pressed her into the mattress. She readily parted her thighs, letting her body take over in this natural timeless function. Brett's hands slid down her body, curving gently under her hips. He lowered himself, easily finding Jane's feminine warmth and sheathing himself slowly and deeply. He groaned and lay motionless while they both adjusted to this ultimate contact.

Jane's throat went dry. She felt possessed and invaded, but the knowledge that it was Brett relaxed her completely. She had never known it was possible to feel so complete with another person. With another groan Brett began to move, very slowly at first, just enjoying the incredible delight of feeling his body against hers. But the movements quickly escalated until his control was strained and pure need took over. Jane easily went into his rhythm and pace, her body responding in a way she'd never thought possible. Suddenly her mind was invaded with the memory of a past time, another man. She closed her eyes tightly, trying to block out the blurry image. *No. Please, no!* her mind screamed.

A throbbing sensation was building in Jane's body with each of Brett's movements, but this awful memory threatened to overwhelm it. Jane feared the lovemaking was going to be over before she'd had a chance to absorb all the physical stimulus that was changing so quickly. "No..." she pleaded weakly and tightened her arms around Brett. He didn't understand what Jane meant, but he became more gentle with her and kissed her repeatedly.

The image in Jane's mind didn't change, however, and this other man completed his needs, leaving her body still unfulfilled. Then the image began to fade as Jane realized there was no ending. The feelings were still spiraling inside her. The man in her arms, the one who was real seemed to know exactly what to do. He wasn't going to stop until she'd reached that magical peak. And it began to happen.

The pleasure achingly sweet, grew until Jane had to clutch at Brett and gasp for air as she felt herself virtually catapulted into space. The strength of his arms, his weight were the only things preventing Jane from falling apart. The lovely feeling seemed to explode in waves of ecstasy that flowed to every part of her.

"Oh, Bre—" Jane attempted to say before her voice failed. It was then that Brett knew she had completely surrendered to their passion and he thrust his hips to let Jane finally know his own. The ride was dizzying. The speed held them suspended until everything gradually came to a stop and they were welded together, breathless on the bed, giddy and helpless.

Jane lay stunned and limp, her arms wound in a near death grip around Brett's shoulders, her quivering thighs a vise around his hips. She struggled for breath and to overcome her shock. She felt an indescribable exhilaration. She thought of the memory that had plagued her as she made love with Brett, and how this moment with him had dispelled forever any further comparisons to the past.

Shaky fingers tenderly stroked the fine hair on Brett's nape as Jane melted into his incredibly caring embrace. They had not only dissolved sexual tension between them, they had also shared a feeling of trust and warmth that she had never known before. For all that she had hitherto missed or been denied, Jane wept.

Brett came first to his senses. Slowly he turned his head and planted loving little kisses along Jane's neck to her shoulders. His mouth formed a drowsy pleased smile. He felt contented, peaceful—and relieved. Brett felt Jane tremble beneath him and moved the weight of his body so he could hold her comfortably in his arms.

"Are you cold?" he whispered against her ear.

Jane uttered a muffled "No," but continued to tremble.

It was another minute before Brett realized that she was shaking from silent tears. "Jane?" Brett whispered, both surprised and anxious. But when he tried to see her face, she only pressed closer against his chest. Brett could feel her tears dampen his skin. All he could do was hold her tightly and let her cry. She had been completely responsive to him, accepting his demanding body with a raw need of her own. He'd thought Jane had been as sated as he was. But now...Brett wasn't so sure. "Sweetheart..." he tried again. Bleakly he stroked her back and shoulders, murmuring soothing words.

It was a long time before Jane quieted and the trembling stopped. She lay motionless for so long that Brett thought Jane had fallen asleep. And then he felt a tender little kiss against his chest. He lay still while her lips traveled up his chest to his throat. He smoothed back her damp hair, exposing a flushed face with wet cheeks and spiky wet lashes.

"Jane?" he asked in a hoarse voice. "Are you all right?"

She looked at him for a long second, realizing that her love for this man had not been misplaced, and then she smiled slowly, nodding. She didn't know if she could tell him of her utter surprise, of the overpowering feeling about what had just happened between them.

"Are you sure?"

"Yes, I'm fine. I...I just never knew it could feel so...personal," she whispered shyly. "I never thought it was possible to feel so humble, so...so alive!"

Brett closed his eyes briefly in relief. He held her tightly to him, enjoying her softness. "Sweet heaven... I thought I'd hurt you. I thought I'd..."

Jane smiled. "I'm just overwhelmed. Brett, it was so... beautiful." She put her arms around Brett's neck and coaxed his head toward her. She kissed him lightly with little butterfly touches. It was the most aggressive she'd ever been on her own with him.

Brett willingly accepted her offering, squeezing Jane tightly as her meaning sank in. "Is this the first time you've known fulfillment?" he asked in a curious but gentle voice.

Jane nodded silently. Brett bent to kiss her shoulder. "Then you're not disappointed, Lady Jane?" He didn't actually wait for an answer, but slid down her body a little, kissing her throat. He began to stroke her warm body slowly, feeling her writhe under his touch as his hands covered a breast and his lips pulled at a nipple.

Jane's eyes drifted shut and her body arched against him, immediately evoking a pulsing response from Brett. "Oh, no. But I was afraid you would be...."

Brett chuckled deep in his chest. "You've got to be kidding!" he growled seductively, sliding his body over hers once again. Brett watched the transformation, the glorious awakening in Jane and felt something come to fruition he'd never thought to know. He gathered Jane to him, beginning to kiss her with a quickly renewed passion... prepared to make her feel wonderful forever.

Chapter Eight

Jane awakened slowly, and a secret smile came to her lips. She opened her eyes and realized that the morning was well advanced and sunshine prevailed. The sudden sunshine was also a culminating high note after several days of strong spring winds and rain. It marked a full week of Brett's presence in Montauk and a week-long journey into a magic world with just the two of them. But even more, it marked one of the happiest weeks of Jane's life. With the unfolding of spring she'd found love. A chance to start over and write a story differently this time...perhaps with a happy ending.

Jane wondered what had become of Oliver. In all truth, it was the first time she'd given any real thought to her neighbor, and she felt a momentary guilt that her mind and attention had been so consumed with Brett that she hadn't. He had simply disappeared sometime last week during Brett's arrival. Now she knew that Oliver was also being sensitive to her need to work out whatever she and Brett needed to resolve, and it had to be done privately.

The smile on Jane's mouth curved to greater warmth as she let her head roll against Brett's shoulder. She glanced with both tenderness and amazement into the strong masculine face now relaxed in sleep. He was showing no inclination to leave for Germany. He had not spoken about his departure, although Jane realized that it had to be soon. And she didn't ask. She was content to let the days pass, one into another, selfishly holding on to her fantasies.

Brett's heavy arm was anchored around Jane's waist. Her fingertips gently brushed through the soft hair on his chest. Jane's green eyes wandered lovingly over his features. The dark line of his brows, the strong prominence of his nose and the grooves in his cheeks were by now very familiar. Her glance dropped with a sultry drowsiness to his firm mouth, remembering all too well the feel, taste, power and erotic tenderness of his expert kisses. With a sigh Jane let her fingers lightly comb through Brett's springy peppered hair, enjoying the thick texture and surprising softness. The gesture caused Brett to move in his sleep, to roll more toward Jane with a sleepy groan, to bury his nose and mouth in her hair. Jane smiled and her eyelids closed.

The week had seemed a magic eternity, yet still not long enough. And as perfect as it had been for her, Jane could not help having a fatalistic premonition that time was running out. She didn't want to be greedy, she'd received more from Brett than she would have ever imagined possible before from anyone. But this week had crystallized for Jane what she'd been missing in her life.

Fully awake now, Jane removed herself from Brett's arms and slipped out of the bed. She grabbed one of her oversize sweaters and moved gingerly toward the bedroom door. As she passed the bureau mirror, she caught a glimpse of a woman she'd never seen before this week with Brett. Her hair was a wild fiery tangle of corkscrew locks, one falling provocatively over one eye. Her eyes themselves seemed rather dewy and soft, and her mouth more expressive from having been taught and schooled by Brett's own. Her breasts were boldly round, fitting so perfectly into Brett's hand and responding freely to his fingers and tongue. Jane recalled how, for several days earlier in the week, her arms and the muscles of her thighs had been sore. She acknowledged that the week had been used well. Jane lifted a hand to explore her face, noting the subtle difference, still surprised that love could make such a difference. Brett twisted on the bed and Jane caught the motion reflected in the mirror. Thoughtfully her smile began to fade. With an odd sadness she donned the sweater and quietly let herself out of the room.

Jones, ever present and hopeful of someday being readmitted to the sanctum of his mistress's room, rose at once to greet Jane, waiting for his customary good-morning pat.

"Poor baby..." Jane crooned in understanding. "I've been ignoring you shamelessly, haven't I, boy?"

Jones whined in agreement and thumped his tail on the floor, then followed Jane downstairs. In truth, a lot of things had fallen by the wayside. Her P.C. had not been turned on once. She'd gone from a feast of unused firewood to a famine of just a few remaining logs as she and Brett continued with new rituals in front of a glowing fire. Even mail had piled up unopened and messages been left unanswered as she and Brett hungrily lost themselves in each other. They'd managed to continue with their morning jog, partially because they discovered that after returning to the house and showering together, they had a tendency to tumble right back into bed for an additional hour of lovemaking.

Jane got the coffee maker going and realized with even more guilt that there had been no time for further investigation into the condition of Harry Lindsay. And while so much in her life had changed in three months, indeed in just the last week, the facts of and questions about her past were irrefutably the same. Harry Lindsay was never far from her thoughts. Neither was Jimmy Cochoran, nor his whereabouts. They had merely taken a back seat to her own personal discoveries with Brett.

At first the discoveries had all been physical. There had been a delicious urgency to their lovemaking. It became a poignant experience that Brett had never had before, one which Jane had always believed herself incapable of. Brett had quickly dispelled that myth. Together they had created a passion so moving and fulfilling that the entire first Saturday afternoon had passed in the bedroom upstairs. It had been after seven when Brett had awakened to the darkened room and the sound of unexpected rain outside, and the feel of a feminine back pressed into his chest, spoon fashion. He'd swept aside Jane's wavy hair to kiss her nape. Jane had finally stirred, awakening to the touch of Brett's lips and hands and the evidence of his highly aroused state. It had been another hour before they'd left the four-poster bed to shower and go in search of food. What had been meant for a lunch much earlier in the day became a late-night dinner.

Jane smiled now at the wholly pleasant memories, loving Brett in a tender way for giving them to her. Dreamily she put mugs and spoons onto a tray as she recalled them in vivid detail. Jane had been nearly speechless at Brett's skill and patience in finding and igniting the sensual fires within her. The first time they'd made love had surprised Jane with what was intimately possible between a man and woman.

Jones looked up from his food dish as Jane began to hum some tuneless song softly to herself. The dog watched her in curiosity, knowing that a lot about his mistress had changed recently. Jane put the prepared coffee onto the tray and with a grimace added the stack of mail. She didn't think any of it could be of much importance....

Upstairs Brett had awakened. With a grunt and muscular stretching of his long hard limbs, he yawned and settled back against the pillows. He put his hands behind his head and in the momentary silence of her room gave thought to the fair lady who was much on his mind. His week of discoveries had been no different from Jane's, however. He had found that she was completely giving and responsive to their lovemaking, displaying a capacity for deep passion. This was of particular importance to Brett, who saw it as a sign of Jane's total trust in him. It also made Brett feel, for the first time since Carolyn's death, that he had not failed in his first marriage after all, but that he and Carolyn had simply been emotionally unsuited to begin with. It made him sad to think of how much time had been lost in trying to find his own happiness.

It came as no surprise to him that he was in love with Jane Lindsay. Jane's personal strength and pride, which Brett had found admirable right from the start, had made her decidedly unlike any other woman he'd known. There had also never been any question that he was physically attracted to her. No doubt Jane had figured it out, as well. Keeping him at arm's length for so long had been merely a way to find out if there was anything more than a physical attraction between them. Until a week ago when all facades and pretenses had come tumbling down.

Brett's thoughts since last week had all been about the future. But he suspected that Jane would have to be coaxed into each new step, as the stranglehold that her past held her in was slowly released. He wanted her free, because in Jane's freedom lay the possibility of happiness for them both.

Brett turned his head and looked thoughtfully beyond the adjacent window to a tree budding with fresh new leaves and life after the winter. In a way he thought of his meeting with Jane as a similar thing. Only since Jane had there been that fresh rush of possibilities and hope. Since Jane there had been this new tumultuous need for love and commitment. He'd even been thinking of more babies with her. But was it possible for him to really penetrate Jane's protective walls? His eyes swung to the photo of Harry Lindsay.

The door opened slowly and Jane came in with the tray of coffee, chuckling as Jones swept roughly past her and settled on the floor by the bed. Jane steadied the tilting tray as several envelopes slid off the edge to the floor. At once Brett was out of the bed to stride naked to meet her.

"I'll get those," he said, reaching to kiss her quickly as she continued to the bed with the tray.

"I wouldn't worry," Jane said as she set down the tray and climbed onto the bed to begin pouring coffee into the mugs. "It's probably all bills and junk mail."

Brett grinned as he rejoined her on the bed. "There could be a very fat check in all this stuff. Or a notice of some literary award." His eyes twinkled at Jane as he took the offered cup of coffee and handed her the envelopes. Jane smiled skeptically at him, but carelessly tossed the envelopes aside. "You really should take a look at those," Brett suggested easily.

With a shrug, Jane began to leaf through the stack. At the first one she laughed lightly. "I told you they were probably all bills!" Then she lifted the next envelope from the pile and gave Brett a sly sidelong glance. "Okay, so there was also a check, but I'm telling you—"

Jane's voice faltered and she stopped talking. The smile faded from her lips as she gaped openmouthed at the envelope now in her hands. She turned completely bewildered eyes to Brett, lounging next to her.

"Brett!" Jane moved suddenly, nearly upsetting the tray. "This really *is* a notice. It's from the Pulitzer board!" She waved the envelope under his nose. "I don't understand why they'd be writing to me...."

He grinned. "Wouldn't it be easier to open the envelope and read why?"

"Oh..." she murmured dumbly, causing Brett to laugh softly. Her fingers were clumsy and shaking as she demolished the envelope and extracted the sheet of stationery. A second smaller piece of paper drifted to her lap unnoticed.

Jane's eyes flew over the printed words. Brett carefully watched her face for reaction. When she'd finished reading Jane turned her head toward him; her green eyes were bright and swimming in tears. She didn't know if she could explain how sadness was mixed with her gratification and thrill at the letter she held. How wonderful it would have been to share the moment with family, to call her parents long-distance and hear the pride in their voices! She had reached a professional pinnacle most writers only dream about.

"I've been selected to receive this year's Pulitzer Prize in journalism for—for a story I did on abandoned children," she said tonelessly.

Brett looked at her for a long moment, and Jane would have been startled to know he fully understood what she was feeling. That the award mattered very much to her, but in another way... almost not at all. He moved the tray away. Jane lifted the second sheet of paper. "There's a check, too. It's for a thousand dollars."

Brett smiled into her face. "What are you going to do with it?"

Jane frowned thoughtfully and gnawed her lip. Then she looked at the check and smiled secretly to herself. "I've always wanted to have a really corny trip to Hawaii," she began softly. "But I'm going to treat us to a very expensive dinner complete with champagne, just to celebrate." Her eyes flew once more to Brett's face. "I...I mean, would you have dinner with me to celebrate?" she asked shyly.

Brett laid his hand on her cheek, his thumb stroking the skin. "I would be very honored to celebrate with you. After all, how many people get to have dinner with such a distinguished author?" he teased her. Brett gently kissed her mouth. "Congratulations, Lady Jane," he said, gathering her to him as he drew her sweater over her head and tossed it aside. "And I congratulate the Pulitzer committee," he whispered, sliding down in the bed and bringing Jane with him. "We seem to think alike."

"What do you mean?" she asked as Brett lifted his thigh over her legs.

"We have demonstrated good taste and excellent wisdom in our choice," he said as he began to kiss her in earnest.

"Oh, Brett..." Jane sighed in delight, welcoming the arms that held her with such care.

JANE FINISHED applying her lipstick and set the tube on the marble surface of the vanity. She fluffed her hair and adjusted the shoulders of her black dress. The deep V of the plunging neckline was provocative, teasing and hinting at what was covered. The gold belt at the waist gathered the sheaved skirt as it tapered to her knees. The fabric widened from the waist dramatically only to narrow at the wrist, the dolman sleeves of the crepe dress like wings.

Jane smiled in amusement as she recalled Brett's reaction to her dress as he waited for her to appear for their celebratory dinner at the Montauk Yacht Club. It made her feel fully a woman to watch Brett's hazel eyes darken and his lips purse in a silent whistle of appreciation as she'd descended the stairs in high-heeled pumps with rhinestone clips on the top. Jane's hair was glossy and soft and clipped back over one ear with a rhinestone comb and there were diamond bobs in her ears.

To Brett she had presented an image of quiet elegance and feminine sexiness. "You look like spring," he'd said softly, reaching out to take her hand and help her down the last few steps.

From a magic suitcase of clothes intended for the trip to Germany, Brett had dressed in a charcoal-gray suit and pale pink shirt with a coordinated tie. Seeing him so formal again reminded Jane of the events that had originally brought them together at Christmas. How much she had changed because of this extraordinary man!

The door to the ladies' lounge opened and an attractive blonde, elegantly dressed in a beautiful turquoise dress came in. Her eyes settled pointedly on Jane.

"I thought it was you," a sultry voice said.

Jane looked into the mirror and found the blond woman was standing just behind her. She looked vaguely familiar, but Jane noticed more the spark of cold antagonism that radiated from the woman's blue eyes.

"I beg your pardon?" Jane asked automatically. The woman arched a brow and slowly seated herself on a cushioned chair next to Jane, regarding her steadily in the mirror.

"You look a little different. Better, actually. The make-up department never did you justice," the blonde commented in a grudging tone. Jane began to frown at her, taking exception to the examination and the woman's bold opinion.

"I'm sorry, but I . . ."

"You're Johanna Lynn, aren't you?"

Jane lifted her chin, feeling wary. "No, I'm not. Johanna Lynn was a stage name."

"Protecting your identity?" the blonde ventured flippantly, but painfully close to the mark, nonetheless. She smiled vacantly at Jane. "I'm Carla Kantor. I was at the station just before you left. What was it, four years ago?"

"Three," Jane responded. Her eyes now strove to recognize the woman. The blonde laughed.

"Oh, I doubt if you'll know me. I was a lowly news researcher three years ago."

Jane shrugged apologetically. "I don't remember you, I'm afraid."

"That's all right. Back then I probably wasn't important enough to notice."

"I remember everyone I worked with," Jane found herself saying defensively. "You probably weren't on my team."

"*Your* team," Carla responded with a subtle kind of insulting smirk. She turned to examine her near-perfect features in the mirror and smoothed a slender finger over her cheek. "*Your* team doesn't exist anymore. Things change, you know." She eyed Jane in the mirror. "I'm no longer a researcher. I now report the news."

Jane almost smiled at the other woman's smug tone. She remembered that well, the fierce competition to move up, be seen, be popular. She didn't miss any of it. And she suspected that Carla was more interested in her own image than in the news.

"Congratulations," Jane said lightly, although she wanted to add a warning to beware. All glory was fleeting.

"You know, the first time I saw you at the station I thought you were related to Harry Lindsay. His daughter, perhaps? You resemble him."

Jane stared silently at the other woman, feeling a rush of heat to her face and neck. "You're not the first person who's thought so," she answered carefully.

Carla shrugged at Jane's answer, but didn't challenge it. She removed a lace handkerchief from her evening purse and dabbed at imaginary moisture on her chin and forehead. "I always thought he was responsible for getting you your job in New York."

Jane couldn't begin to guess why, but this woman didn't like her. It was a shock, since she didn't know her at all and couldn't imagine what she might have done in the past to warrant such hostility from a near stranger. "You were wrong," she said, replacing her comb in her own evening bag. She wanted to leave, to get away from this woman. "I was asked to join the station. And you?" Jane confronted her softly.

Carla laughed again and a chill swirled up Jane's spine. "My father knew someone who knew someone," she readily admitted.

"Sooner or later you're going to have to prove how good you are," Jane offered.

"If you were so good, then what happened three years ago? Why did you drop out?"

Jane looked at the other woman. She could be the same age as herself, maybe a few years younger. Certainly more beautiful, poised and self-assured. But cold. "TV journalism was limited, and it's not an end in itself. I wanted to do other things." She got up to leave. "If you'll excuse me…"

"How did you meet Brett Chandler?" came the silky voice behind her.

Jane stopped short and looked over her shoulder. "Do you know Mr. Chandler?" she asked with careful curiosity.

Carla tilted her head and regarded Jane with a superior smile. "Very well. We used to see quite a bit of each other several years ago." Carla lifted a shoulder. "Then I got very busy with my career. How did you meet him?"

Jane smiled coldly at the blonde. "It's a long story," she said easily. "And it's private." And she quietly left the lounge. Her heart pounding in anger, Jane went to find Brett.

He stood when he saw her, but concern filled his eyes at the tight, strained expression on her face. "Are you all right?" he asked, seating her and taking hold of a cold hand.

Jane tried to smile at him but, an image of the lovely Carla with Brett was undermining her attempt. "Yes, I'm fine." She looked earnestly into his handsome face, amazed that but for a sheer accident their paths would never have even come close to crossing. Again she felt how tenuous her relationship with Brett seemed to be. "I met someone from your past. Her name is Carla Kantor," Jane said, watching him. For a moment Brett looked completely blank, then recognition filled his eyes.

"Oh, yes . . . Carla."

Jane withdrew her hand from Brett's and reached to take a sip of champagne. "She said you two knew each other well." Jane kept her eyes averted, not aware that Brett's questioning gaze was slowly turning to one of amusement.

Brett leaned toward her across the table. "I hope that's jealousy I hear in your voice," he teased, and watched as she blushed with uncertainty. Again Brett captured her hand. "Let's say *I* knew Carla very well. She and I dated for a while some years ago. It was casual. No doubt she embellished the facts somewhat."

Jane's eyes flew to Brett's face and she felt relief at his smile.

"Her father is a prominent banker and had dealings with my family for many years."

"She's beautiful," Jane said by way of comment, not aware that her voice and eyes expressed a vulnerability that Brett only found endearing.

Brett grimaced and arched a sardonic brow. "Yes, she is. But I also remember Carla as being a flirtatious little tart well on her way to being spoiled and manipulative. What is she up to now?"

"She says she works at a TV station in the city, doing the news."

Brett chuckled softly in dry amusement. "Don't worry. The secrets of the city are safe. I don't think it's the news Carla is interested in. But she's probably found her calling in front of the camera."

"What?" Jane asked.

"Adoration," Brett said wryly.

A feminine voice interrupted. "You left this on the vanity. . . ." A lipstick case was held out to Jane.

Jane reached to take it, and the woman's eyes focused on Brett with feminine guile.

"Hello, Brett. It's been a long time," Carla cooed as Brett stood politely. When she leaned forward in an obvious invitation to be kissed in greeting, Brett merely brushed his lips near her temple.

"Hello, Carla. Jane told me you'd introduced yourself to her."

Carla raised her brows and finally looked down at Jane. "Jane?" she questioned. "How old-fashioned," she said and turned back to Brett. "Yes, I did. I almost didn't recognize her. TV cameras can be very unflattering to a lot of people."

"On the other hand they can exaggerate a great deal."

Carla frowned, confused by Brett's words. "I'm here with some producer friends of my father's. They might be interested in putting together a show of my own on one of the local networks. Why don't you come over for a moment, Brett?" she suggested, possessively taking hold of Brett's arm.

Brett carefully released his arm. "I'm afraid not. Jane and I are having a private celebration." He gave Jane a warm, knowing look and she basked in the attention. "We'd like to keep it that way."

Carla turned a condescending blue gaze on Jane. "What are you celebrating? Three years of unemployment?"

Jane looked deeply into Brett's hazel eyes. A very private smile passed between them. "Spring..." Jane whispered softly.

SOMETHING STARTLED JANE awake in the middle of the night. But at once she felt the reassuring pressure of Brett's arms around her and relaxed. Somehow she knew that today Brett would leave. A week ago she'd lived in dread of being left alone again. Now, in the dark, Jane realized with calm that it was time for Brett to go.

Somehow Jane felt that the very love she held for Brett had in some ways made her strong, given her confidence. Her time with him over the past few months had healed many wounds. She had only one more secret to share with him. Whatever the outcome was, she owed them both the complete truth.

Jane felt Brett's hand glide gently up her back. Jane sighed and tilted back her head to gaze into the shadowed planes of his face.

"What's the matter?" he asked in a sleepy voice.

"I didn't mean to wake you."

"But something is troubling you. Want to talk about it?"

Jane smiled. She loved the way he always seemed to know when something was on her mind. She loved the feel of his body next to hers in bed, his deep voice rasping in the dark . . . his security and care. "You know that Harry Lindsay is my father, don't you?" she asked in a soft small voice.

Brett was stunned. She'd never once made reference in any way to her family, particularly her father. Brett was greatly relieved and thankful that she was at last sharing her past with him.

"Mmm-hmm," he murmured lazily.

"When did you know? How?" Jane asked.

"I guessed almost from the start, when I saw the photograph," Brett admitted.

"And yet you never said anything."

"I promised you I wouldn't probe into your life, Jane. And it's not important whether or not Harry Lindsay is your father. It doesn't change anything."

Jane was silent for a moment. Closing her eyes, she sighed. "But it does matter. More than you realize. I've never known my father. I only know what I see on television. You know as much about him as I do. He didn't want me. He and my mother never shared a life." The painful grabbing at her heart that Jane had known all her life did not recur.

Brett gently began to stroke her hair. "And yet you wanted to be like him. You studied journalism. You did TV news."

"Maybe I thought he'd notice and be impressed. Funny, I used to think I couldn't wait to grow up so I could see him, show him...show him..." *What?* That she was worthy to be noticed and loved? "Anyway, everything just got so complicated."

Brett wanted to make her realize that it was over. But he didn't want to make light of the tremendous pain she'd endured. He wanted Jane to know as well that the decisions her father had made had nothing to do with her. Sometimes people didn't have control of the choices they made. They were simply the best ones for the moment. And while Jane might have suffered for her father's actions, Brett felt sure that Harry Lindsay had not gotten away scot-free either. No one ever did.

"Jonathan was only three when his mother died, but he was very angry with Carolyn for leaving him and he acted out his feelings for months. Of course, now he has no memory of her at all. She's a stranger to him in much the same way that your father is a stranger to you...and you are to him."

Jane was silent, and Brett couldn't tell what her response was to his words, whether she understood his point or not. But he also wanted to tell Jane that when someone didn't find love in one place or with one person, he or she searched out another. He, after all, had found his true love in her. He desperately wanted Jane to find it in him.

Suddenly Jane pulled away from him and climbed gracefully out of bed. She walked to the window and stared silently into the black night. The room was chilly. She hated the cold. She never wanted to be so cold and alone again. She heard Brett follow her and come to stand behind her. Slowly he slid his arms around her smooth naked body and hugged her to him. Brett kissed her cheek and rubbed his chin across the top of her head.

"Jane, lots of people have trouble being parents. They don't want or aren't prepared for the responsibility. Sometimes I wonder if I'm really doing a good job with Jonathan. Sometimes people get selfish . . . or scared."

Jane began shaking her head. "Brett . . ." She turned in the circle of his arms. "You don't understand. My father never—"

"Jane, listen to me. Lindsay could have had a daughter to be proud of, and you could have had a father who was worthy of your love and devotion. But *he* blew it. Not you."

Jane stared at him, struggling to see his eyes in the dark, struggling for the right words. Maybe she was wrong. Maybe it wouldn't matter to Brett that she was illegitimate. Then Jane just blurted everything out.

"My parents never married, Brett. As a matter of fact, they didn't even know each other very well at all."

Brett became very still—and slowly very angry. Jane watched as his eyes grew cold and his jaw tensed as he clamped his teeth together. Slowly the life began to die out of her. She'd always known that she had to tell him the truth. It had only begun to be important once she realized she loved Brett Chandler. And because she had been honest, she knew she was going to lose him.

Brett released Jane abruptly; now it was his turn to stare out into the night. She felt numb.

"I can't even say I was a . . . a love child," Jane said in a quavering tone. "There wasn't any love between my mother and father. There was only ambition and a battle of wills. My mother lost."

"*You* lost. You got caught in the middle," Brett said.

She sighed. "No, not caught. I was the fly in the ointment. The cog in the wheel of two promising careers. My mother had hopes of—"

"Dammit!" Brett said so violently that Jane jumped.

"Brett, I'm sorry. I should have told you sooner. I tried to. I told you I wasn't right for you."

Forcefully Brett grabbed Jane's arms. She faced him wide-eyed, frightened by the storm clouds in his eyes.

"Don't be sorry!" he said through clenched teeth. Jane could only stare at him. "I don't give a damn who your parents are. They don't matter to me. *You* do!" Jane gasped, her heart squeezing tightly in her chest. "How could you think that you're any less a person because they didn't care enough for each other? How could you think it would make a difference to *me*!" Brett's voice was raw with emotion.

He released Jane and began to pace, running his hands through his hair. He took a deep breath and stepped in front of her, bending a little so he could see into her eyes. "All that time...all those years of believing that marriage would have made things all right. It doesn't always work that way. I did the *right* thing and married Carolyn, and it was the *wrong* thing for both of us. Your parents probably made the right decision, Jane. Marriage wouldn't have changed the people they are."

Jane began to weep. "It wouldn't have made things any different for me, but it seems so important to the rest of the world. Judgment was passed from the very start."

Brett slowly straightened. "Not by me," he whispered softly. And it was true. He had always accepted her just as she was.

When Jane raised her face her cheeks were wet with tears. Brett grabbed her roughly to him.

"Lady..." He groaned softly. "It's not going to work. There's nothing about you that's going to cause me to disappear from your life. And from now on—"

"Please don't say anything about the future!" Jane interrupted quickly. "Let's not make promises or plans we might not keep."

Brett indulged her and said no more, but then bent to kiss her on the mouth. He looked into her face and smiled gently. "I think it's time I get on to Germany. The sooner I leave, the sooner I get back."

Jane was confused. "And then?"

Slowly Brett began to smile. "You're a smart woman. You'll figure it out."

Jane sniffled through her tears. "Is this some sort of test?"

"No. But my returning from Germany is something you should give a lot of thought to."

Jane just looked more confused, and Brett realized that he should have told her sooner. But when he came back, everything would fall into place.

"Let me give you a hint," Brett said as he cupped her face and used his fingers to wipe away the tears. His eyes looked deeply into her own. "I'm in love with you, Lady Jane," he whispered.

JANE'S HANDS FLEW over the keyboard and her eyes were trained to the screen. She was unaware that Jones was carefully strolling from the den to the door. Jane was aware, however, that Oliver was due soon. He had taken a very authoritarian position with her ever since Brett's departure for Germany weeks ago, declaring that all work and no play made Jane a dull girl, and had set about seeing to it that communicating with nature was part of her daily routine. But in all truth, Jane knew now that staying in the house hard at work all the time would have driven her mad. It was something she never would have concerned herself with before Brett came into her life.

Actually, work had been a saving grace. It had served to divert some of her thoughts from dwelling on Brett's absence, and from anticipating too often his return. The extra work was a direct result of the recent posting of the newest Pulitzer awards. The downside was that somehow people had gotten hold of her phone number; for a full week after her name was listed in the *New York Times*, the phone never stopped ringing. There were calls requesting interviews, congratulations from editors and publishers, and even one caller who, when Jane identified herself, promptly hung up, once again reminding her of the threatening elements that were still at large.

Then there had been the telegrams, even one from her mother. She'd gotten very little sleep, but not all of it was due to the ringing of her telephone. She missed Brett terribly. He had been gone nearly a month, and Jane had received a postcard or scribbled note from him almost every day. The first message came just two days after his leaving and read, "Oh babe...I hate to go...." Another had been folded into a paper airplane, complete with instructions on how to fly it across the living room.

The article she'd written about the land dispute with Brett's father-in-law was printed and Jane sent Brett a copy. She also sent him a card with Jones's paw print on it, because she didn't have the nerve to send a photograph of herself. Jane knew Brett would see the humor in it.

Over the clicking of her computer keys Jane heard the knocking on the door. "It's unlocked, Oliver!" she called out, but continued typing. "I'm almost finished," Jane said at the sound of footsteps. "I know I said it would only take an hour, but you know how—" Jane turned her head to smile at Oliver—and stopped abruptly, her mouth open.

It was not Oliver who stood there but a young boy with Jones standing next to him. Jane got up slowly, her eyes riveted to the boy's face. His coloring was fairer, but there could be no mistaking the boy as Brett Chandler's son. At thirteen, he was thin and already an inch or so taller than Jane. His dark blond hair had the thick wiry look of his father's, and he had his father's direct gaze.

Jane took in the slim-legged blue jeans, the bottoms of which bunched around his ankles in a pair of high top heavy sneakers. The tongues of the sneakers were flapped over the loosened shoestrings. He wore a white shirt with a thin navy and red tie pulled askew around his neck and a woolen school blazer with the insignia of a prep school on the breast pocket. His green duffel bag was lumpy, its shape distorted by its contents.

Jane returned her amused gaze to the boy's face and saw that he was nervous and unsure. She smiled warmly at him.

"I guess you're not Oliver."

"No, ma'am," he said in a voice that was a telltale mixture of the adolescent and the future young man. "My name's Jonathan Chandler," he said, offering Jane his hand after wiping it down the leg of his jeans.

Her smile broadened and she continued to stare, feeling an odd and unexplainable catch in her throat. She took the offered hand. "Hello, Jonathan. I'm Jane Lindsay."

"Yes, I know," he said, putting down his duffel by his feet. "My father told me all about you."

Jane blushed. "He did?" she asked softly, although she wondered what Brett had told his son. He was dressed for school, although he looked as if he'd been traveling all day. Jane suddenly wondered not only what Jonathan was doing on Montauk, but how he'd got there. She did suspect that whatever the reasons, neither Jonathan's father, grandmother nor school knew of them.

"Did you come by yourself?" Jane asked.

Jonathan stuffed his hands into the front pockets of his jeans. "Yeah. I . . . I hitched a ride from Manhattan," he freely admitted.

Jane frowned. "All the way from the city? Why?"

"Well, Dad's talked so much about you and . . . and well . . ." Jonathan began to blush and became tongue-tied.

"And you were curious." Jane supplied softly.

"Yes, ma'am," Jonathan said politely. He looked down at the Labrador sitting patiently by his side. "This is Jones." He stroked Jones's silky head.

Jane couldn't help laughing. "Your father told you about Jones, too?"

Jonathan beamed. "And Oliver!" Slowly his smile faded and he again became uncertain. "I . . . I read a book by you once. Dad and I talked about it. He said that . . . well, that maybe I'd get a chance to meet you someday." He looked at Jane openly, doubt reflected in his eyes.

"I'm afraid that I'm to blame for that, Jonathan, not your father. You see, I've been very busy this year," Jane said weakly. She couldn't very well tell him that she'd been afraid to meet Brett's son for fear he wouldn't approve of or like her.

Jonathan nodded in understanding. There was another knock, and the door opened abruptly to admit Oliver.

"Ready, Jane!" he shouted. Both Jane and Jonathan turned to him. In some relief, Jane went to take his arm.

"Oliver, come in. There's someone here you should meet." Jane introduced them and watched as Jonathan stared somewhat in awe at Oliver's huge presence. "Jonathan is here to . . . well, he's here because . . ." Jane blinked. Actually, she wasn't at all sure why he was here.

Oliver, watching the lad carefully, had already drawn his own conclusions as to Jonathan's sudden appearance. "I tell you what," Oliver began, taking charge for the moment. "I was going to take Jane out for a sail, but why don't we go for some lunch? Then Jonathan can tell us all about being here. Are you hungry, Jonathan?'' Oliver asked.

''Yes, sir. A little.''

''Okay then, let's go.''

The subject of Jonathan's visit was avoided at lunch. Jane was concerned that something had happened that the boy wasn't telling them about. But Oliver, instead of rushing things, set about putting Jonathan at ease. And then, after a series of complicated signals, Oliver left the table on the pretext of having spotted a friend. Jane tried once more to find out Jonathan's intention.

''How are things at school?'' she began, noticing that Jonathan didn't meet her gaze.

''Fine,'' he mumbled.

''Are you finished for the year?''

Jonathan shifted on his seat and drank half his soda before answering. ''Well . . . almost. I mean, there's only one more week left to the term. But it's really not all that important to be there,'' he added hastily.

Jane felt her apprehension rising sharply. ''Then . . . you're supposed to still be at school?''

''Sort of,'' Jonathan admitted reluctantly.

''Jonathan, does anyone know where you are?'' she finally asked softly.

Shyly the boy met her gaze. It may have been on the tip of his tongue to fabricate a story, but he gave up at once, fiddling with his silverware. ''No, ma'am,'' he quietly said.

''But why?'' Jane asked, bewildered. ''Why did you leave? You're not running away, are you?''

''No, not really. It's just that I don't like being away at school.''

''But there was only one more week to go.''

He shrugged. ''I know, but all the other guys had their moms and dads coming to get them and I don't have a mom, and my dad's in Germany on business. He's supposed to come and get me next week...."

Jane's eyes grew warm with understanding. He was feeling all alone. "And you couldn't wait?"

Jonathan nodded. Jane gnawed on her lip. She mulled over this unexpected turn of events and how best to handle it. She had never thought to meet Jonathan quite this way and it bothered her that he had managed to reach her on his own without his family knowing. What could Brett have said to his son that would have provoked Jonathan to take matters into his own hands? Did he resent his father's interest in her? How much had Brett told his son about that?

"Jonathan, why did you come all the way to Montauk? Why didn't you go to your grandmother's?"

"Nana would only send me right back to school."

When Jane continued to wait, Jonathan began to blush.

"Well, I just wanted to meet you. That's all," he said earnestly.

That's all. So simple. And yet she felt uneasy. "But Jonathan..."

"Well, now," Oliver said as he returned to the table. "Is everyone finished? How about the sail?"

"We're finished. And we seem to have a slight problem."

At Jane's words Jonathan quickly stood, mumbling, "Excuse me..." and escaped to the men's room.

Jane sighed heavily and turned to Oliver. "He's left school, Oliver, and didn't tell anyone. He says he wanted to meet me."

Oliver's eyes crinkled at the corners. "Like father, like son..." he offered softly.

"What does that mean?" Jane asked in exasperation.

"It means that he's checking you out, looking you over. And it's somewhat understandable."

"You mean he wants to find out if...if I'm okay?"

Oliver merely nodded.

She frowned. "Oliver, I love Brett Chandler. I admit it. But I'm still not sure what's happening between us. What if his son doesn't like me? Then it's really all over, isn't it?"

"Now, now. Let's not go off the deep end. I think he's going to like you fine. He's here, isn't he? Why don't you let him stay for a few days?"

"Stay? With me?" Jane frowned. "But ... I don't know anything about children."

"Then it's time you learned. You're way overdue, anyway."

"Overdue?"

"You should have had some of your own."

"Oliver..." Jane pleaded in a whisper; he'd touched a sore nerve.

Oliver put up his hands. "Look, you managed well enough with Brett, and Jonathan is only a third his size and age!"

"Very funny," Jane said dryly.

Oliver regarded Jane thoughtfully. "Let him stay. I think it's important for both of you. Besides, it could be fun."

Jane was sure she was much too nervous to have fun. Jonathan came back with an almost painful expression of anticipation in his gray eyes.

"You're going to send me back," he stated rather than asked.

"Maybe not yet," Oliver answered.

Jonathan turned to Jane for confirmation and she smiled at him. "I still have to call and let someone know where you are. Do you understand?"

"Yes, ma'am," Jonathan said, brightening.

"Well then, let's go back to the house and make a call."

But when they returned to the house Jane reconsidered. She was no relation to the boy and legally the school was responsible for him. She asked Jonathan and Oliver to take

Jones for a walk, an idea that didn't appeal to Oliver and only left the dog confused, so that for a moment he resisted going. Once alone, Jane, as she had months before, placed a call to the Chandler house in Bridgehampton.

"Hello, Mrs. Chandler. This is Jane Lindsay calling," Jane began when the phone had been answered.

"Jane Lindsay. Jane Lindsay..." the other woman repeated. "Oh, yes!" Then she gasped sharply. "Good heavens! Don't tell me there's been another car accident!"

Jane chuckled. "No, no. I'm calling about Jonathan."

There was another gasp. "Has *Jonathan* had an accident?"

"Jonathan is fine, too," Jane hastened to assure the older woman. "It's just that he's...here!"

"Here? You mean with you in Montauk? What on earth is he doing there? He's supposed to be at school."

Jane smiled at the obvious bewilderment in Priscilla Chandler's voice. "Visiting," Jane responded in amusement.

"*Visiting?* Do you mean to tell me he simply up and left school and came to your house?"

"I'm afraid so, Mrs. Chandler."

Jane went on to tell Jonathan's grandmother all that she knew. In the end she was glad that the older woman could laugh at the resourcefulness of her grandson, as she now merrily did.

"One would think you were running a halfway house for wayward Chandler men!" she said with a chuckle.

Jane grinned, feeling at ease with her. "I am sorry. I always seem to be calling you with bad news."

"I'm just grateful both my son and grandson found someone so understanding," Mrs. Chandler sighed. "Well, poor Borden will have to come and retrieve the young rascal and get him back to Pennsylvania before he's counted as missing."

Jane wet her lips and interrupted. "Mrs. Chandler, I...I think I have another idea. I realize that you don't know anything about me and we've never met, but could Jonathan stay? At least for a day or so? Would it matter to his school?"

There was silence on the other end. "No...I'm sure the school would understand an early departure for the term, but...it's a terrible imposition to you."

"Oh, not at all."

"Well, let me be frank, Miss Lindsay. Brett has mentioned you with...admiration and a great deal of affection. And I know he's spoken to Jonathan about you. However, I am a little concerned as to how Jonathan might be reacting."

Jane flushed deeply. "I appreciate your honesty. I'm a little concerned, too. But Jonathan said he wanted to come and I think it's important to him. I realize it's very irregular, and certainly I'll abide by your wishes. But I'd consider it a big favor if you would let him stay with me," Jane thought quickly, trying to think now of anything that would persuade Jonathan's grandmother. "I'll drive him back to you myself in a few days."

Priscilla Chandler raised her brows. For almost five months she had wondered a great deal about the woman who had not only captured her son's attention but now her grandson's, as well. She was hardly going to pass up a chance to meet her. "It's a deal!" She responded cheerfully. "But you tell Jonathan, if he gets out of hand you have my permission to put the fear of God into him!"

Jane laughed, knowing that wouldn't be necessary. She looked over her shoulder as the door opened and Jonathan came in behind Jones. Jane gave him a thumbs-up sign.

Chapter Nine

"Jane! Have you seen my polo shirt? The one with the green stripes?"

Jane frowned over the sandwich she was putting together. "I think I saw it this morning in the upstairs bathroom," Jane called out. A second later a tousled blond head and bare bony shoulders appeared behind her in the kitchen doorway.

"Thanks!" Jonathan said and quickly disappeared up the staircase two steps at a time, with Jones right behind him.

Jane was constantly amazed at the amount of energy at work in an adolescent of Jonathan's age, as well as at his prodigious appetite. She hoped three sandwiches, two pieces of fruit and chocolate chip cookies were enough for an afternoon boating trip. Jane was also concerned as to whether or not Jonathan should take along an extra sweater, or a slicker in case the weather changed for the worse. She admitted there was a lot to learn about the care and feeding of thirteen-year-old boys, and she'd been nervous and unsure at first. Jonathan, however, was polite and touchingly deferential.

Jane was never quite certain how Jonathan was responding to her in the four days they'd spent together. Oliver would have honestly told her that Jonathan was very taken with her. And if Jane had been asked about her young charge? Simply put, she thought he was wonderful.

Jonathan was knowledgeable and inquisitive, funny, irreverent, rambunctious, caught in that curious youthful limbo, no longer a child but nowhere near being a man. Never before had Jane felt so severely the loss of never having married, of not having children of her own. All her accomplishments did not change that. No one had ever asked her—but, *yes* she would have loved having children of her own.

With a sigh, Jane packaged Jonathan's lunch and took it into the living room, which looked as if a hurricane had cheerfully swept through. Never had it looked so lived-in as it did now with a tangle of bed linen and the contents of Jonathan's duffel scattered here and there. *How odd,* Jane thought as she absently picked up one of Jonathan's socks from the floor, that father and son had done more to bring joy to her life than any other people she knew. Life seemed so incredibly full and rounded with the two of them. Jane turned her head to regard the rangy youth as he returned, tugging the polo shirt over his head. She loved this boy's father. Jane knew she'd have no trouble loving the son, as well.

"All ready?" she asked.

"Yep," Jonathan answered, using his fingers to comb his hair. Jones came to sit by his mistress. The animal had been caught between his love for and devotion to Jane and his obvious fascination with the tall young boy who ran with him through the brush and over the rocky beaches and sandy dunes.

Jane reached to pet the dog behind his ears. She handed Jonathan the lunch. "Now if you get seasick, make Oliver bring you back to shore."

Jonathan laughed. "I never get seasick."

"And tell Oliver you have to be back by six. I promised your grandmother I'd have you back in Bridgehampton in time for dinner."

Jonathan grimaced. "Can't I stay until tomorrow morning?"

Jane laughed softly. "That's what you said yesterday morning. Your grandmother is going to get the idea you don't want to come home."

Jonathan blushed and shrugged. "It's not that. It's just that I'm having more fun here with you. I like it here," he admitted simply, and Jane was deeply touched.

"Well . . . I like having you here. But it's probably time to get you home."

Jonathan nodded, looking less than enthusiastic. "Could I come for a visit some other time? I don't mind sleeping on the sofa."

The question completely threw Jane. She hadn't the first idea if there would be a chance for another time. "I don't know," she answered honestly and saw Jonathan's disappointment. "You'd better go get your jacket. Oliver will call in a minute." And even as she said so, the phone rang and it was Oliver instructing Jonathan to meet him at the end of the road.

With a slamming of the door he was gone, and Jane was plunged into the most profound silence and loneliness she'd known since Brett's departure.

"You don't know what you've wrought, Brett Chandler," Jane murmured to herself in irony as she set about gathering Jonathan's belongings and pulling the room to rights.

The four days with Jonathan had been fun. He showed curiosity about her writing and Jane told him that she was considering writing another children's book, perhaps the sequel to the one he loved so much. He showed playful and affectionate wonder toward Jones; it was clear he'd never had a dog of his own and had missed the experience. Jonathan tried to be helpful in the house and Jane loved that he didn't want to feel a burden, but she quickly suggested that he just relax and enjoy himself. It had taken her a full day to persuade him to call her Jane, and then he did so with abandon and ease. While she tried to plan interesting outdoor activities for him, he seemed just as happy to be quietly in her company. They watched TV together, Jonathan introducing Jane to a host of harmless sitcoms, which they watched while eating freshly made popcorn. She began to teach him how to use her computer. After a short time she forgot to be nervous.

And it was clear that her relationship to Brett interested his son a great deal.

"Do you like my father?" Jonathan had asked one night over dinner.

Jane fingered the ends of her hair. "Yes," she admitted very quietly.

Jonathan thought this over. "A lot?"

Jane swallowed and lowered her gaze to her plate. "Yes," she repeated in an even quieter voice.

There was no immediate reaction from Jonathan. Finally she hazarded a quick glance at his face. "That's good," the boy said lightly.

Jane didn't know why he felt it was good, and she wasn't about to ask.

The afternoon was quiet and long without Jonathan's chatter, but it allowed Jane a chance to soberly consider her future in the light of the present and recent past. Jonathan and Brett, and in his own direct way Oliver, had shown her what life and love were really all about. It had nothing to do with her parents, although she had been hurt and confused by their indifference, and it had nothing to do with Jimmy Cochoran. Her encounter with him had only been a catalyst to reexamine her life and redefine it. And now that she'd had so much time to do just that, she came to realize that in many ways she had been very lucky. The afternoon turned warm and Jane sat on the steps to the house with the door open, Jones roaming near at hand. Without the aimlessness with which she'd lived for three years, Jane gave serious thought to where she'd move once the summer was over, so she could get on with her life....

IN THE EARLY EVENING Jonathan cheerfully related every detail of his day to Jane as they drove west along Montauk Highway toward the township of Bridgehampton. Jones sat in front seat of the car between Jonathan's feet while the boy affectionately stroked the dog's neck, as if knowing he'd be saying goodbye to the animal soon.

Perhaps he was tired from the long day in the sun, for Jonathan lapsed into a thoughtful silence during the final twenty minutes of the drive, absently navigating Jane to the Chandler estate, which was every bit as grand as Jane thought it would be. Insecurity attacked her again and made her hold the wheel tightly as she maneuvered the car up the driveway.

Borden met them at the door. Jane had only thought to see Jonathan safely delivered and to be on her way, since it was already getting late. But Priscilla Chandler suddenly appeared under the entrance lamp, smiled at Jane and grimaced playfully at her grandson.

Jonathan dutifully kissed his grandmother and waited for the scolding.

"You and I are going to have a serious talk, young man," Priscilla Chandler said with mock sternness. "I notified the school that you were home. I *knew* you wouldn't want the officials to worry needlessly...."

Jonathan blushed at the sarcasm.

"If you weren't my only grandchild, I'd murder you."
Then Jonathan's grandmother winked mischievously at
him. "Did you have a good time?" she asked with a smile.

"Yeah ... it was *neat*," Jonathan replied, relaxing.

Mrs. Chandler gently patted Jonathan's shoulder and
turned to Jane.

Jane knew the older woman was in her sixties, but something was incredibly youthful and warm about her, with her
white hair and fashionable outfit of slender black slacks and
bright yellow print sweater. The presence matched the voice
Jane had heard twice on the phone, but seeing Brett's
mother in the flesh doubled Jane's insecurity.

Priscilla Chandler was quick but precise in her assessment of the young woman before her. She immediately liked
the freshness of her. Everything about her bespoke a lady of
strong personal presence. But Priscilla was also aware of a
hesitancy about the younger woman.

She smiled warmly at Jane, extending her hand. "You
know, my son promised he'd let me know when he found
you. I'll have to call him to task for waiting so long!"

Jane stared blankly. "I beg your pardon?"

Priscilla grinned. "Don't mind me. I was just thinking out
loud. Come on inside. I've been looking forward to meeting you."

"I'm sorry," Jane began. "I have my dog with me,
and...I really don't want to intrude. It's getting late, and..."

"Nonsense!" Mrs. Chandler brushed the excuses aside.
"We'll put your pet in the kitchen, and you're staying to
have dinner with us. Right, Jonathan?"

Jane had to smile at Mrs. Chandler's shameless use of her
grandson to get her own way.

Jones went complacently to the kitchen with the housekeeper, Maggie. Priscilla Chandler led Jane into the house
and the comfortable den, talking all the while. It was an attempt to put Jane at ease, and Priscilla could see she was

succeeding, when she turned the conversation to Jonathan's escapades and avoided mentioning Brett too often. Whenever she did, however, she noticed that Jane had a tendency to blush unconsciously, which convinced Brett's mother that this attractive young woman was in love with her son.

It was nearly eight-thirty when the three of them sat down to dinner. It was a very informal and light meal. By the time they had finished with a dessert of apple tart, Jane felt as though she'd known Priscilla Chandler for a long time. She almost regretted having to leave so soon, but was concerned about not being on the road so late at night by herself for the return drive to Montauk. Priscilla tried to persuade Jane to stay the night and start back the next morning, but Jane declined, feeling that it was inappropriate under the circumstances.

Jane was about to begin her goodbyes when there was a small flutter of sound and commotion in the entrance hall. Priscilla Chandler excused herself and left the room. A curious Jonathan stood slowly, silently disappearing after his grandmother. Jane didn't know who the new arrival was, but decided this was the appropriate time to leave. She left through a second door in the dining room and went to retrieve her handbag from the den. She was about to recross the room when she heard the door close behind her. When Jane turned around it was to see Brett in the shadowed darkness near the door.

There was a moment of stunned silence. Brett's eyes grew dark with longing as he gazed at Jane, a slight smile curving his wide mouth. Jane's eyes filled with instant joy and wonder, as if Brett were an apparition. Perhaps it was the welcoming warmth of Priscilla Chandler and the pleasant coziness of having had dinner with her and Jonathan, but Jane knew such delight, such happiness at seeing him so suddenly that instinctively she went forward and into his outstretched arms. She wasn't thinking or rationalizing at that moment. Only feeling intensely, completely, exhilaratingly alive.

Their lips came together out of a mutual longing and hunger that surprised them both. They clung to each other, Brett clasping Jane tightly to him, his large hands boldly outlining her buttocks, stroking her hair and cheek. His tongue plundered her mouth, claiming her, startling Jane with his possessive eagerness. And she was equally fervent, pressing closer to his hard lines. When she realized where they were, she hastily but reluctantly pulled back, her mouth tingling from his hard kisses. Jane's eyes were glowing as she regarded him.

Brett took another brief kiss from her before settling his arms loosely around her waist. He arched a brow and grinned down into her face.

"Maybe I should go out and come back in again. I like the welcoming committee."

Jane's eyes devoured him. "Don't you dare!"

His smile was still complacent, but his eyes roamed her features with serious intent. "Can I take that to mean you missed me?" Brett asked hoarsely.

With the point of a finger she stroked his hard chin. "Yes..." she answered softly.

Brett put a hand under her chin and lifted her face. "I would like to demonstrate how much I missed you. But this isn't the time or the place."

"Brett..." Jane breathed in a whisper of desire.

Brett used his thumb to stop her. "I love you, Jane. Quite frankly it's been hell without you. I want you to believe that."

Her eyes were bright. "I... I do."

"Then we have to talk...."

Jane smiled and kissed his chin. With an inward sigh she pulled out of his arms. "Later. When you've had a chance to relax from your trip, take care of business and see your family."

Brett frowned. "What's this about you bringing Jonathan home from Montauk? What's been going on?"

Jane shrugged, reaching again for her handbag. What had happened was between Jonathan and herself. "He just hitchhiked out one day," Jane began carefully. "We spent some time together, and I brought him back home."

"That's it? Just like that?"

Jane fiddled with the strap of her purse. "Just like that."

But Brett wasn't buying so simple a story. A grave apprehension grabbed at him suddenly. "Jane, did Jonathan...did he give you a hard time?"

Jane's eyes flew to meet Brett's concerned gaze. "Oh, no! Jonathan is a wonderful boy. I loved his company. He's a lot like you," she said wryly. "Your mother is gracious and lovely, and..."

Brett came toward her, taking her purse, putting it aside and again taking Jane into his arms. She didn't resist. "Mother says the exact same thing about you."

Jane laid her hands on his chest and shook her head. "She's just being kind."

Brett squeezed her to him. "Well, I'm not," he said with a dry chuckle and slowly bent to kiss her again. Jane savored the taste of him, the firm manipulation of his mouth that was so erotic. With a moan of pleasure she pressed into the safe strong harbor of Brett's arms. She wanted to stay there forever. She heard Brett groan as he pulled her hips against the tautness of his own.

Brett's mouth began a slow sensuous withdrawal that teased and stroked at Jane's mouth and tongue. His lips nipped and nuzzled down the corner of her mouth to her jaw. "Jane," he barely whispered into her skin with a kind of reverence that sent a thrill up her spine. "Won't you stay the night?'' he asked suggestively, causing her knees to weaken.

Jane sighed. ''No. I have to go back to Montauk.''

He held her for a moment longer, knowing in that instant, the way he'd known when he was leaving for Germany that he didn't like being away from her. At some point in the recent past Jane had become an integral part of his life, and he didn't want to be without her again. With a groan of frustration Brett released her, looking into her face. His inclinations warred with common sense.

''There are a few things I have to take care of here and in Bethpage. When I'm done I'm coming to Montauk to get you.''

His voice was very firm and Jane smiled at the sternness in his tone. ''This sounds serious,'' she teased gently. But Brett didn't return the smile.

''It is,'' he answered. He let Jane get her purse and together they left the den and went back into the grand foyer.

Jane's color was heightened and she wore a rather soft, gentle look from her brief encounter with Brett in the den. Priscilla Chandler gave no indication that she felt their sudden closeting was out of line. Still, Jane found it difficult to face Brett's mother and son again. Jonathan had retrieved Jones from the kitchen and the dog gave Brett a familiar welcome by sniffing at him and swishing his tail in recognition. The Chandler family escorted Jane and the dog to her car, and Priscilla extended an invitation to visit again.

Jonathan suddenly walked up to Jane, put his arms around her shoulders and gave her a warm hug that left her speechless. She quickly recovered and returned the embrace, as her eyes also met the alert gaze of Mrs. Chandler. Jonathan kissed Jane's cheek and stood back awkwardly.

''I had fun. I sure hope I can come again,'' he said.

Brett's mother and son stood as a watchful audience, but Brett showed no hesitation in leaning over the open door of the car and giving Jane yet another kiss that could hardly be described as a friendly goodbye peck. It was personal and passionate, no matter how brief.

"Drive carefully. I'll see you in a few days," Brett said before stepping back.

Jane merely smiled because her throat was too constricted for a single sound to pass. She waved and quickly got into the car with Jones. She was at the very end of the driveway before Jonathan, his grandmother and father turned back into the house, and as the door closed behind them Jane's emotions overwhelmed her. Tears rolled freely down her cheeks, while Jones put his head against her thigh as though in understanding.

Never had the Montauk house seemed less like a home than after returning from the Chandler estate, because there were people living there who projected warmth and love and caring for each other. They embodied the true meaning of "family"; Jane knew she couldn't stay and intrude on something so personal.

In a way that was really too bad, since Brett had long since come to a decision that Jane should become part of the family. But first he had to find out what had happened in Montauk between Jane and his son. He didn't get the full story until the next morning at breakfast. Jane would have been mortified to learn she was the primary topic of conversation, with Jonathan a close second, and Brett's trip to Germany trailing behind in third place. Brett didn't have to say much at all, actually. He just sat and listened happily to the glowing reports about Jane Lindsay. Since he also knew Jane to be a somewhat private person, he wondered anxiously how she'd reacted to being taken by storm, so to speak, by the Chandler household.

Brett could easily interpret his mother's opinion of Jane simply by what she *didn't* say. She wouldn't mince words despite her claims never to interfere in her son's life. Nonetheless Brett made it very clear that he loved Jane Lindsay and intended to ask her to marry him. Brett also carefully related some of Jane's fears as to her own eligibility, not because he thought his mother would care, but because he wanted to avoid any sensitive questions in the future. He need not have worried. Priscilla had never been one for believing that the sins of the fathers were visited on the children.

Jonathan, on the other hand, hedged a little about Jane. Brett cornered him as he was about to leave to bike to a nearby friend's home, and suggested that they sit and talk for a while. Jonathan acquiesced with a kind of fatalistic gloom.

Brett began with his son's highly irregular departure from school the week before. It was a familiar story. Brett had great hopes, he said, of changing Jonathan's school situation, although he was not ready to say how or when. He spoke calmly but firmly about Jonathan's behavior, then turned to the subject of his surprise visit to Jane.

They had returned to the dining table, where Brett nursed another cup of coffee. Jonathan had always been close to his father and knew he could talk to him about most things. But just now he eyed his father with trepidation. There were some things between adults he sensed to be private, and he knew he had overstepped his bounds by going to see Jane Lindsay without his father's knowledge or permission.

"I understand you made a trip to Montauk," Brett began again, as if by way of making conversation.

"Yes, sir," Jonathan admitted. His voice cracked over the words and Brett hid an understanding smile.

"Why?"

Jonathan shrugged and blushed. "I . . . I guess I was just curious."

Brett arched a brow. "And did you satisfy this burning curiosity?"

Jonathan nodded.

"Did you like it there?"

Again Jonathan nodded. "I really like Oliver. He barks a lot but he's really okay. He took me fishing."

"And what do you think of Jane?" Brett's tone was carefully cool...but he was anxious.

Jonathan glanced quickly at his father, and then away. "She's okay."

Brett's heart sank.

"I mean, she's more than okay," Jonathan hastened to add, flushing even more deeply. He looked at his father. "She's really neat, Dad," he said earnestly.

Brett relaxed and slowly began to grin. That was one way to put it. "You sound like you're trying to convince me."

"No. I mean, yes! I mean...well, what do you think?"

"I think Jane is really neat, too," he said smoothly.

"Really?" Jonathan questioned in his typical way.

"Really," his father assured him.

Brett finished his coffee and watched his son digest his words. "Dad?" Jonathan began very quietly. "Are you going to marry Jane?"

The question was thoughtfully asked, and Brett knew one of the moments of truth was at hand. "I've been thinking about it. Why?"

"I think you should."

Brett was amazed and his expression probably showed it. It was the very first time that Jonathan had ever hinted at thoughts of his father remarrying, or of the possibility of having a stepmother.

"I think that's an excellent idea," Brett answered softly.

Then a lopsided grin broke out on Jonathan's face. "Gee, that's great!"

Brett held up a hand. "Wait a minute. There's still one more person I have to convince."

Jonathan frowned. "Nana?"

"No. Jane," Brett said with a wry chuckle.

IT WAS ALMOST A WEEK before Brett could even consider going to Montauk. There were days of meetings with Grumman engineers. There was a one-day trip to Washington to NASA. His wing design for the glider competition was an innovation, and although scoring well in performance, the Germans won again, remaining virtually undefeated. Brett's new design, however, was bought outright by Grumman to be used in production. Brett's thoughts were dominated by Jane and the need to see her, yet constraints of time and business conspired to keep them apart.

Jane had also worked herself into an emotional state, missing Brett desperately. She didn't want to love him this much, to need him this much, that her future seemed a barren stretch of years unrelieved by love or happiness. Nonetheless Jane believed she could not ask anything more from him. Not because she thought he wouldn't want her, for she knew Brett to be innocent of duplicity, but because she felt he *shouldn't*. She had learned that sometimes when people most desired something or someone was when they had to think of just letting go. So Jane began to consider seriously taking an instructor's position that had been offered her before the announcement of the Pulitzer. It would determine where she'd move to and live.

JANE'S SUDDEN INTROSPECTION lent her the nerve one morning to call the Washington hospital where Harry Dean Lindsay was being treated, only to learn he'd already been released. Jane had thought to make one more attempt at contact, even against her better judgment, perhaps because in her loneliness that week she could still feel and remember the closeness offered by Brett's family. But on finding Harry Lindsay no longer at the hospital, the last of Jane's hope and courage died and she didn't try again.

It was Wednesday evening of the second week of May. There had been a sudden rush of warm days. Jane had opened the windows in her den to let the sweet breeze sweep through the cottage. The days made her feel alternately giddy and light-headed with hope and weighed down by doubt. They either made her sleepy and languid, or filled her with so much energy that she walked miles along the beaches with Jones, her imagination active and fertile. She'd been working out an idea for the sequel to her children's book.

While she worked, Jones lay asleep in contented abandonment in the living room, occasionally making his way to the den as if making sure she was okay, before retreating to his rug. Jane's thoughts ran swiftly as the story idea took form, and she worked on into the early evening as the sun dimmed. She got up from the computer and leaned across the desk to look out the window. In the fast-fading light there was only the breezy movement of the leaves on the trees. She drew back inside and closed the window.

Her attention span broken, Jane began to feel the hollowness in her stomach and realized she hadn't eaten all day. She thought to just make a salad and feed Jones before coming back to her computer. She recalled with a grimace Oliver's threat that he'd have to resort to feeding her intravenously if she didn't remember to eat properly. Oliver had also added that Brett was going to hold him accountable if anything happened to her, at which point Jane had snapped she didn't need anyone to be responsible for her.

Thinking, as she was, of Oliver and Brett at the same moment, Jane didn't hesitate to answer the light knock on her door as she was about to enter the kitchen. If it was Brett, she would welcome him lovingly. If it was Oliver, she was going to send him back home. She really wasn't in the mood for lectures, teasing, frivolous observations or Oliver's irreverence toward everything in general.

But when Jane opened the door neither Brett nor Oliver stood on the doorstep. It wasn't anyone she knew or recognized. Jane went stiff as her mind fought to conjure up the caution with which she'd lived her life before Oliver had befriended her and Brett had gotten past her barriers. But it was too late for caution. The man who faced Jane was of medium height and husky. His face was rough and square, with hard cold experience buried behind his close-set brown eyes. His hair was cut short and gray over his ears. But despite his middle-aged markings this man was muscled and fit. And he looked dangerous.

Jane felt her stomach tighten with an odd bunching of her muscles and nerves that was almost painful. Her eyes assessed the stranger in a mere second, as he did her. He began to speak in a strangely soft, gravelly voice.

"Evening. I'm looking for N. Jane Lindsay."

N. Jane Lindsay. How did he find out that was her real name? Who had bothered to search hard enough until it was found? Was Jimmy Cochoran *that* determined? And who was this man who knew whom to ask for?

She just stared. She heard Jones come awake and alert behind her at the strange voice, but she didn't even pay much attention to him. She could only think that this was it. Somehow she'd been found, tracked down. Jane's green eyes stared unflinchingly at the strange man, trying to decide if he was capable of following out an order to carry out revenge.

"Who are you?" Jane asked in a voice so calm and reasonable that it surprised her.

The man squinted thoughtfully and looked her over. Jane suddenly noticed his broad hands and short fingers. They were opening and closing restlessly at his sides.

"Are you Jane Lindsay?"

Jane gripped the door handle. What if she said yes? What if she said no? He'd found her. She began to close the door, shaking her head.

"You'll have to tell me who you are and what you want first."

The man smiled. But the flash of his uneven white teeth only tautened Jane's spine, and the apprehension grew to a threatening lump in her chest.

"You're right. There's no reason to trust me, is there?"

He opened the flap of his inexpensive sports jacket as he reached with one powerful hand to an inside pocket. Jane saw a holster and a gun.

"No!" she shouted in a panic, and caught the flash of sudden surprise in his eyes before she attempted to slam the door on him. Jones started from the living room with a deep-chested growl and began to bark. Jane had all her weight against the door in an attempt to shut and lock it, but the man on the other side was quickly applying his own counterforce.

"Dammit!" he grunted against the impact of the door, his hand gripping the edge and pushing against Jane.

She knew she couldn't possibly close the door against his superior strength, but she wouldn't give in. She gritted her teeth, feeling not so much fear right now as a determination to survive. It never occurred to Jane to scream or to even yell for help, and she struggled in a desperate silence as Jones continued to bark and growl and brush against her legs excitedly.

"Come on! Open the door, lady! What do you think I'm going to do to you?" Then with one shove the door slammed against Jane's side and chest and threw her completely off balance. She went flying backward and landed hard on the floor, her right forearm and thigh taking the impact. She was momentarily stunned, and her stomach protested the ill treatment. It began to churn alarmingly.

The door swung back on its hinges and the stranger was outlined with a disbelieving frown on his harsh features. Jane was still trying to catch her breath, when Jones came running past her and jumped to snap with open jaws and exposed teeth at the man, who put up an arm to protect his face. The large dog crashed with full force into his chest and clamped his jaw to one arm. The stranger yelled something incoherent and struggled to keep his balance. Jane pulled herself to her feet and ran to the door, biting her lip against the pain.

"No, Jones! Down, boy!" Jane commanded, but Jones was enraged and paid her no heed.

"Call him off, lady!" the man grunted through his teeth, trying to shake the animal free.

Jane grabbed the struggling animal, but every sinew and muscle in his body was tight and lending Jones's body weight and force. Jane held on to his neck and shoulders. "Let him go, Jones! Let go...."

Jones suddenly obeyed, although he still bared his teeth and snarled, watching the man intently. Jane pulled the dog back into the house and once more tried to close the door while the stranger stood confused, cradling his arm. Suddenly he was propelled forward through the door. Jane gasped and grew wide-eyed as the man landed clumsily on his stomach—with Brett on top of him. She watched dumbfounded as the two wrestled briefly until Brett forced the man's face and head flat to the floor, immobilizing him.

The man on the floor gave up the struggle as he realized he was at a disadvantage. Brett reached under his chest, deftly removing a small .38 revolver from a shoulder holster. Jane was mesmerized by it. All she could see were small explosions of light and she heard a sound like firecrackers. All she could feel was summer heat overwhelming her and she could smell of fear and danger. All she could remember were the threats hurled at her—and someone dying. Jane suddenly felt sick to her stomach, and she clutched at it, feeling the bile rise in her throat. She swallowed hard.

She still had a firm hold on Jones, who strained in her arms to be released as he continued to bark angrily at the stranger. Brett then twisted one of the man's arms behind his back and began to apply pressure. His control assured, he then glanced quickly but thoroughly at Jane to make sure she wasn't injured.

"Who the hell are you?" Brett ground out the question as the man winced from the pain of having his arm held at an unnatural angle.

"Hey, take it easy! You're going to break my arm!"

"Your *name*!" Brett prompted.

"*Weeks*, okay? Roger Weeks."

"What is it you want, Roger Weeks?"

Oliver appeared, bulky and intimidating behind the two men on the floor. He looked over the scene quickly then touched Brett on the shoulder. "See after Jane. I'll take care of him," he said.

Brett relinquished the man to Oliver and rushed to Jane, who couldn't have spoken or moved in that moment if her life had depended on it. Brett noticed she was dazed and her face was unnaturally pale. Jones had stopped barking and stood with his attention still trained on the man lying flat on the floor.

"Look, I'm not going to hurt anybody. Let me up."

Jane stared blankly at Brett, and he gently tried to help her stand. She grimaced.

"So help me, if you've touched her..." Brett said menacingly. Jane drew in her breath sharply when Brett squeezed her injured arm too tightly. "Jane. Are you all right? Did he hurt you?" But he got no answer. He brought her to her feet and took her limp body into his arms, holding her tightly.

Brett experienced a fear and anger he'd never known before. He was unreasonably angry with himself that he'd not been here to save Jane this trauma. Now he held her close, his heart in his throat. If anything had happened to her...

"What are you doing out here?" Oliver asked the stranger. "Who sent you?"

"Who are *you*?" the man challenged.

Oliver was relentless. He put his knee against the man's lower back. "You first!" he shouted. Jane jumped in Brett's arms.

"Okay! Okay. I...I'm a private investigator. I was hired to find a Jane Lindsay. I can prove it!" he added when Oliver's knee dug into his back.

Slowly Oliver released the pressure and stepped back. The man dragged his body into a standing position, grunting at the pain in his arm and looking to see who these two men were who'd come out of nowhere. When he stood up, Jones began to growl deep in his chest, prepared to come to Jane's defense, but he made no move toward the man, who eyed him warily.

"Quiet down, Jones," Oliver ordered the dog and the big Labrador sat down. Then Oliver looked at Brett, who was holding the silent Jane. "You better sit her down, Brett. She's going to pass out, otherwise. And get her something to drink. Quick!"

Brett slowly led Jane to the living room sofa and sat her down. He knelt before her and chafed her hands, which were icy cold. He checked her pulse and found it much too rapid, even though she seemed so languid. He cursed under his breath when he saw the bluing of her skin where her arm had hit the floor, and gently touched it with his fingers. Brett left Jane to go to the kitchen and came back with a glass of water.

In the meantime Oliver had closed the door, retrieved the gun and motioned to Roger Weeks to move into the living room. Oliver brought one of the straight-backed chairs from the kitchen and placed it in front of the fireplace. The husky stranger sat in it, still rubbing his abused arm and trying to put his clothes to rights.

Sitting next to Jane, Brett held out the water to her, but Jane shook her head and turned away. Brett forcibly turned her back to face him and set the glass to her lips. "Come on, Jane. Drink it." Jane willingly took sips from the glass, her eyes focusing now and recognizing Brett. He set the glass down and watched as some color came back into her face. Brett smiled in relief.

"Brett..." Jane whispered and came forward into his arms, sighing with released tension. Brett was here.

Brett hugged her and nodded at Oliver over Jane's shoulder. "It's all right, darling," Brett whispered to her.

"Look, I wasn't going to hurt her," Roger Weeks said.

"That's not how it looked, Mr. Weeks."

The man was incredulous. "Hey! *I* was the one who was attacked! That dog is dangerous."

"He's supposed to be, to strangers," Oliver answered.

Jane had come to her senses and from the safety of Brett's arms turned her head to watch Oliver's interrogation with more interest. She was just as curious about Oliver's reaction as she was about that of Roger Weeks.

"Who hired you?" Oliver asked.

"I can't tell you that. That's information for the right person."

"Was it Jimmy Cochoran?" Jane asked softly, drawing all eyes to her.

The man only blinked at Jane. "Jimmy who?" he asked, so puzzled that Jane believed him instantly. In that moment she also knew she need never fear Jimmy's threat ever again.

"Look...all I know is I was hired to find Jane Lindsay. Are you her or what?" he asked impatiently.

"Prove it!" Oliver ordered, not giving Jane a chance to answer. Slowly the man reached into a pocket and withdrew a sheaf of papers secured with a rubber band, and a bent and used manila envelope. He handed everything to Oliver. Oliver scanned the sheets but without his glasses couldn't read much. With a disgruntled sigh he gave everything to Brett.

There were pertinent facts about Jane's early life. Dates, names, people she'd worked with or known briefly in the past...an old lover. Her mother's name but no address. Questions written and then crossed out. There was a P.I. license with Roger Weeks's picture staring blankly back at a camera. There was another piece of ID with a New York Police Department number on it. Roger Weeks was also an ex-cop.

There were pictures of Jane from magazines and old newspapers. The man stared at Jane while she and Brett looked through the bits and pieces of her life, all stuffed into a soiled manila envelope. It seemed a sad commentary. Jane looked across at Roger Weeks.

"You dialed my number a few weeks ago and then hung up."

He shrugged. "I was checking out a lead. I was pretty sure I'd found you."

"I'm Jane Lindsay," she said smoothly. Brett reached to take her hand and held it.

The investigator began to smile. "You're much prettier than your pictures."

"Why are you looking for me?" Jane asked, but her voice was filled with exhaustion.

"I was only hired to find you, give you a message, and report back to my client. For the record, Miss Lindsay, you were damned hard to find. There are a lot of people who are willing to protect your whereabouts." He glanced at both Brett and Oliver. "If I hadn't heard you were a Pulitzer

Prize winner, I'd still be looking. But a secretary at the committee board had a helpful and loose tongue." He grinned.

"You're avoiding the question, Weeks," Brett interjected dryly.

Roger Weeks looked to Jane. "The message is . . . 'I have few recriminations, but I do owe you the reasons why.'" He looked around at each person and spread his hands. "That's it. That's the message."

Brett and Oliver exchanged brief noncommittal glances. Only Jane held her breath, her eyes glazed. She gripped Brett's hand tighter.

With a certain degree of satisfaction Roger Weeks could see he had complete control of the situation once more. "May I use your telephone?"

Jane slowly nodded. "It's over there." She pointed to a corner.

Mr. Weeks got up, straightened the front of his jacket with a tug on the lapels and cautiously sidestepped the huge black dog. He turned to Oliver and with a strange little smirk held out his hand. "Don't worry. It's licensed. And I hadn't planned on using it."

Oliver handed him the gun and Weeks reholstered it before walking to the phone and dialing a number. Only Brett and Oliver were watching. Jane was staring into the dark, cold fireplace.

"This is Roger Weeks. I'm on Montauk, Long Island, in New York...." He turned to look steadily at Jane. "Yes, sir. She's here, Mr. Lindsay."

Chapter Ten

Jane heard the door close. Brett came back to her side on the sofa. Oliver was heard to let out a long tired sigh.

"Well, that was certainly interesting," he commented dryly.

Brett sat down next to Jane. He was still concerned about her lethargic state and lack of response. But then, how should he expect her to react? With joy? Surprise? Hope? Gratitude? Her silence was self-explanatory. She was numb and bewildered. Brett sat close to her, his strong arm urging Jane to rest against the support of his chest and shoulder. She did so, responding from sheer physical exhaustion rather than from any need for comfort. Brett understood that somewhere deep inside herself Jane was processing this new and unexpected turn of events.

Jones approached Jane on the sofa. Tiredly she put out a hand to stroke the black Labrador's head. "Thank you, Jones. You're a good friend."

Brett squeezed Jane's shoulder. "And I apologize for ever thinking him a marshmallow. Remind me never to make him angry."

"He's a smart dog. He knows who he can trust," Oliver said.

Jane regarded the doctor with curious eyes. "And you, *Dr.* Seymour...can you be trusted?"

Jones settled on the floor by Jane's feet. Oliver merely sighed, but there was no surprise, no indignation at the implication behind Jane's words. He crossed his arms over his chest and looked patiently at her. Brett watched, a glint of keen awareness in his hazel eyes.

"Okay, Jane. Let's have it. What's on your mind?"

Jane looked at the man who had been there for her when she'd first moved to Montauk Point. The one who had been father confessor...and protector. Jane stood up and walked to Oliver.

"Who are you, Oliver? I mean, really. Are you truly a retired doctor? Or are you a retired New York City cop as well? What's been going on here for the past three years?"

There was a calm and analytical thoughtfulness to Jane's question. Oliver didn't pretend not to understand what she was asking. Oliver knew he couldn't get around it now, and perhaps the truth would finally free this woman, whom he'd come to care for a great deal, so that she could find love and live the life she deserved.

"Well, I hope I've been your friend, Jane. I hope I've been here for you when you needed me, and made myself scarce when you didn't...." He glanced meaningfully at Brett. "I'm everything I said I was. A retired pediatrician. And maybe a few other things I never mentioned." He sighed in resignation. "I'm also Norman Rosen's brother-in-law. His wife is my sister."

Jane stood staring at Oliver. Immediately everything fell into place. All the seemingly insignificant things Oliver used to do or say...all the ways he seemed to know so much about her, when he really shouldn't have.

"Norman believed you after the shooting involving Jimmy Cochoran. He believed Cochoran capable of trying to hurt you. I hadn't planned on moving to Montauk when I gave up my practice. But Norman asked me to kind of hang around Long Island for a while. Get to know you. Be here, just in case.''

Jane shook her head. ''You mean, all this time you were watching out for me? Protecting me? I was a complete stranger to you.''

''I might not have known you at first, but I came to. Norman told me he thought you were very bright. And he knew he was one of the few people you'd told about your childhood and your relationship to Harry Lindsay. Norman thinks very highly of you. He said he'd never known you to be bitter or angry or revengeful about how Harry Lindsay denied you. That took guts and character. And it got me curious. I've seen a lot of abandoned and neglected children in my work. I wanted to see how one had grown to adulthood. I wanted to be someone you could trust and talk to. Someone you could see as—'' Oliver stopped abruptly. Jane watched as an uncharacteristic flush colored his face. And then the great man, who'd always seemed so invincible to Jane, so totally self-sufficient and independent, looked at her with a soft kind of longing that melted her heart and made Jane aware of a part of Oliver she'd never seen or considered before. His own loneliness.

''As a father?'' Jane supplied in a low voice.

For an answer Oliver cleared his throat, and looked down at his boat shoes.

How could she not have seen that this man was needy, too? That there was much missing from his life, as well? Jane turned her head to consider Brett and saw that he knew very well what had happened. Somehow that didn't surprise her. She turned back to Oliver. Slowly she approached him, feeling a flood of love and affection for this man, who had indeed been a father to her.

''If I could have picked my father, out of everyone I'd ever met...he would have been you, Oliver. I mean that with all my heart.''

Oliver's face grew as soft and vulnerable as anyone was ever going to see it. Awkwardly he gave Jane a rough quick hug and released her. "Thank you," he said in an emotional growl.

Turning around in front of Oliver, Jane regarded Brett once again. "And you, Mr. Chandler... what were you up to?" Jane asked with a small teasing smile. But Brett knew there was a real question being asked.

"Me?" he exclaimed with feigned innocence. He stood and came to gather Jane into his embrace. "Once I found out I could trust Oliver to take care of you, I spent my time just falling in love with you. I had the easiest part." He kissed the top of her head. Jane's eyes drifted closed in relief.

"What?" Oliver burst out. "You mean to tell me you... you investigated me?" he said affronted.

"I certainly did. When I found out about the shooting and the threat to Jane, I wanted to make sure you were everything you said you were. If I'd suspected that Jane was in any danger, the last few months might have gone a lot differently."

Jane looked at Brett. "What do you mean?"

"I'll tell you later in private."

"You had a hell of a lot of nerve, Chandler! I didn't have *you* checked out!"

Brett grinned wickedly. "You know you didn't have to, Doctor. I made my intentions clear at the beginning."

Jane laughed almost giddily. "Are you two fighting over me?"

Brett and Oliver exchanged looks. "Not in the same way, sweetheart," Brett replied.

On the floor an inert Jones stretched his body and settled back into sleep with a snort.

"And then there's Jones," Brett said dryly.

Jane looked from him to Oliver and chuckled. "Forget it! I'm not going to believe that Jones is an undercover agent."

"Mmm...no, but he was gotten and trained just for you. I supervised it myself," Oliver said smugly.

"But I never thought you liked Jones," Jane said.

"Jones is a great dog. But I didn't want him getting too friendly with too many people, even me. I wanted him to remember his real job was to be a companion and protect you." A sly glint came into Oliver's eyes and he laughed. "It's a good thing he took a liking to Brett, or you wouldn't have had a love life these last few months."

"Oliver!" she exclaimed indignantly.

Brett laughed. "That's okay. Jones and I came to an understanding last December. He knew I wanted Jane and that I was going to take care of her."

Jane blushed. "Brett!" she protested. The two men laughed.

And then everyone sobered, remembering suddenly the events of the evening. Jane supposed it was a testimony to how much she'd changed since knowing both Oliver and Brett that the news she'd received didn't seem at all devastating.

"Well..." Oliver sighed, moving slowly toward the door. "I'm going home. It's late and I'm getting too old for these middle of the night adventures."

"Oliver," Jane called out behind him. He turned and Jane put her arms around his neck to kiss his cheek and hug him to her. "Thank you, Oliver. Thank you for caring and believing in me."

Oliver returned the embrace, but quickly put Jane from him. "Look . . . let's not make Brett suspicious. One thing I don't need is to fight off a jealous lover."

"Not for long," Brett drawled.

"I didn't think so," Oliver responded.

Jane looked back and forth between them. "I don't think I understand."

Brett kissed her temple. "It's all right, darling. I'll explain that later, too."

Oliver opened the door. "Let me know what you decide—" he glanced quickly at Jane "—and you better make it soon." Then he was gone.

Brett looked down into Jane's tired face. "Come on, Lady. You've had enough excitement for one night. Let's go upstairs."

Jane didn't demur. She allowed Brett to turn off the lights and settle Jones down. It felt wonderful to have Brett here with her. But each of them knew they were avoiding a significant part of the evening. Perhaps not avoiding so much as just letting alone the fact that, after a lifetime of denying her very existence, Harry Lindsay was now seeking her out. She didn't know what to think or to feel, except that gone was the empty void she'd lived with so much of her life, and gone was the sense of somehow being incomplete. Brett had given her that, and Jane acknowledged now that in a backhanded sort of way her father had contributed, as well.

No more was said between Jane and Brett. First of all, every bone in her body begged for rest. She was tired beyond belief, and her stomach had yet to settle down. Jane stood pensively in the middle of the bedroom. Brett closed the door and walked up behind her. He slipped his arms around her, letting himself finally relax to fully feel and enjoy the soft curves of her. His hands roamed slowly, rubbing her midriff through her blouse, kissing her ear down to her neck. He slid both hands erotically over her hips, but it was not a sexual gesture, just a need to assure himself of her presence—and to assure Jane that he would always be here for her.

Jane sighed, telling herself for the first time that the only thing that mattered was belonging to someone who could accept her and love her just as she was. She leaned her head against Brett's shoulder realizing, all things considered, she'd been more fortunate than she knew. Brett had freed her, and so had Harry Dean Lindsay.

"Brett? What did you mean before? When you said the last few months might have gone differently?"

Brett hugged her, enjoying the airy fragrance of her soft hair. "I mean I might have been more aggressive in my pursuit of you. If I had believed you were in real danger, I would have found a way of getting you out of Montauk. I would have pushed the point of you coming with me to Germany. Believe me Jane, I would have found a way."

Jane smiled. "It might have been interesting to see how you would have handled me."

"I'm glad I didn't have to. I wanted you to take your time and get to know me. Be sure about me. I would have just loved you sooner."

"How could you have been so sure?"

"I was sure I wanted you the first time I came back to Montauk. After that I never had any doubts at all."

Brett turned Jane in his arms and with stirring tenderness kissed her for a long moment. He released her mouth and heard Jane breathe out softly. She regarded him for a long moment, her green eyes drowsy.

"I love you, Brett," Jane said in a whisper. She watched as a spark lighted his eyes. "I was sure, too. But I was scared."

Brett gently cupped her face. "Thank you. I've waited a long time to hear that. And it was worth every minute." His mouth opened to capture her lips briefly.

Jane snuggled into his arms again. "I've never felt like this before. It almost hurts."

There was a rumble of a chuckle deep in his chest. "Sweetheart, if it hurts, then I must be doing something wrong.'' Then Brett set about demonstrating how it should feel.

In the darkened room without benefit of light or reflection from the moon, Brett began to touch Jane. His fingers began with the buttons on her blouse. The fluttering touch of his hands on the skin of her throat, chest and stomach sent waves of delicious anticipation over her. His mouth was equally busy tasting at her mouth, drawing air and breathy sighs from her. He encouraged Jane's lips to respond and she met him with challenging touches of her own.

She paid no heed to the blouse slipping down her arms, her breasts jutting into Brett's chest where the contact made her nipples swell with desire. She drew in her breath, utterly surprised that such a small motion could evoke such enormous pleasure. Brett's fingers touched her spine, and pressing her closer slid up to the clasp of her bra. With a gentle movement Jane's breasts were freed. His hands were there instantly to add dizzying stimulation to the already turgid peaks.

Jane could hardly breathe now, and she pressed forward into his arms, their lips finally ending the game of hide-and-seek and consummating the darting courtship of their lips and tongues. While they were so occupied, Brett's hands found the snap and zipper of her jeans, and forcing his hands into the waist, drew them down along with her panties. The clothing lay bunched around her ankles as they clung to each other, Jane's now-naked body against the rough fabric of Brett's sweater and slacks. He was a lot quicker about removing his own clothing; then they were flesh to flesh, and she moaned deep in the back of her throat.

Brett's body began to push Jane backward, his lips still keeping her a willing prisoner, his hands stroking and touching until she trembled and felt her knees weaken. When the back of her knees hit the bed, Brett held her tightly with one arm and came forward, bracing his other arm on the bed as he eased them both down. Brett quickly adjusted his weight over Jane, settling enticingly between her thighs. But he held off completing the deeper contact as he bent to cover Jane's breast with his mouth, his tongue rough and warm, stroking the sensitive nipple, sending swirls of exquisite pleasure shooting through her body. Her hands began their own restless exploration, enjoying the powerful movements of his thighs and flanks. Her mind began to fly, absorbing this miracle with both wonder and gratitude. She and Brett were lovers in the true sense of the word.

Brett transferred his attention to the other breast and Jane ran her fingers through his hair, urging his mouth to ravage and delight her body. She felt as if she were floating upward from the bed. He slid a hand provocatively down her right thigh and felt Jane's body stiffen. Brett lifted his head and tried to see her face in the dark.

"Did I hurt you?"

"It's where I fell," she said softly.

Brett kissed the bruised spot, and the touch only stimulated Jane all the more. She quickly forgot about the pain. Brett's fingers danced over her highly sensitized skin, kneading her body until she lifted her hips against him suggestively.

It was then that Brett lifted his body slightly and slowly thrust forward. The exquisite feeling stripped Jane of breath until Brett began to move against her. After a moment, Jane began to match him. The slow stroking and thrusting pushed them both to the edge of an emotional abyss, balancing them on the brink until Jane's head rolled back and an unbelievable joy toppled her right over. Brett whispered encouragement, moving still to keep the pleasure going until he too joined her in a free-fall, their arms wound tightly around each other like a lifeline.

The room was filled with sweet murmurs and the sounds of their loving until Brett lifted himself free to lie next to Jane. He pulled her limp body against his chest and kissed her damp cheek.

"There, Lady Jane," he drawled. "Does that feel better?"

THE NEXT MORNING Brett smiled as he stretched languidly and reached for her. He began to make love to her before she was fully awake. The loving this morning was slow and easy, and they took time to savor each touch or whispered endearment. This time when they were replete, they rolled on the mattress in play, and then just cuddled quietly together.

"You know," Brett said lazily, "Jonathan seems real determined on having you for a stepmother." He turned his head to watch the many emotions racing over her face.

Jane hid her face against his chest. "And . . . how about you? What do you think?" she asked quietly.

"I'm not the least interested in having you for a stepmother. I had a wife more in mind," he teased.

There was silence for a very long time. Jane put her arm around Brett's middle and sighed. "You're asking for an awful lot of trouble. My life's a mess!"

"You've had some unkind things happen to you, but that doesn't make your life a mess. And I'll tell you what trouble is." He half sat up and turned to face her seriously. "Trouble is the possibility of having to live without you now. I couldn't and I don't want to. I love you."

Jane looked at him, catching a glimpse of the faint scar, a reminder of what had brought them together.

"Marry me, Lady Jane."

Jane smiled gently at his pet name for her. She stroked his hard bristled jaw.

"There are still so many things that need to be settled in my life."

"They are not going to make a difference. I'm not going to change my mind about the way I feel."

Jane smiled lovingly at him. "You *are* a wonderful man, Brett Alexander Chandler."

"Does that mean yes?" he asked, sliding his hand along her spine.

Jane arched a brow. "That means I'll think about it. I'm not trying to be coy, but—" her eyes were suddenly thoughtful "—there's something very important I have to do first."

Brett leaned over to kiss her mouth lightly. "I thought there would be."

"I have to see my father," Jane finished.

THERE WAS NO ONE prevailing emotion at work as Jane set off to meet Harry Dean Lindsay for only the second time in her life. She'd said to Brett that she had to see her father, but Jane was not really sure why. Perhaps to close a chapter on her life before she began a new one with Brett. There was a fluttering in Jane's stomach and with a sigh she pressed her hand flat against her middle to control it. She was beginning to suspect it was more than mild apprehension.

Brett had wanted to accompany her to Washington, but a hearing date had been set in Suffolk County Civil Court on the question of the property dispute with Stanley Hastings. Brett was understandably annoyed at the untimely coincidence, but Jane thought it just as well that she'd have to manage this encounter alone. And so here she was...alone. Like the last time she'd seen Harry Lindsay.

She'd called the Washington number that Roger Weeks had left with her. Her entire conversation had been conducted through a business manager. When Stephen Halliday, the business manager, had said he'd wire a plane ticket for her, Jane had informed him she'd come, but she'd pay her own way.

She left a reluctant Jones with Oliver, and Brett drove her to the airport. He held her in a gentle embrace and looked into her face.

"You only need to remember that I love you and need you. I'll be here waiting."

Now as Jane stood in front of the gray Georgetown house with its white shutters and trim, she could only hope this wasn't a mistake and that she wasn't going to be humiliated again as she'd been at eighteen. Jane rang the bell. The door was opened at once by a robust man in his early forties.

"How do you do," he began at once and held out his hand. "You're Jane," and he smiled faintly at her.

"Yes," Jane murmured, taking the fleshy hand with the firm grip.

"I'm Stephen Halliday, Mr. Lindsay's business manager. Come in."

Jane was left for a moment to look around at the quiet elegance while Mr. Halliday went into another room. The impersonal atmosphere reminded her of the cottage at Montauk. When Mr. Halliday reappeared, it was with a middle-aged woman who smiled kindly at Jane.

"This is Mrs. Taylor. She's a private nurse who's been retained to look after Mr. Lindsay."

The introductions thus taken care of and with Mrs. Taylor's okay, Jane was finally taken upstairs, her luggage left by the stairwell. Jane couldn't help but wonder how much they knew about her. Had her father kept his secret? Jane had no time to reflect on the endless possibilities as she found herself outside a set of double doors. Mr. Halliday knocked quietly and gestured Jane inside. She didn't even have a second to compose herself, and quickly tried to smooth her hair and straighten the seams on her white summer dress. Mr. Halliday left and closed the door. She found herself in a sitting room. There was a floor to ceiling double-paned French window with light flooding into the room. Next to it was placed a high-backed chair. In the chair sat Harry Dean Lindsay.

Jane was vastly surprised by the change in him. His once-abundant hair looked rather thin and wispy with the light behind it. His face was very pale, the eyes alert but shadowed. He'd lost considerable weight and while a slender man before, was now gaunt and spent by his sickness. Whatever it was had taken a tremendous toll, robbing him of vigor and strength, stripping him of the magic that had always made him seem much larger than life, almost immortal.

Harry took in the dignified, gentle presence of the woman before him. He saw little of that hopeful teenager with the wild reddish hair who'd so boldly met him years ago. And there was none of the overeager young reporter who'd surprised everyone with her journalistic abilities. This woman had matured, grown older and wiser.

"This is every bit as awkward as you thought it would be, isn't it?" he asked in a soft, deep voice. It held much more strength than he appeared to have.

Jane shook her head. "I'm not sure what I thought it would be like."

"Sit down. Over here in the light." He pointed to a French provincial chair with a padded brocade seat.

Jane quietly followed orders, thinking that this was like having an audience with royalty rather than a father. She sat a little stiffly, Harry watching her intently all the while. Jane met his gaze openly.

"You're grown into an accomplished, beautiful lady." A thoughtful glint shone in his eyes and he leaned a little toward her. "You would have done me proud," he said with a great deal of irony.

Jane regarded him for a moment. She was remembering Brett and Oliver and Norman Rosen, who'd always believed in her. "I've done myself proud," she said.

Harry Lindsay raised his brows, and slowly sat back in his chair. "Well put," he conceded.

It was a strange exchange. They talked for nearly an hour, but nothing of real consequence was said between Jane and Harry. She felt as though they were only spending time searching each other out.

"I want you to come back, Jane," Harry said.

"If you like. I'll come back tomorrow."

"No! I didn't intend for you to stay at a hotel. There's a guest room down the hall."

Jane was very uncomfortable with that. "It . . . it's not necessary."

"I insist." His presumptuous tone caused Jane to lift her brows. He was still a man who wanted his own way.

"It will help if you stay close at hand," he said gruffly. "I don't have a lot of time for niceties or sparing of your feelings. You will remember that I have never been known for that."

Jane felt herself blush.

"There is a lot we have to say to each other. But it has to be done quickly."

Finally Jane fully understood. Harry Lindsay was putting his house in order.

"All right. I'll stay."

THE STAY STRETCHED into nearly a week. Jane felt an odd companionship and challenge in Harry's company. They were not as father and daughter and never would be, but there was a grudging admiration based on similar streaks of stubbornness and pride. They did not speak of Jane's mother at all.

Once they got into a spirited argument on politics and government until Jane realized that he'd deliberately baited her, testing her mettle and convictions. She found that he had read everything she'd ever written, including her children's book. He'd followed the story of the campaign coverage that had embroiled her in tragedy, but he'd never taken Jimmy Cochoran's threat seriously and had been disappointed that Jane had let it end her career precipitously.

He seemed surprised that Jane was not angry or bitter at him for the past. In truth she was an interested but impartial participant in their time together. Jane had learned months ago to accept reality. That had been more due to Brett's belief in her than her own. But she had also come to see that her existence was her own responsibility. She had Brett's love and faith, so it ceased to matter what anyone else thought about her... even Harry Dean Lindsay.

During the week of her visit Harry began to deteriorate physically. But despite advice to the contrary, he insisted on Jane's visits. Even Jane began to feel strange, however, and to have moments of highs and lows. She felt languid and dreamy.

"You must be in love. Are you?" Harry observed.

Jane never hesitated. "Very..."

Surprisingly, Harry roared with laughter until he was overcome with a paroxysm of coughing that sapped his strength and left him looking pensively at Jane. "I envy you having learned what love is. Don't ever believe that work is enough. Is he an innocent man?"

Jane frowned in puzzlement. "What does that mean, an innocent man?"

Harry smiled reflectively. "Oh...someone capable of love unselfishly. They're a rare breed, you know."

"They shouldn't be. It shouldn't be so hard to love," Jane replied.

Then Jane knew she wanted to go back to Brett. Being with Harry had only made her lonely, because he was a lonely person. For all his career and fame, there was no one in his life to care for and love him beyond his loyal staff. Jane felt sorry for him. Harry Dean Lindsay had settled for so little. But before she could go, she had to ask the question that had sat at the back of her mind, not just for the past several days, but all her life. Would it really have been so terrible, having her for a daughter?

Harry's eyes grew distant. "I didn't like being tricked. The decision to be a father was not mine to make or even to take part in. I resented that." He was weak and tired and filled with the past himself. "When I learned that Margaret was to have a child, I was furious. As far as I was concerned it was *her* baby... not mine." There was a curious mellowing in his face. "Make no mistake, Jane, I was never sorry for my decision. I was selfish and vain to a degree, but I was also young and not ready for the responsibility of a family. My career was just getting started. Frankly, that was more important.

"But death is a great equalizer. Death puts all of life into proper perspective. I missed the process of you growing into a strong young woman who did very well for herself. And I've made you an innocent victim of two foolish young people. For that... I've always wanted to beg your forgiveness."

Jane didn't realize that she was crying. Harry's weakened body suddenly seemed to shrink before her eyes and to blur through her tears. The room was silent and heavy with memories.

"I forgive you," Jane said in a thin ragged voice, but she was never to be sure if Harry heard her. He seemed to be asleep all of a sudden, and in a panic Jane hurried to summon Mrs. Taylor.

Harry Dean Lindsay was rushed to the hospital that very evening. Jane accompanied him and called Brett to tell him of the latest development. The tired confusion in her voice threw Brett into anxiety over her own welfare.

"Just take it easy, sweetheart. I'm on my way down to you."

"Yes . . . please hurry!" She didn't want to be alone anymore.

BRETT HAD BEEN PACING in the lobby of the Washington office building for well over an hour. Anyone spotting his tall, handsomely suited frame would have thought he was waiting for a client, like any of the dozens of men and women attorneys who were bustling around him. In truth Brett's outward air of a preoccupied businessman disguised his inward concern. He was concerned about how Jane was holding up under the emotional stress. First the encounter with Roger Weeks, then there was the trip to Washington for the brief reunion with her father. Sitting vigil over him until he passed away quietly in his sleep, ending a relationship that had never actually gotten started. And now being closeted with Stephen Halliday and half a dozen lawyers for the last hour or more.

When Brett had arrived two days ago, it was to find that Harry Lindsay had already come to the end of his futile battle against his illness. Brett remembered Jane walking to meet him as he waited then by a nurses' station.

"Are you all right?" he'd asked in a deep concerned voice.

Jane had looked up at him with eyes that were tired but clear and bright. She nodded.

"And how's your father?"

"It's all over," she whispered. "It was quick. There was no pain."

"So in the end he was still all alone."

Jane sighed. "Not quite. There were reporters who'd been called by his business manager. There was a prepared statement from Harry, supplemented by the doctor's report. He'll get a spot on local and national news tonight and he'll be eulogized by the press corp and his colleagues for a while. He'll have condolences sent by the President of the United

States, and there will be statesmen attending the service. I won't be there . . . but he won't be alone. That's the way he wanted it.''

Brett hugged her quietly as they stood in the middle of the hospital corridor. "I'm sorry, sweetheart," Brett said softly.

Jane held on to him. "So am I."

But with the passing of Harry Lindsay all was *not* over. Whatever claim he'd refused in life, he seemed determined to pursue in death. No one had been more surprised than Jane when she'd been summoned to the law offices of a prominent Washington firm to hear the reading of Harry Dean Lindsay's will.

Jane didn't want to attend, but Brett had persuaded her otherwise. He wanted the business of the past with its guilt and disappointment to be over. He wanted Jane and himself to begin their own life together.

When the elevator doors finally opened and Jane stepped out in her summer dress of pale yellow linen, she was like an odd beam of bright light in a sea of dark suits and attaché cases. Jane's face was rather serene and a soft smile curved her mouth. Brett was mesmerized. He knew for sure now what that look meant. He'd never seen it on Carolyn's face, which had been a shame. Brett felt a tightening in his chest and throat. He felt awe and elation and overwhelming love for this woman who, by loving him and letting him love her, had fulfilled more than one of his own dreams. Jane had never looked more beautiful than she did right at that moment, as her life fell into place at last.

Jane felt herself bursting with a need to share with Brett, to give to him in return all he'd been to her and more. There was a lot to say, though that moment of meeting in these surroundings was not exactly conducive to love and romance.

"Come on," Brett said, taking her hand, his eyes looking deeply into Jane's. "Let's go someplace private where we can talk."

That turned out to be the hotel where Brett had taken a room two nights ago, and where only today he'd been able to transfer Jane and her things. When they reached the cool interior of the spacious modern room, Brett and Jane came together for an embrace and kiss of welcome, of grateful endings and joyous beginnings that naturally led to slow, gentle removal of clothing. They didn't bother to draw the draperies, letting the afternoon sunlight filter through sheer white curtains to play over their heated skin, to create shadows and an air of secrecy. Their kisses were languid and sensually thorough, connecting them in one way and erotically hinting at the more intimate other.

Brett and Jane were still slow and gentle with each other in the huge bed, as if now they had all the time in the world for each touch and caress, even for the ultimate possession that brought them to a breathless dizzying explosion of their senses. Finally they were one. Then, curling up afterward in each other's arms, both had a sense of total peace.

Jane let her fingers roam, first stroking Brett's throat and chest, letting her hand rest for a moment over the sure beating of his heart. The hair on his chest and stomach tickled her skin and she dreamily closed her eyes, loving the masculine firmness of his body.

But now that they'd had this moment, Jane knew it was time to tell Brett the rest of her news about the afternoon.

"All the lawyers seemed to know I was Harry's natural daughter. But it was...all business. They weren't interested in the details. I told them I wanted nothing from him," Jane began softly. Brett silently stroked her hair, encouraging her on. "I said it wouldn't be fair and very inappropriate."

"Did they understand?" Brett asked.

"Yes, but it didn't seem to matter. They had very clear instructions and a counterargument for everything I said. He left specific gifts for a few colleagues and staff. He bequeathed money for a scholarship fund at Columbia School of Journalism in his name...." Slowly Jane sat up, allowing the covers to drop to her waist. Then she leaned foward to hug her legs, resting her chin pensively on her raised knees. "He gave large sums to a few charities, but...he left the Georgetown house and his other assets to me. He said they were for Noel Jane Lindsay, who had achieved in her career the tribute he'd always sought," Jane said in a mere whisper. She shook her head. "Poor Harry. He just didn't seem to understand his love and respect would have meant more to me than his assets."

"But maybe that was all he really had to give, Jane," Brett suggested softly. He sat back against the pillows and drew Jane against his chest.

"The last few weeks have been so crazy, and I've been so tired," Jane murmured.

Brett hugged her. "I know, darling. I've been very worried about you." He grinned suddenly. "Jones sends his love. He wants to know when you're coming back."

Jane laughed lightly. "I miss him, too. I realized several nights ago how much I rely on his companionship. But I also miss Oliver, and—" she stole a shy look at Brett who waited for her words "—and I desperately missed you."

They took several silent moments to enjoy just being close before Jane spoke again. "How did the court case go with your father-in-law? Was it hard?" she asked.

Brett shrugged. "Not really. As a matter of fact, it had a few surprising twists and turns. First of all, the judge chastised my father-in-law for wanting to take back a gift that he assumed had been given with love. Actually, by giving the property to his daughter, Stanley Hastings had given himself an enormous tax advantage. But he'd obviously hoped to persuade Carolyn at some future time that the la should be developed. Of course, he hadn't counted on C olyn putting the land in Jonathan's name, or on her timely death.

"The judge has ruled that the land legally belongs Jonathan, and he asked Jonathan what he thought sho be done with it."

"He asked Jonathan?" Jane questioned.

"Actually, I thought it was a pretty good idea," Brett s thoughtfully.

Jane frowned. "But Brett, don't you see? If the judge that, he's putting Jonathan in a terrible spot. He would want to do anything to offend his grandfather...or you

"That's true. But Jonathan seemed to think he had a lution that was best for the land, rather than what was for his grandfather or me." Brett smiled down at Jane quirked a brow. "It seems my son read an article recer about how a certain species of turtle that used to be qr common around the ponds of the Hamptons is now thre ened with extinction. If the land in question is allowed to developed right now, the drain on the water supply and change in foliage will have an effect on the survival chan of the turtles. Jonathan suggested than an environmer impact study be done. Then he turned to Stanley and sa 'I'm sorry, Grandpa, but I think we should be concerr about the animals and wildlife already on the land.'"

"Oh, Brett," Jane said as her frown deepened. "I th Jonathan got that information from my article."

"I wouldn't be a bit surprised. But don't worry. The juc didn't seem to feel that the information prejudiced the ca at all. I think he was surprised and impressed with Jor than's arguments."

"And what about your father-in-law?"

"Well, after the shock wore off, he got a good laugh out of the situation. He told Jonathan he was proud of the way he'd carefully thought out his point of view. And he said, far be it from him to displace endangered turtles. The land remains with Jonathan unconditionally."

"Good for Jonathan," she said warmly.

Brett looked at her with his own special regard. "And good for me."

Jane looked puzzled.

"For having a brilliant son...and wife." Jane blushed profusely. "I still want to marry you, Lady Jane."

When Jane made no immediate response, Brett gently stroked her arm and began to talk to her in a caressing whisper. "I think you'll like the Boston area. I have a house there. I'm taking an instructor's position at M.I.T., and I'll continue to consult now and then with NASA and Grumman. You can continue to write and do whatever else it is you want to do...as long as we're together."

"Are you sure?" Jane asked plaintively.

Brett chuckled richly. "Sweetheart, I can't remember when I've been more sure of anything. Mother has even promised to give you the family recipe for our fruitcake. This is serious!"

Jane smiled.

"And she's threatening me with bodily harm if I don't return with you."

Jane pulled back so that she could see Brett's face clearly. "Harry said you were an innocent man, you know."

Brett smiled wickedly. "Did he? He was wrong. I'm guilty as hell for conniving and plotting to be with you. I wanted you to trust me and to love me, Lady."

She smoothed a hand over his chest. "I do love you, Brett," she said and sighed.

"I'll take that to mean yes, you'll marry me." Jane suddenly buried her face against his chest.

"Jane..." Brett said in gentle amusement at her sudden tears. He pulled her closer. "Darling, don't cry. Talk to me. Tell me why you're crying."

"B-because everyone has been so sweet."

"That's because everyone cares about you. Jonathan wants to know if, when we get married, he can live with us and not go away to school. And poor Jones has gone into a decline. So... are you ready to come home with me?"

Home. The word alone evoked a sense of peace, a vision of family that was unbearably sweet. Jane put her arms around Brett's neck, laying her damp cheek against his. Her eyes drifted shut and she smiled.

"Yes. I'm ready to go home."

Epilogue

Jane leaned over the railing and looked down into the foaming rush of water. She was hoping the sun behind them would cooperate and reflect through the misty spray to create a rainbow. She leaned over farther.

At once Brett's arm circled her waist to hold her secure. He smiled at Jane's eagerness.

She sighed. "I can't see anything yet."

Brett gently pulled her away. "Be patient. These things take time." Taking her hand, he led Jane along a foliage-rich path, one of many that wound throughout Waimea Canyon on the island of Kauai. This was the third island they'd visited on their two-week honeymoon and the one they liked the best. It was called the Garden Isle, and justly so. Kauai lived up to Hawaii's reputation as a tropical paradise.

They were married two weeks after returning to Montauk Point from Washington. But it had been another two weeks before they could leave for their honeymoon. Brett had wasted no time in having Jane's meager possessions moved to the house in Boston where they would live, and while wedding plans were made he'd deposited Jones with Jonathan, much to the joy of both boy and beast.

Jane had insisted on a week to finish obligations to several publications. And she'd also discovered that her solitary existence had left her with an embarrassing lack of clothing, which necessitated a shopping spree. Priscilla Chandler had the time of her life ushering her future daughter-in-law in and out of outrageously expensive boutiques, offering free advice on what Jane should purchase. Jane allowed herself to be led through several days of this before Brett, sensing her growing wariness, put an end to the expeditions, declaring he'd rather have a naked wife than an exhausted one. Jane had enjoyed the chance to know better Brett's irrepressibly cheerful mother, but was nevertheless grateful for his intervention.

All the excitement played havoc with her system, sending her rushing for the bathroom at the mere sight of food, and once she broke into tears after speaking with her mother long-distance. Jane believed it was all premarriage nerves and prayed for a speedy end.

The wedding was small and unpretentious, which suited Jane and Brett just fine. Oliver escorted her down the aisle, Priscilla was matron of honor and Jonathan best man. Norman Rosen and his wife were present as witnesses. After the ceremony, Oliver immediately declared first rights as godfather. While everyone laughed, Jane blushed, but not in embarrassment. Brett hugged her, and Jane didn't have to ask him if he wanted more children. The positive answer was in his eyes and his satisfied smile.

She slept through the first two days on Oahu until Brett teasingly asked if she was ever going to recover from jet lag. She did, in sufficient time to enjoy seeing the historical sites of the island, yet finding some of the exotic local cuisine too rich for her. They'd then moved on to Maui, staying in a quaint old guest house just outside the old whaling village of Lahaina. Brett watched Jane carefully, but made no more references to her latest physical eccentricities until one morning before dawn as they waited for the sun to rise over the dormant volcano of Haleakala.

They'd driven to the top of the crater, ten thousand or so feet above sea level, at four-thirty in the morning, because the tour book said the trip was not to be missed. For entirely different reasons, Brett would later wholeheartedly agree.

Jane and Brett huddled against the predawn chill in a ranger's station. Brett wrapped his arms around Jane for warmth as a rosy dawn began to creep along the open crater edge, and slowly the sun made its appearance.

"Oh, Brett!" Jane gasped in undisguised wonder. "It's beautiful!"

"So. Was it worth getting up in the middle of the night for?" he asked, feigning a yawn.

"Don't you think so?" she asked, stroking his cheek.

Brett grabbed the hand and kissed the palm. "It was worth it just to see you so happy."

Jane smiled warmly. "It's not the sunrise that's responsible. It's you."

Brett kissed her forehead and Jane snuggled closer to him, watching through the station window as the warm sun burned off the night clouds still hovering over the crater.

"Now I know what's meant by birth of a new day," Jane murmured.

"I never thought of it that way before."

They were silent for a long moment until Jane said quietly, "I guess this is as good a time as any to tell you."

Brett smiled to himself. "Tell me what?"

"That I...I think I'm going to have a baby," she said very softly.

Brett let out a deep sigh, crushing Jane to him. "Darling, *we're* going to have a baby," he corrected her emotionally. "I wondered when you were going to tell me."

Jane looked up at her husband. "You knew?"

Brett grinned. "I began to suspect when we were in Washington. I've been through this once before, sweet-

lent. I recognized the symptoms. But I knew it hadn't occurred to you yet that you might be pregnant."

She shook her head. "It hadn't. Not until a few days before the wedding when . . . when . . ."

"When breakfast became very unappealing," Brett said, amused.

Jane grimaced and nodded. "This wasn't planned very well. I mean, maybe it's too soon. Maybe we need more time to . . ."

"It doesn't matter. Believe me, Jane," Brett said lifting a brow, "it would have happened sooner or later." As Jane made to protest, he silenced her with a brief kiss. "I know what you're thinking, and you're wrong. This is not anything like what happened to your parents. We love each other and that happened first. And it's different because I want you and our baby."

Jane shifted her gaze to the glory of the sun that was bringing with it the promise of a magnificent day. "I suppose that's why Oliver was so quick to make himself future godfather."

"Mmm-hmm. He guessed, too. He is a doctor, after all."

Jane furrowed her brow and gnawed on her lip. "Brett, do you think your mother will . . . ?"

"No, I don't. Besides, she'll be delighted that there will be a new Chandler to indulge. She'll probably thank you. But not half as much as I do. . . ."

Jane bent to pick a bright red hibiscus blossom from one of the shrubs that grew wild on the islands. She turned back to Brett and he helped her attach it to the wavy ponytail her hair was gathered into.

"That should solve the problem of which ear it should go over," Jane laughed, her green eyes bright with love. Brett regarded her as he picked a fallen leaf from her shoulder. "How are you feeling?"

Jane beamed. "Wonderful and happy. Very, very happy."

Brett's hand rubbed her stomach intimately. "And how's our national treasure?"

Jane covered his hand with her own. "Keeping a low profile for the moment. I'll see a doctor as soon as we get home."

He put his arm around her and they walked slowly back toward the overlook and the waterfall.

"I suppose you and Oliver have already decided if it's a boy or a girl."

Brett lifted his brows. "I had to leave some of the work for you. I'd love a little girl, though. As a start, you understand."

"You probably planned for this all along."

"I'm innocent...."

"Well, you'll get your wish and—" Jane gasped "—Brett, look! It's a rainbow!" She held her breath and watched the spectrum appear through the reflected light.

"Well, you've gotten one of your wishes, too."

"Are you responsible for this?" she teased.

Brett gathered her close. "Again, I'm innocent. I've never been able to perform miracles." He looked down at her. "Well...maybe just once. Winning your trust and love," he said, as he bent to kiss her gratefully.

Harlequin American Romance

COMING NEXT MONTH

#281 ONE WHIFF OF SCANDAL by Judith Arnold

For weeks Griff had been on the trail of the worst sex, money and power
scandal ever to hit sleepy Rhode Island towns. Then Jill Bergland
stumbled onto the story and made Griff wonder—could love
survive scandal?

#282 KISSED BY AN ANGEL by Kathy Clark

Guilt had changed Kristi Harrison's life and made her seek solitude at a
Florida beach house. When nightmares drove her from her bed to the
quiet of the moonlit beach, she met Scott Sanders, who was driven by his
own midnight demons. They each had their secret guilt—but could they
find peace in each other's arms?

#283 SIDE BY SIDE by Muriel Jensen

As children, Janessa and Clay had promised to be united forever. It was a
bond they vowed would never be broken. But could their childhood
dreams anticipate their adult realities?

#284 LADY'S CHOICE by Linda Randall Wisdom

Whoever called it "midlife crisis" was right! At forty, Abby's life had
gone haywire. Her grown children continued to give her problems, and
now her best friend suddenly decided he wanted *more* than friendship.
Zach's timing was perfect, for they would need their combined strength to
weather the crisis to come.

Harlequin Temptation dares to be different!

Once in a while, we Temptation editors spot a romance that's truly innovative. To make sure *you* don't miss any one of these outstanding selections, we'll mark them for you.

EDITOR'S CHOICE

When the "Editors' Choice" fold-back appears on a Temptation cover, you'll know we've found that extra-special page-turner!

THE

Temptation

EDITORS

Have You Ever Wondered If You Could Write A Harlequin Novel?

Here's great news—Harlequin is offering a series of cassette tapes to help you do just that. Written by Harlequin editors, these tapes give practical advice on how to make your characters—and your story—come alive. There's a tape for each contemporary romance series Harlequin publishes.

Mail order only

All sales final